T0154951

f'antastical

edited by
Lucy Sussex
& Judith Raphael Buckrich

sybylla

Sybylla Co-operative Press and Publications Ltd
1st Floor, Ross House
247–251 Flinders Lane, Melbourne 3000
Australia

First published by Sybylla Feminist Press, 1995

Cover art: 'St Martha' by Deborah Klein
Design: Kerri Valkova
Typeset in Arabian and Bernhard Modern by Caz Brown

Printed by the Australian Print Group

She's Fantastical
   ISBN 0 908205 12 0

This project has been assisted by the Commonwealth Government
through the Australia Council, its arts funding and advisory body.

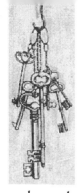

contents

acknowledgements

the Editors and Sybyllas appreciate the invaluable assistance given in the making of this book. Thanks to Juliet Peers, Phillip Morrissey, Antoinette Birkenbeil, Ken Endacott for his on-line systems management, Mary Dabrowski, Samantha Lovrich, Victor Stojćevski, Queenie (aka Beans) for stress management, and the English Department of the University of Melbourne.

Extra special thanks to Dale Chapman for letting us hog the computer and for curry and endless supplies of port.

'Maydina' and 'Alinta' by Hyllus Maris first appeared in the television series *Women of the Sun* (Episode One 1824–1834 and Episode Two 1890s respectively), Currency Press (1983); 'The Master Builder's Wife' by Lisa Jacobson in *Stand Magazine* (vol. 34, no. 4, Autumn 1993, UK), reprinted in *Best Short Stories 1994* (Heinemann); 'Angel Jacko' by Gabrielle Lord in *The Times on Sunday*, 15 March 1987; and 'Our Mother Land' by Daisy Utemorrah in *Do Not Go Around the Edges* (Magabala Books, 1990). 'Aubade' by M. Barnard Eldershaw is taken from the Virago 1983 edition reprinted with permission from the copyright owner, Alan Alford, c/- Curtis Brown. Maurilia Meehan's piece is an extract from her novel *The Sea People* (Penguin, forthcoming).

saint martha according to deborah klein: cover art

Sister of Mary (sometimes identified with Mary Magdalene) and of Lazarus. The Bible represents Martha as being totally dedicated to domestic duties, and her sister as being more sociably inclined. Martha was present on the occasion of the raising from the dead of Lazarus. She served supper to Christ at her home in Bethany. It was then that Mary annointed the feet of Jesus. There is no early tradition about Martha's death. However, after the death of Jesus, mediaeval legend has it that Martha, Lazarus and Mary were cast off in an unseaworthy boat without sails or rudder. Miraculously, they landed at Marseilles, France. Martha subsequently converted the people of Aix to Christianity. In Tarascon, she tamed a fearful dragon – the Tarasque – that was laying waste the countryside. Legend has it that she aspersed him with holy water, wrapped her sash around his neck and led him to Arles, where he was killed.

Saint Martha is invoked as the Patron Saint of Housewives. Her attributes include a ladle, a bunch of keys and a broom. She is sometimes portrayed with a dragon. My image is based on the painting 'Saint Michael' (1469) by Piero della Francesca, which hangs in the Sainsbury Wing of the National Gallery, London.

foreword

Until a few decades ago, the world of fiction was mostly the world as men imagined it to be, described (as Virginia Woolf noted) in sentences shaped by men's minds and voices. Men ran the publishing houses and all the machinery of evaluation and criticism. Editors seldom print and critics seldom praise a work outside the conventions they uphold, and teachers can't usefully discuss a story they don't understand; in order to be published and read, serious writers wrote as men. Writing 'for women' was a subliterature, trivial by definition, and even the most serious writer who avowedly undertook to write *as* a woman was suspect and liable to be relentlessly marginalized, like Virginia Woolf herself.

In the last thirty years or so, as women have taken to writing as women, not as honorary or artificial men, it's become clear that they see a rather different world and describe it by rather different means. The most startling difference is that men aren't at the center of it – sometimes indeed are quite peripheral to it. Relationships between women, familial, sexual, or social, often fill the whole field of vision. Children are likely to be integral to the story and to appear as human, rather than supernaturally percipient or demonically nasty. Heroism is redefined;

violence is not assumed to be of compelling inherent interest. The male experience of sexuality is not the defining one. The story is often told by a voice or voices that have no absolute authority. And so on. Of course all these characteristics turn up in fiction by men, increasingly often indeed; but I think there is still a genuine difference, the result not of some biological imperative but of the different upbringing and expectations we have for men and women. When these expectations change, the differences will change. When the expectation of gender difference lessens, the differences will lessen.

Right now, women writers enjoy a singular and probably temporary double freedom. A generation of feminists has given women permission to write as women, freed them as artists to be themselves. And this combines with the paradoxical freedom women have always had, the underdogs' privilege of not having to support a society they don't run.

Women in power, PMs and Congresswomen and CEOs, are still almost universally honorary or artificial men, required to behave in a manly fashion; they don't count as women. Women as such still don't set the terms of society, profit from it less than men do, and usually work more. So long as the 'division of labor' (a term that conceals the fact that it concerns gender) gives women the unpaid or low-paid or domestic-dependent jobs, women will remain a partially dispossessed element within the society, whether socialist, capitalist, or hunter–gatherer.

The dispossessed are of course the potentially rebellious. They seek change who might profit from it. They watch the powerful who depend on the powerful. Tonto knows a whole lot more about cowboys *and* indians than the Lone Ranger does. The view from below, from outside, from behind the mop-bucket, is a view through the illusions and collusions of the ruling class.

It is, in fact, the novelist's view. We know who to go to for truth about life on the plantation, and it ain't Massa.

So it isn't surprising that we are in the midst of a great flowering of fiction by women, or that most of our finest novelists and story-writers writing in English are women – many of them Lesbians and/or women of color, doubly disadvantaged by white society and therefore, paradoxically, doubly free as artists.

Even straight, white, male artists often assume the liberties of the outcast and berate their society for not valuing them while declaring all its values false (just like a bunch of feminists.) Writers may choose to work in outcast forms such as 'genre' fiction, just because they're considered to be beneath the conventions and judgmentalisms of the critics and the academics; I think one reason highly respected women writers such as Atwood and Lessing write science fiction is that they delight in the freedom of not being responsible to the Canon of Literature.

There are areas of society, however, where women do run things, and take responsibility or have it thrust upon them: 'home,' however constituted, 'family,' ditto; all responsibility for pregnancy; most of the care of young children; and most of the ordinary relational functioning of society, in which women's role is that of wife, secretary, volunteer, etc. Men leave day-to-day control of these areas to women while retaining hierarchic superiority as paterfamilias, boss, chairman, etc.

But instead of looking with the clear, powerless, observing eye of the outsider at these areas where they're not directly in charge, male writers tend simply to overlook them. They ignore them, especially the regions where women relate principally to other women or children. Like Tolstoy, they flee in horror from the nursery. Our information on many such areas comes solely from women telling tales.

In thinking about these areas of women's lives, I thought of that familiar novelistic figure the governess, and as a sort of exercise tried to imagine *Jane Eyre* as written by a man. The central relationship might well be much the same, though Jane might not win quite so many arguments and Rochester might not be punished so mercilessly at the end. But I think we'd know very much less about Jane's school, and her conversations and relationships with Bessie, and Rochester's housekeeper, and his daughter, and St John's sisters – all of which are central to the book's plausibility, the broad, realistic, humane foundation that so firmly supports the romance. And a male writer might have handled Jane's extreme vulnerability – the fact that she is in almost all respects as much in Rochester's power as is his first wife – with a different slant, the way Flaubert sees Emma Bovary's feckless helplessness as a natural condition, inevitable – anatomy as destiny. The choice Jane finally makes might not really have been, as it is in Brontë's book, *her* choice.

These are illegitimate suppositions; but legitimacy is not really a woman's concern, is it?

In the areas where women are given or have taken social responsibility, women writers don't portray themselves as dependent on men, and they do regard these areas as important, often as central, whether to the society or to the story. Women like to write and read about their realm. Men too like to write and read about the areas where they are solely and totally in charge – sea stories, war stories, male-bonded adventure stories, and so on. Women often seem to enjoy such exclusively male preserves quite as much as men do; I certainly will not be driven out of the Seeonee wolf-pack or the Company of the Ringbearers, or ordered off the deck of the *Pequod* or the *Surprise*. It must be men's need to keep establishing their masculinity that prevents so many of them from reading woman-centered fiction, or even being civil about it. Men's power is greater than women's, but most of them live in a smaller country than women do. As a poet once said to me when I asked him why poets were so cruel to one another, far worse than even British novelists – 'Well, the smaller the territory, the oftener you have to spray the boundaries.'

❧

Fantasy has always been a rebel's mode, a means of sneakily saying unwelcome or disturbing things about one's society, or of offering a more or less plausible alternative to it. The stories and poems in this book are all in one way or another fantastic, and all are rebellious, subversive, critical, or teasing, cheerfully or fiercely knocking the posts out from under the Status Quo.

One, only one of all these stories, brings a man and a woman together at the end in traditional, nay wedded, bliss. It does so by the most amazing, entirely supernatural – perhaps preternatural? – means, which I cannot divulge here, but can only praise as being far more convincing than most contrivances intended to get the prince and the princess together, including the telepathy in *Jane Eyre*. But then, there's a story here about the Prince and the Princess themselves, which in good Richian re-visionary style deconstructs the fairy-tale into tatters a derridean would not recognize and sends the Princess off on her own towards a distant reconciliation, not with the Prince, not with Faithful John, but with that figure so feared by timorous freudians, the Big, Bad Mother.

Several of these stories are concerned with a woman's discovery that she's independent (is this the Ewige Weibliche Bildungsroman?) – her discovery of the power or powers proper to her, as herself and as a woman, hence her abandonment or escape from male control. Other stories tell of a failure to find female power or resist male power, leading variously to a series of murders completed by suicide (now there's a real male tradition), to a literal and endless process of discreation, or to the creation and loss of an impossible male dream-figure, an angel. But in another story, the angel is a man-made monstrosity whose sacrifice frees the two colluding, rebellious women, a mother and daughter.

Mothers and daughters, women friends, women lovers, women and children, women and animals – the book is full of pairings, interweavings, minglings, transformations, transgressions of boundaries between generations, between species, between realms. Borders which we're used to seeing well sprayed and marked with neat piles of scat become crossings, trysting-places, meeting-grounds. The camera eats the child. The woman is the falcon. Woman is other.

Australia itself is other. The landscapes of these stories are familiar and strange, whether to the Australian or the outsider reading them. Daisy Utemorrah's infinitely quiet and moving poem closes,

> The moon shines on the water, all is ended –
> and the dreamtime gone.

But beneath every time, every landscape, lies a dreamtime. These poems and stories are signs, ways, roads leading into that time, our shared country.

Ursula K. Le Guin
1995

introduction

traight she's fantastical, they all do cry
Yet they will imitate her presently

So wrote Margaret Cavendish, Duchess of Newcastle, in her *Nature's Pictures* (1656), which provided the title and inspiration for this anthology. A feminist, a writer in many genres, and also a stylishly avant-garde dresser, her words seem appropriate for this garland of fantastic(al), speculative, surreal and magically real writing by Australian women: *She's Fantastical*. Moreover, as the author of *Description of a Blazing New World* (1668), a book regarded both as proto-science fiction and source matter for Coleridge's 'Rhyme of the Ancient Mariner', Margaret Cavendish was fanciful not only in dress, but in subject matter. Thus, this Fantastical She is a literary ancestor of the women collected here, writers from a sunburnt – if not blazing – country.

Cavendish's voyage to a new world could only be in the imagination, given her era and gender. Her male contemporaries, most famously William Dampier and the Batavia mutineers, were the actual visitors to Australia. How prosaic, in contrast, is the discourse of their discoveries! She wrote of lands of ice, inhabited by spider-men and satyrs – they merely delineated the rim of the continent or created horrors on its outlying isles. Earlier cartographers had filled the blank space at the edge of experience with the words 'Here be Dragons', or by drawing monsters such as the Tarasque of St Martha, depicted in the *She's Fantastical* cover art by Deborah Klein. Yet the imaginative truth behind the null space of Terra Australis was a domain where roamed not dragons, but the far stranger bunyip and quinkan, creatures of a belief system dating back to the Ice Ages.

While *She's Fantastical* was never intended to be an anthology organized on historical principles, the ancient tradition of women wording the fantastic on this continent is recognized by the inclusion of poems by Hyllus Maris and Daisy Utemorrah, the former beginning with the first dawn, the latter concluding the many 'dreamings' of this book. In between is as wide a selection of contemporary Australian women's writing as the editors could lay hands upon, with the common ground being anti-realism. And while it proved impossible for reasons of space to include selections from all the notable Australian foremothers of fantasy, two outstanding examples have been chosen: Henrietta Dugdale's polemical *A Few Hours in a Far-off Age* (1883), and a text which it may possibly have influenced, M. Barnard Eldershaw's *Tomorrow and Tomorrow and Tomorrow* (1947). The latter has been widely reprinted, but the former appears here for the first time since its initial publication over a century ago. Both being novels, they appear in extract form.

Dugdale's and Eldershaw's works are Australian contributions to an important and venerable literary genre, the utopia and its converse, the dystopia. It is a reflection on our interesting times that, while imagining the ideal society was the predominant form until the end of the nineteenth century, in this century writers have preferred to consider the worst of all possible worlds. Jane Routley's story in this anthology, 'The Goddess Wakes', utilizes a blend of fairy-tale and movie myth against the background of a devolved future; a recent novel-length Australian dystopia was Gabrielle Lord's *Salt* (1990), although Lord is represented in this volume by another style of fantasy altogether.

Another category of writing that has been a haven for the fantastic has been children's literature. Though often discounted as caterers for immature tastes, authors writing for this audience face readers singularly demanding in their low boredom threshold and intolerance of pretension. Two contributors to this anthology, Nadia Wheatley and Isobelle Carmody, are winners of the Children's Book Council Award, incidentally the only literary prize in Australia that sells books in quantity. These writers leap the boundary between readerships with grace, but then, as Ursula K. Le Guin has noted in the preface to *The Language of the Night* (1989), the refusal to 'accept rules we don't make and boundaries that make no sense to us is a direct expression of our being women writers'. In a similar spirit, *She's Fantastical* ignores the frontiers between genres, proving that they have, in fact, more commonality than is recognized by current literary marketing.

Ursula K. Le Guin very kindly agreed to contribute a foreword to the anthology, thereby providing a linkage to another Australian literary tradition, science or speculative fiction. In 1975 Le Guin was Guest of Honour at the World Science Fiction Convention, held in Melbourne, and she also taught a writer's workshop, whose attendees included Philippa Maddern and Petrina Smith. The success of this venture meant that other workshops were held, at the third of which, in 1979, the *She's Fantastical* editors met. Another notable writer at this workshop was Leanne Frahm. While not all Australian women authors of speculative fiction benefited directly from Le Guin's visit, it was inspirational to this small but significant minority, and yet another thread in the sampler of *She's Fantastical*.

Until recently, the freeing of the imagination provided by taking one step sideways from the real or throwing it completely out the window, as does Ania Walwicz in her 'Flight', was not part of the Australian literary mainstream. It was in 1958 that Patrick White decried the Australian novel as being 'the dreary, dun-coloured offspring of journalistic realism'. Nearly forty years later, his words are no longer applicable, partly due to the influence of magical realism – the canonical and acceptable face of fantastic literature. Maurilia Meehan, Carmel Bird and Gabrielle Lord are writers whose work is not pigeon-holed into genre, and yet they write in this anthology of the surreal – the nuns of St Mary Magdalene, a preternatural disappearance, an angel lover – with no signs of strain, indeed, positive zest!

To leaven the mix of writing in *She's Fantastical* even further, some experimental writing, namely Walwicz's 'Flight' and berni m. janssen's *SAW*, has been included, as well as poetry. The only current form of Australian women's writing within the subject criteria under-represented in our selection is horror, although this area was covered by the recent Women's Redress Press anthology, *Shrieks* (Sydney, 1993). It may also be considered that some of the subject matter of these stories is quite sufficiently horrific, an incidental hazard in the compilation of an anthology of feminist bent.

So to conclude, while the original quotation by Margaret Cavendish referred to female fashions, or specifically to the Duchess being ridiculed for her elaborate and imaginative garb, it is equally applicable to literary modes. Styles of literature can be as fickle and proscriptive, if not quite as rapid in their turn-over, as this year's hat or hem-line. The literary mode showcased in this book is, to pun upon the Duchess, the fantastical; a coming trend, it may be, as is showcased by the *She's Fantastical* designers, writers and artists. Margaret Cavendish deployed patches, velvets, and ermine in her outward display, decried as a raree-show by her contemporaries; we have similarly eschewed the drab and dun-coloured. As the Tarasque on the cover indicates: Here be Monsters, also witches, angels, princesses, time-travellers and other inhabitants of the land of anti-realism. Enjoy them!

L.S.

We certainly enjoyed the process. There's nothing quite like the pleasure of 'making a book', especially reading the stories for the first time and finding the wonder of diversity. Making decisions about who and where and how is at times not so pleasant, but still interesting. The final ordered selection seems like a magical result indeed when what seemed like such a short time ago there was nothing except Lucy and Judy talking over cups of coffee at the Melbourne University Union House.

If anyone had told us in 1979, when we met at a science fiction writing workshop in a hot and possum-ridden boarding house in Cremorne, Sydney, that we would one day be putting together this anthology of women writers, I think we would have been incredulous to say the least. We came for such different reasons and went away to live very different lives. Yet it is just such meetings that make life more than just the facts of waking, sleeping, eating, making a living. You never know what the future will bring or where a seemingly finite occurrence can lead.

To have been part of making this book was a great opportunity. We believe it has great historical significance – however, this is hardly something we can control or know – we may be 'science fiction buffs', but we don't have a crystal ball. Still, we hope that readers will be inspired by these pieces, see something in them that they have not seen before, or understand something that perhaps was not clear.

We hope that this book will inspire writers and anthologists to make more books and write more stories. In other words, let this first anthology of Australian women's fantasy, science fiction, magical realism and experimental writing be just that – the first of many.

J.R.B.

alinta – 'the flame'

from women of the sun

there, on the first dawn, before time
The mind was pure sustenance
   Born long ago
   Before body
It moved freely, yet with purpose
It knows boundless space
   Having come from there
It spans this web of the universe
   From which the planets hang suspended
   Ever turning
   Stars glittering in the velvet darkness of forever
The sun, through it, is giver of warm Life
The rain (from that same source it comes) is messenger
    of Life
Wind is its voice, telling the earth always of Life

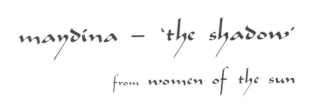

maydina — 'the shadow'

from women of the sun

Our culture is like a great bird
It was born aeons ago in the mists of Creation
On the winds of Heaven it came to this planet
Its eyes are the stars
Its feathers are golden like the sun
Its legs great trees of the forest
Its claws are like the rocks
Planted firmly in the earth
Its breaths are the clouds
That turn to rain
And when it sings!
It is the sound of Life itself

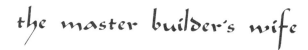

the master builder's wife

If you ask, 'Why is Thekla's construction taking such a long time?' the inhabitants continue hoisting sacks, lowering leaded strings, moving long brushes up and down, as they answer, 'So that its destruction cannot begin.'
— Italo Calvino, *Invisible Cities*

First, I should tell you about the house, which was once ordinary enough. It had, as my husband put it, seen better days. When the auctioneer's silver hammer finally fell and the place was ours, he took out his grandfather's pen and signed his name across the creamy sheaf of paper that was the contract. After that, when all the men in their dark suits had departed, we drank champagne and made love in the kitchen on the rough, hard floorboards.

The roof of our house was at this time covered with a tapestry of overgrowth — blackberries, wheat grass, moss. The external walls had been slapped so often with quick coats of paint that even the most recent layer of ivory was already peeling back to reveal earlier colours — apricot, strawberry, aqua, violet. Inside, the walls leant on all angles into themselves, so that none of the doors ever closed properly, and we would wake in the mornings to find great cracks clawing their way over the plaster where the night before there had been none. On top of that, the bathroom was almost unendurable. We were dirtier after we had used it than before. The first time I tried to take a bath there came out of the tap a stream of mud and leaves and tiny, unnameable insects. And I was reminded of the princess in the fairy-tale who, cursed by a witch, spewed out of her mouth toads and tadpoles every time she tried to speak.

We did not waste an hour or even a minute. We moved into the kitchen as soon as possible. It was the only room not threatening to collapse under the weight of weeds and silt and crumbling rafters. One hundred and twenty-two cardboard boxes lined the hallway, and I had labelled each one so that the material contents of our lives together were as neatly organized as possible into such categories and sub-categories as 'silverware', 'woollen socks', and 'Christmas decorations'. Then we set to work with hundreds of buckets of soap and water. We stirred plaster into a creamy paste, we sunk silver nails into the buckled walls. We polished the windows until they disappeared into the clarity of their own surfaces. How our arms ached! At night I would prepare for our supper a few boiled eggs, some bread and butter, and a little wine. Then we would lie on the old mattress listening to the sounds of each other's breathing, too tired to talk. Behind us, in the dark, the garden stretched on for miles, and the back fence reached right across the horizon in a thin wooden line.

All of this took place back in the days of the seventy-hour week, when we had so very few moments to share with each other. After all, the necessary details of life seemed to take up so much time! One stacked up tasks like so much bricks-and-mortar. Even the act of filling up a glass of water and placing it by my husband's bedside table became something which had to be carried out with haste; so precious had the price of a minute become that it assumed the status of an hour, or even a day. Then, you see, my husband was employed as a builder; paid plastic money to build on some bare, loamy mound some other person's ordinary dreams. Hallways for the children with their coloured hoops and balls, windows through which the sun blazed like a single yellow eye or the centre of a giant flower. I am sure that some have said we make a curious couple – I, with my careful rounded vowels and he, with a certain roughness in his hands and at the corners of his mouth. Yet he never could erect the foundations of cement and wood without seeing in them some far more intricate structure, a palace perhaps, or some sprawling mansion, its roof peaked as a mountain range. He could have been paid in gold and silver coins, or even a paper bill, thin and brown as a leaf, had he been so inclined. The value of such artefacts has soared now that plastic is the common currency. My husband could have been in high demand ...

He would often bring home for me miniature masterpieces carved from a door handle or window-sill; the hoary head of a lion, a peacock with its tail spread out and, once, a church with turrets, domes and even a bell tower, so tiny I could place it in the palm of my hand! Sometimes, long after everyone else had left the site, he would lean against the new raw wood of a verandah post or an unfilled doorway and wander, trance-like, into the private city of his own ideas. Late at night I would find him there, stiff and cold, with a look of vague surprise in his walnut eyes. But when the new government introduced the fifteen-hour week and the country was at leisure, my husband was the first to go. It is true that the strain of his occupation was beginning to show. He had worked on building sites for so long that the very extremities of the weather imprinted themselves upon his body. Even now there are red streaks of sun on his back and arms and an almost permanent sheen of liquid, which might be rain or perspiration, on his face. I thought he could do with the rest. I had no idea ... I am, perhaps, more at ease with leisure, with the hollow hours through which the wind moves like an ocean. He, on the other hand, is not comfortable without his instruments – his battered measuring-rod, still in metric, his ancient levelling pole. The first thing he did with his empty hours was to fill them up.

※

My husband cannot seem to stop building. It is as if the pattern of his working days has been so deeply inscribed in his mind that he cannot help but act them out. No longer must he stand propped against a verandah post dreaming up his imaginary edifices. Now he may build precisely what he wishes. On the first morning after he stopped work I rolled over in our bed and my hand met nothing but the cotton sheets and cold dawn air. Then I saw his dark shape framed for a second by the doorway. He had his overalls on and a hammer in his hand.

Approached from the front, our house is much improved – the paint is a clean, hard white and we coloured the glass in the windows ourselves so that the sky is green as leaves or blood red, depending on which pane you are looking through. If you happened to be walking past and paused, say, while your dog snuffed the grass or your child handed you a chocolate wrapper, you might perhaps see the place as a cottage, as the home of a young couple with no children. We have no children, but that is beside the point. Do not, however, be fooled by first appearances. Our house is no longer what it seems. For a start, it's so much larger than it was. And the back garden, that huge sprawling forest of a garden where once I could wander for hours and not see anything but trees; well, now it's so much smaller. Looking in from the front you'd have no idea. But it is no longer possible, for instance, for me to change my daily clothes for I am unable to find the bedroom closet. Room after room appears – sometimes, it seems, overnight – and often one will take the place of another. I have no idea any more where this house begins or ends.

What was once the laundry is now the lounge and what was once a bedroom is now a bathroom. I have counted at least twenty-seven separate bathrooms, with their gold and silver, crystal and mahogany taps. Sometimes I am certain that I have walked through the same house twice, only to find a different view out of the windows, for some rooms are completely identical at first sight. But then there will be the slightest change of colour on the walls, from lemon, say, to peach, the almost imperceptible change of pattern on the tiles, from pentagons to hexagons, and I will know that I have moved on. There is an entire wing of nurseries although, as I have already said, we have no children. And in these rooms everything – the doorways, the built-in wardrobes, the height of the lavatory seats – is scaled down to the size of a child. There are other rooms too, but these ones frighten me; long and narrow as coffins, they are, with all the walls painted black.

Except for our daily breakfast together I often do not see my husband for weeks at a time, though he is no longer at work. We take our breakfast in the old kitchen. It is the only part of the house that is, strangely enough, easy to find and every morning I stumble into it to prepare some kind of meal from the diminishing stocks – tinned tomatoes, spaghetti, chicken soup. On the kitchen wall I mark down each day with the blade of a knife. My husband sits in the yellow chair and eats whatever I put in front of him. I do believe if I were to mix up some dirt with a little water he would eat that too. It may soon come to that. And he will insist upon conducting a normal conversation as if everything were still the way it once was, as if it were a summer's morning in, say, early February, and he was just about to, any minute now, push his chair out from the table, wipe the bacon fat from his chin, and go off to work. It is impossible to get any sense out of him. 'Is there anything I can do to help you?' I say, meaning the question in several different ways at once. 'The silver could do with a polish,' he says, rustling last month's paper in his dusty hands. 'I cannot find the silver,' I say. 'I cannot find the dining-room where the dresser that holds the silver is kept.' 'What do you mean?' says he. 'It's down the hall where it's always been, first on the right.' But there is no left and right in this house any longer, as I have told you.

What if I were to try to leave here? I have often considered it. But the last time I unbolted a window the air rushed through in a such a vertiginous wave that I felt as if I were drowning. Once a bird flew in, just some dun-coloured sparrow, and it took all my energy to chase it about the room. It crashed into the walls, left feathers clinging to the cornices, and splayed its wings up against the green and red glass until at last, quietly, carefully, I cupped my two palms over its wings and felt its heart pound beneath my fingers. Then I opened the window the slightest crack and released the bird.

I have taken to trailing about with me a long piece of yellow ribbon, like the ones my mother used to tie my sisters and me together at the zoo so we wouldn't get lost. That way I can find my way around, although only yesterday the ribbon caught beneath a doorway and broke, and I lost all sense of direction. North, south, east and west mean nothing in this house any more. Last night, while I lay down to sleep on the floor in a room painted all over with cornflowers, the sun set behind my head; today, it has risen in exactly the same spot. I have a recurring dream in which I tie my yellow ribbon to the leg of an enormous bird the size of a horse. I am outside the house. I am actually outside! There is no fear, no dizziness. The bird soars up above the trees and, suddenly, I am soaring with it. My feet brush the leaves of the tallest oaks. Below me the house sprawls and I can see how it has dug itself deep, deep into the earth. The wooden stumps thrust down through the dust, the soil, like the countless arms of some great wooden beast. Straight through the rock they plunge and do not stop for breath. But I am thousands of feet above the house and as long as the cord does not break I am free.

∽❦∾

Not long ago (I can no longer be precise about the names of days, the numbers of hours) I discovered a room filled entirely with goldfish. What wonder! The walls in this room were made of glass, double-glazed, and within their narrow confines fish swam like tiny jewelled stars. The sofa, too, was made of clear plastic and there were fish inside it, each with a strip of lightning across its back. Even the crystal vase, the face of the clock and the glass floor were swarming with the things, gold as nuggets and a strong rusted red, like the earth in the centre of this wide country. I lay on the floor with no shoes on my feet and watched the fish in the water below me. Just like ants, they were, making their incomprehensible journeys to and fro in water so clear it seemed they were swimming in air. I have never looked at fish so closely before. I noticed how the fins on some were eaten away, and how others had several scales missing, so that the skin shone out in a moony silver. I considered my own flesh. I scratched at the dry surface of my forearm, so that flakes of skin fell to the floor. I tugged at a finger-nail until the crescent of nail itself peeled away. I picked at a loose thread in my shirt, which I have not changed for months now, until the entire sleeve gave way. I began to notice, you might say, the unravelling of things, and the fist of an idea slowly uncurled itself inside me.

I have allowed myself to become the engineer of a plan in which, little by little, I shall take away from this house the most minute amount – say, a single floor tile, a ceramic doorknob, a strip of paint from a bedroom wall – until there is nothing left at all. In fact, I am surprised that I have not thought of it before. I am used to undoing things. As a child, my broad, square hands must for some strange reason have signalled the talent of a seamstress to every aunt and uncle in our large family. At Christmas I unwrapped my shiny parcels to find embroidery sets and knitting needles. That's all they ever gave me. They were wrong about my talents, but not about my persistence. For every stitch that I sewed, knitted, or crocheted, I undid another. I was the shy girl sitting cross-legged in the centre of some aunt's drawing-room, unpicking a thread of cotton or wool with eternal patience.

The plan that I have engineered swings round and round like some well-greased cog. I like the sound of the word 'engineer'; it brings an oily taste to my lips, and the smart crimson panels of a fire engine or a train. Did you know that you can almost spell the word engine both ways? Forwards and backwards? If you swap the letters 'g' and 'i' around, that is. There is a term for that kind of word, but I cannot recall it now. The plan that I have engineered stops me from sleeping, and it is true that I have been sleeping far too much lately. Even before I open my eyes, my dreams slide away from me, their edges blurred, and all I can recall are dark, unspecified colours with the texture of an old serge coat. But now I am kept busy day and night.

To begin with, I took the diamond ring from my hand and made an almost imperceptible crack in the glass wall of the goldfish room. The glass began to emit its drops of water, one at a time, until finally a pool of the stuff had formed, the size of a rose petal, near my right foot. Then I pierced the plastic couch in the goldfish room with the point of a safety-pin, so that slowly, slowly, water leaked out of it, too. There is no hurry, you see. The speed at which I do these things is not nearly as important as the fact that they are done well. But that is not all. I have also wrenched out all the nails I can find from the floorboards with a fork from the kitchen cupboard. Later, when I am rested, I shall rip away some of the skirting boards, and that will be enough work for the day. My husband, you see, is a very hard worker. He was never one to break for lunch. But that is what we have in common. And so for every ceiling rose and plasterboard that he puts up, for every strut and prop, lintel and louvre, I will tear one down.

⚜

My hands are embossed with cuts and scars. One wound never seems to heal before another one is made. My finger-nails, too, are chipped, and beneath each nail I have a black crescent of dirt that I can never get rid of, no matter how hard I scrub. Amidst the coffee grains and the canned tomatoes my finger-nails stand out against the white cotton cloth on the table where we eat.

When I passed my husband his plate this morning I left a dark circle, like a bruise, on the white china rim. Meanwhile, the floorboards clank beneath my feet, flakes of plaster stick in my hair. I keep a stack of unhinged doors and broken four-by-twos beneath the beds, behind the sofas, in the cupboards – although the furniture, too, will eventually have to go. The goldfish room must surely be demolished by now. Sometimes I can almost hear the faint tinkle of glass falling into water.

My husband has begun to comment upon my hands. It is the only thing he has noticed about me for what could be months or even years. My husband once had an eye for detail. So I tell him about the garden, though we must have very little garden left, scarcely a patch six feet by five. I tell him my hands are not used to such hard work, for I must tangle with the thorny stems of roses to make them fat and pink, and plunge my fingers into the rich, dark soil so that the daffodils open yellow as butter. I think that he believes me.

the goddess wakes

the Movie Goddess woke slowly, layers of drugged sleep peeling away from her like heavy blankets. Dream merged muzzily into a kind of reality. Hollywood reality. When at last she opened eyes gluey from long sleep, it was to the fairy-tale scene of an exquisite boudoir hung with swathes of white muslin tied with pink ribbons. For the usual dim moments, the Goddess wondered where she was and slowly remembered that this was her own bedroom. Candlelight filled the room with warm golden light and deep velvety shadows. Candlelight? Was it night then? Still night or another night? And why was she alone? She never woke alone now. Bathsheba, her maid, was always there in the background, flicking the switches that powered down the Venus Machine and coiling up the tubing. Where was she? The drugs in the Machine's nutrient fluid would not let her wake unless the flow was turned off. Unless … Oh God! The Machine was broken.

May Her light shine on all my words

1   Long ago the Children of Earth sinned. A great fire swept the face of the Earth so that even the rocks burned and screamed out in pain.

2   In the time afterward, the few Children of Earth who still lived continued to sin, a great sin; the sin of despair. They lived like animals amidst the grey shells of empty houses, wresting what substance they could from the waste that the greasy scum sea smeared upon the land, and preying upon each other. Their hearts and bodies were sickened by the poison of the great fire.

Meanwhile Irena watched Tally in the firelight. She hated him. Him and his iron-hard fists and his beefy dick that he was always shoving into her. Sometimes she thought of running away from him. She had been twelve years old when the Apocalypse had happened. For almost two years she survived by herself among the ruins. Then she had fallen in with Tally and his tribe. Now she was starting to doubt she'd survive Tally.

It wasn't the beatings that were the problem. It was the rapes. In fact she could even have lived with the rapes if that had been all. But the results terrified her. The women of the tribe couldn't have children. Instead, they squeezed out bloody masses of jelly, hair and finger-nail; squeezed them out in agonizing pain. Irena had seen several women die of these 'births'. She herself had sweated through the birth of her third a week ago. She'd felt its jagged edges ripping at her privates and had feared that it would kill her. It made her think.

Alone among the ruins there would be no further chance of such births. Maybe she should run for it. But could she still face the packs of wild dogs, the constant exhausting vigilance, the aloneness? Loneliness had made her join forces with the tribe in the first place. It was what kept her with them. And she knew, because she'd seen it, that there were much worse tribes to belong to than Tally's.

The rest of Tally's tribe – four other women and two men – were losers. They feared the poisoned wasteland they lived in so much that putting up with Tally's blows was easy for them. Tally was a big lean bully of a man, an office manager before the war. Irena could imagine him humiliating the secretaries. Now he was free to carry out his cruelties any way he liked. Irena tried to hide how much she wanted to escape, but Tally watched her and knew she had disloyal thoughts. He saved his worst for Irena.

So the tribe survived, grubbing food from among the muck washed up by the greasy sea. When the earth shook, as it often did, the sea became dangerous and they moved inland in a nomadic circle, through the sick vegetation and the broken houses of what was all that now remained of the rich and famous. The endless sickness and the hunger left all of them weak and listless. Their bodies were red with sores and twisted and lumpy with growths.

3   Time comes in cycles and brings with it change. The Blessed Seven were then lost Children of the Earth, roaming the land in degradation. And with them roamed the terrible eighth, the Evil One in his human form, who held them in thrall, who deceived and enslaved them. Always he sought the Goddess that he might destroy Her.

4   They did not know that they were living at the beginning of one of the great cycles; that the Goddess was about to take pity on their sinful desolation, manifest Herself among them as flesh and lead them out of despair as She had before and will again.

Blessed be She who brought life forth

Sluggishly the Movie Goddess rolled her heavy head. The panel beside her twinkled with reassuring yellow lights. The Machine was faithfully doing its work. The Movie Goddess let herself doze again, but her sleep was troubled by anxious half-dreams.

After a time she noticed the thin trickle of blood along her wrist. There was moisture under her elbow. The tube of the Machine ... it must have come out of her wrist ... the tube of the Machine was oozing fluid onto the silk sheets. Vaguely she was glad again for the sleeping drugs that the Machine's Beauty Fluid contained. Otherwise that wrist would have stung.

It did sting and so did her other wrist. And her face. Her nightgown was gone. Ooze trickled from between her legs. As consciousness blurred and cleared again, she was disturbed by fleeting memories of men's bodies thrusting into her, memories like landscapes glimpsed from a train, memories mixed in with a shattered kaleidoscope of other thoughts, yet more persistent than the rest. She could not work out if these men were real or phantoms brought back by the drugs.

Finally, she heaved herself upright and looked down at her body. The torn and crumpled nightgown lying against her thigh seemed to suggest that something really had happened. She hoped to God it was nothing the papers would find out about. She sighed. Wishing she could remember last night, she rose unsteadily from the now sodden bed and staggered into the *en suite* bathroom where she washed herself all over with the bottled distilled water kept there for just that purpose. Nothing was too good for the Goddess's precious beauty wherein lay, she knew full well, her fortune.

She examined her face in the mirror and wondered anxiously,

as she did every morning, if there were wrinkles around her eyes. Her cheeks were red. Had someone slapped her? Thankfully it would not bruise. Her lip was cut. She dabbed at the blood with cotton wool. Big tears welled out of her eyes. At that moment the Goddess knew, as surely as she could know anything in her habitual morning haze, that she had been the victim of an unwilling penetration. She would never have used the bald term rape. Nor did she react like a woman raped. She was merely depressed by the certainty. Security guards and alarms protected her from strangers, so these must have been the tender ministrations of 'friends'. She hoped it had been worth it, that she had not been forced to give away her major currency for nothing.

It was not the first morning she had awoken with the vague, revolting memory of the rough penetration of her unwilling body. She hoped, but did not truly expect, that it would be the last. Years of the casting couch had left her philosophical about all the necessary humiliations of the Starlet's life. Her success promised, but did not deliver, immunity to such interference. Her flesh had become hardened to intruders, not just the appendages of the company executives, the producers, the directors, the backers, the leading men, but all the other more subtle intrusions that fame had brought; the movie cameras, the publicity photographs, the journalists, the costumes, the props, the special effects, the make-up, the wigs, the peroxide, the perms, the false eyelashes, the false nails, the plastic surgeon's scalpel, the silicon implants, the amphetamines, the diet pills, the barbiturates.

In fact, her body had even begun to welcome some of them. Most intrusive of all, and most beloved, was the Venus Machine, invented for her by Dr Karls, who was a Very Big Fan. Its hair-fine nylon needles were inserted into her wrists every night as she slept and without fail (for it had its own biochemical power source utilizing the age-making waste products it removed from her body) it pumped through her veins a fluid that nourished and renewed her treasured body while she slept a drug-induced sleep.

It was worth it. All these things were but the necessary unpleasantnesses that accompanied the life of a Movie Queen. They were the price paid for the moments of power she now had, the ability to make whole movie lots tremble, reduce strong directors to tears and make studio heads beg. Most of all, they earnt those rare ecstatic moments of transcendence, of frenzied audience adulation, of adoring wide-eyed recognition, when she knew herself indeed to be the Goddess.

5   Among the broken canyons and sickened trees, the Goddess lay asleep in Her womb of rock and obsidian, pure and perfect. The shaking of the Earth opened the place where She lay, spilling forth the sweet-scented roses that surrounded Her, sanctifying the land all around. The time was ready for the miracle.

6   In their lost wanderings they came upon the Goddess's sleeping place; the Blessed Seven, five women and two men who, led by Holy St Irena, would become Her first servants and finally bring peace and cleansing to the Earth. Even the thorny vines of the roses saw that the Evil One accompanied the Blessed Seven. They knitted their branches together to form a great wall, but they could not hold long against the Evil One's powers. With the Blessed Seven, he penetrated into the Holiest of Holies.

Roses. So beautiful. Irena had not seen such beauty since before the world had ended. Even now, though she burned with anger inside, part of her still had the heart to touch the petals that had fallen on the concrete before her and to marvel at their softness. Earlier, when the tribe had found the roses poking out of a newly opened crack in the rock, it had been like a miracle. They had struggled through that crack, scratched bloody by the sharp thorns of the briars, and beyond ... an even greater miracle.

The walls of the canyon had leaned inwards and twisted, forming a kind of rock cave. In the rose-filled dimness stood treasure; a low, flat-roofed house, its intact picture windows blinded with curtains. It had a cracked, greying marble balcony. From the balcony a set of wrought iron stairs swept down to the gracious poolside patio with its brick barbecue and rusting garden furniture. The pool itself was empty, its white tiles buckled in a thousand places.

It was evening. There was a fire in the barbecue and the tribe sat around it eating. Eating food from cans they had found in the house. Wonderful food. Delicious food. Enough food. Everyone laughed and drank French champagne from green bottles. Everyone except Irena, who did not care for the flavour of champagne. Instead, she crouched by the fire feeding it with dried branches and rose leaves. She did not laugh, but brooded. Brooded and wished Tally dead with all her heart. Her eye was bruised closed and her guts ached from the most recent blows he had given her. She made herself feel better by dreaming up accidents for him. Accidents happened when people got drunk, but dreaming was all she dared do. The others worshipped Tally, relied on him for their survival.

Usually she got scared when Tally was out of control, but she knew that tonight she was safe. When Tally's thoughts turned to violence tonight, they would turn to the strange woman they had found in the house.

She couldn't understand the reaction of the others to the woman. She had understood how they'd reacted when they'd seen the house all right, how they had stood stock silent and stared. Seeing it had made her sad, too. She remembered the beautiful suburban dream she'd grown up in: the nice houses, the shiny cars and the swimming pools. But then the sadness had passed and she'd become excited and impatient. She had rushed forward to open the doors of the house, to see more, to discover the treasure. Tally had chased after her and beaten her heavily for her impudence.

But the woman. Why had they ...? Till then it had been a fairy-tale. They had explored the house by the light of candles Tally had found in the living-room. It was so beautiful, full of carpets and china and mirrors that weren't broken. Time had brushed over this place, bruising it lightly, while in the outside world it had attacked and smashed with clenched fists.

Finally the most fairy-tale part of all. They had entered the bedroom and, pulling aside white muslin hangings tied with pink ribbons, had found the most beautiful woman Irena had ever seen, lying fast asleep. So beautiful and perfect. She had the face of an angel.

7 Behold the Goddess lay manifest. Her shining beauty
was like a star, all Grace and softness, Love incarnate.
She was the light in the darkness, the sun rising, the
promise of hope. Her skin was fresh and perfect,
clean and white as snow, Her soft cheeks shadowed
only by thick dark lashes, Her rosy lips softly parted to
show pearly teeth. Her golden locks crisped gracefully

across the pillow beneath Her, entwining one delicate white hand.

Her breasts heaved peacefully as she slept. Beside her bed was a little machine covered in tiny yellow lights. It made a tiny beeping sound and tubes ran from it to the woman's arms. Even Tally had been amazed. The tribe had stared and stared at this miraculous being before them. The sight had filled Irena with such joy. But not the others. Their faces had filled with a bitterness that she could not understand. With a sudden roar, Tally had launched himself at the bed. 'Gonna make this bitch hurt too!' he'd yelled. The others had cheered.

8   And then darkness. For the Evil One was there too. He it was who committed sacrilege upon the Goddess's innocent and sleeping body, an act through which he sought to defile Her beyond redemption.

He'd raped her. The men of the tribe had ripped aside the soft muslin curtains, torn off the woman's sheer silk nightgown and splayed open her legs so that Tally could take her. Well, perhaps Irena could see the necessity. As the possessor of all this wealth, the woman herself must be possessed to proclaim Tally's domination and his ownership of this place. But they had turned something so beautiful into something ugly and horrible. And why had the other women watched with such malicious pleasure? Didn't they remember what it had been like for them? Irena could, and the sight sickened her.

Tally could not wake the woman to witness her own despoliation. Even during the act, even though Tally slapped her around, she merely stirred and moaned. She did not actually open her eyes. It seemed to madden him; seemed to madden them all.

The other men clamoured for a go. Tally had backhanded one of them and knocked him across the room, ripping down one of the fragile curtains. Irena had not wanted to see what would happen next. As Tally swore and jerked the plastic tubing out of the woman's arm, Irena slipped away. It was she who had saved the fairy-tale princess from further harm, for she had come upon the kitchen and cried out the word that had distracted them; the magical word. Food!

9   But the Goddess in Her wisdom had foreseen his act, had indeed used it. In the end all actions serve Her purposes, for the Goddess is all powerful and all wise. Nothing happens without Her plan. The terrible sacrilege of the Evil One only showed the Goddess's true might. She took his substance into Her womb, changed it, overcame it, bound it to Her own so that it would in time bring forth only goodness, new life and hope, hope and cleansing for the Children of Earth, who had so long despaired.

In her dressing-room the Movie Goddess glanced for reassurance at the little card of contraceptive pills tucked between the bottles of barbiturates. Abortions were a nuisance. But the card only filled her with greater confusion. What day was it anyway? Bathsheba always knew, but where was Bathsheba? As the drugs slackened their grip and the edges of reality firmed, the Goddess became uneasy, more aware that something was wrong. There was no water coming from the taps or toilet, the electric light would not come on and the make-up bottles on her lacy-skirted dressing-table were dusty and disarrayed. Her thoughts were too confused, however, to formulate more than a vague fear.

Instead, as she always did in moments of disturbance, she

.

sat down at her dressing-table, opened one of the jars arrayed before her and with slow, steady movements began the familiar comforting ritual that would bring the Goddess to life. It was a ritual so regular that she was able to perform it even now, when the residue of the drugs snapped the strings of thought and gave the walls strange, paranoiac angles. Opening the exquisite jars of silky creams, with the care of a priestess, she began to cleanse, tone, moisturize and nourish her translucent skin. Expertly she massaged her face, neck and breasts, tweezed her eyebrows, applied eye gel, eye drops and depilatory cream till the face was ready to receive the Face.

With tender fingertips, she applied the layers one by one, smoothed in the foundation, patted on the powder and, with a delicious little brush, stroked on a hint of rouge. Leaning into the mirror, she beautified her big eyes using pencil and shadow brush with the same skill as a monk copying out a holy text, a shaman his runes of power. Sensuously she smoothed on lipstick and lip gloss and used something that looked like an implement of torture to curl her eyelashes. She patted and smoothed and drew until finally ... There She was in the mirror! Transformed! The Goddess of glamour, the Goddess of beauty, the Goddess of love, the Goddess!

It was dark outside and Bathsheba did not answer the bell. But then, since the lights did not work either, the electricity must be cut off. That would explain why Bathsheba did not come. Perhaps an earthquake had happened. The Goddess had been in Hollywood long enough to think little of these. She was no longer troubled. Her vision was tunnelled into her own creation. She was not going to go and look for her maid in a torn nightgown, was not going to leave her *sanctus sanctorum* until she was quite, quite perfect.

She did her surprisingly tangled hair, painted her nails blood-red and after a long process of selection and rejection amongst the clothing in her special wardrobe room, hermetically sealed against dust and moths, put on exactly the right glamorous gown – a body-hugging creation covered in sequins with a plunging neckline to show off her magnificent bosom. Then at last, after a few final pats and an anxious glance in the mirror, she was ready. She took the candlestick and left the room.

The house was dark and quiet. And odd. The Goddess felt a moment of panic, a certainty that something was not right. The house smelt strangely of rot and roses and the skylight in the hallway seemed to be bulging inward as if it were carrying a heavy weight. Had those voices in the house been just phantoms of the drugs? Was this strange dark hallway just a dream? – she had them sometimes. Strange that she could remember almost nothing about the day before, did not know ... But there was steel in her soul. It hardly mattered if this were real or not. She would put on a performance regardless.

'Give them Hell, honey!' the Goddess told herself and launched into the unguessable as she had so often before.

The lush living-room, designed by Luciano and seldom used when she was alone, was empty, but the curtains were open and a breeze blew through the open patio door. Firelight danced against the glass. She could hear them out there. The audience. Talking and laughing. Her pulse quickened. Once again the familiar rituals reasserted themselves. She checked her hair in a nearby mirror. (Dusty! She really would have to say something to Bathsheba.) She posed with the candlestick, holding it in different positions so as to achieve the right effect, but finally abandoning it for a whole candelabra of candles from one of the buffets. At last, holding the candelabra at the most flattering angle and satisfied with the effect, she stepped through the open door and allowed herself to appear to those below.

10   Blessed is She who brings forth New Life
       For Life is Hope
       And in Hope all things are joined
       And the circle is made complete

An astonishing sight met the Goddess's gaze and turned her mind momentarily from the all-important audience. Instead of the familiar back garden with its pleasant lawns and crystal-clear swimming pool, here was a landscape of rocks and uprooted trees. And what had happened to the pool? It was a great empty hole in the earth. The whole thing reminded the Goddess of the plaster and papier mâché scenery of the B-grade Westerns she had starred in early in her career. Surely this could not be real. Surely this must be some kind of dream? Or was this some film that the drugs had made her forget? No matter what it was, she was still the Goddess. The Show must go on.

The eight who sat around the fire, joyously replete, senses reeling with champagne, turned and saw her; saw a vision at the top of the balcony stairs. A shining, translucent vision with a bright halo of golden hair, a perfect, undamaged body that glowed and sparkled and seemed to hover in the very air, a transcendent, glorious, female being. A miracle. A Goddess.

Irena's spine tingled with the pure magic of the moment. Then Tally broke the spell. He must have recognized the threat.

'Get the Bitch!' he shouted, leaping to his feet and running at the Goddess.

11   Even at the moment of Her transcendence the Evil
       One sought to destroy the Goddess. He lifted his
       hand against Her.

The Goddess thrust out the candelabra in a great sweeping arc, for she suddenly had some inkling of danger.

> And She was filled with righteous anger. She struck him down.

Then, as the vision on the balcony waved her arm in a great sweeping gesture, as if at her command, the earth trembled again. The house shuddered and a great piece of the cracked marble balcony broke away and crashed down on Tally's head. It was large enough to obliterate him.

> She crushed him with Her power as She crushes all who offend Her.

When the dust cleared, the vision still stood calmly at the top of the balcony stairs, like an avenging Goddess, the light in her out-thrust hand still bright. Below her lay the great chunk of marble. A tiny line of dark blood seeped out from under it, trickling down between the buckled white tiles of the swimming pool.

The tribe was awe-struck, filled with terror. How could they bear the death of Tally, who had always been their saviour? It seemed to them that they were in the presence of something supernatural. But Irena's joy at Tally's death overcame her fear. She rushed forward and knelt before the rock to make sure that it was indeed true, that he was indeed gone forever. The tribe must have thought she was kneeling to the being on the stairs for suddenly she became aware that they too had knelt.

With rat cunning Irena's brain scampered back and forth across the possibilities. Tally was dead. She must make sure that no one replaced him. She would make sure of it. She must never have to submit to beatings and rapes ever again. The woman who was to become Holy St Irena lifted her eyes to the Goddess on the steps. The future, that monotonous grey line, unfolded, suddenly opening out before her into a million exhilarating vistas, each filled with possibilities.

And the Goddess saw not the strange, ragged bodies of the tribe who crouched below her in the firelight, but their glistening eyes, every one turned intoxicatingly towards her. Every eye filled suddenly with amazement. And hope. As they always did. She saw too the ambition on the face of one of them. It did not trouble her. She recognized it, having seen it often before on the faces of those who had shaped her career. She knew she could satisfy that as well.

widow wilberforce and the lyrebird

i woke one dawn in the bed of someone new, and there she was on the wall.

Nearly hidden by the forest that swirled around her, she sat towards the left-hand back corner, her hand resting comfortably on her cunt. Naked of course, she was aged about forty, her body still strong, her shoulders at right angles to the sides of the frame, but her belly bearing the slight stretch marks that show the beginnings of age. (Or childbirth? No, she'd never had a child. If she had, this tale would be very different – not better, just not the same. Or might not have occurred at all. But where was I?) Her hair was long, reddish-brown, floating into the vines, and her skin was greenish-white like a plant that lives where it rarely feels the sun. I didn't see the lyrebird at that stage. I didn't notice him at all. But when my companion woke at last and I said I loved the woman on the wall, she pointed out the bird – and I wondered how on earth I'd ever missed him.

'But who are they?' I asked. 'What's going on?' I meant, why was this woman lolling about with no clothes on while she watched a lyrebird parade his tail?

She shook her head slightly, as if this weren't the time for questions, but relented and told me what she knew of the story:

'That's the Widow Wilberforce. She lived by herself in the forest and she was in love with a lyrebird.'

'Is that all?'

'Mmmmmmmm ...' She was still beautiful with sleep. As she curled her face into my neck I forgot about the widow. (Tracing the light that falls like vines across your belly, I think how being with you is like seeing myself in a mirror. Is this your breast or mine? Whose hand?)

Later, as we lay smoking and drinking and telling the stories of our lives, she said, 'I always think – for talking with, for drinking with, for sleeping with, women are best, but for fucking it's usually better with a man.'

'Perhaps,' I said, 'but not this morning.'

'Not this morning,' she agreed ...

Afterwards, when I stayed there, I became so used to the widow and the lyrebird that I barely looked at them. Then as the affair turned into a friendship, I spent more time in the kitchen and less in the bedroom, and after a while I forgot about the whole thing. My friend took up with a new man, I went back to my old one, my friend moved to another house, I left my man for the very last time (I swore!) and, to make sure of the fact, headed out of the city.

ᘓᘓ

When some of the local kids told me a witch lived in the forest down at the far corner of the valley, I just smiled. 'Oh yes? Like some lime cordial? A chocolate biscuit? Oh shit, the bushrats have been at them again.' I was much more interested in finding the waterfall that was said to be down there, at a place where two creeks met. I kept promising myself I'd go and look for it, but that first summer I was flat out building a boundary fence, slashing blackberries, painting the kitchen, patching the roof. The place had been deserted for years before I'd bought it and everything was in a shambles. At night, bushrats came into the pantry and stole muesli, dried apricots, spaghetti, jelly crystals … anything that wasn't in a container. Indeed, they would sometimes even manage to get the jars and tins open, and every morning there'd be a trail of crumbs and havoc.

I decided to get a cat, and the idea escalated. I went down town to the little Saturday market and chose a kitten; but she had a sister, so I took her too. Then my friend broke up with her man, moved to a unit, so she had to send down my old black city cat that she'd been minding for me. Suddenly the bushrats were no more. When I still sometimes found the biscuit tin open in the morning, or bright trails of crystals on the shelves, I blamed Sybil and Olivia and Eugenie. I'd hear them in the night, clattering in the pantry, but I was always too tired from a day of brushcutting to go out and yell.

Looking back now, I could tell you other things that happened: the green blanket disappeared; so did my beloved Cretan penknife; there were often fewer oranges in the bowl than I seemed to remember buying; the enamel mug went too; also my special chipping hoe and my binoculars. Biros and paper seemed to get used up quickly, and I was sometimes sure I hadn't run out of beer but … When books (usually crime or romance) went missing (though there was also the Frida Kahlo biography), I naturally thought I'd lent them to someone, and when my Walkman vanished (with the Freddie Fender tape inside – 'Before the Last Teardrop Falls' – my man's farewell gift to me), I blamed my teenage nephew. All the rest just seemed to be part of the entropy that happens to my things: to tell you about it now is to impose a pattern, a set of clues, onto something that I didn't see as part of anything at the time. (I mean, how many times have you gone to the fridge and found the last beer missing? It seems always to be the one that goes first.)

And so it was getting on for winter when I went to look for the waterfall. My heart that day was in such terrible pain. Bugger it, I thought. I was tired of waiting for him to phone, sick of the silence of the empty line. (Did I say we were back on again by long distance? Well kind of. You know what I mean.) So I flicked on the answering machine and went exploring.

⁂

It was a white day, heavy with a mist that rolled up the valley and made my house disappear when I was only fifty metres or so down the ridgeline. I remember glancing back to check that the kittens weren't following me, and it was completely gone.

That made it easier. In earlier walks I had always stuck to the old sheeptracks that meandered through the marginal grazing country that bordered the old road to town; though these dipped occasionally down into the forest. After a short time they always swung reassuringly back within sight of sagging fences, rutted gravel, civilization. Now, however, with no home to lose, I plunged hard left down a steep gradient that took me – skiing first on the heels of my gumboots and then sledging on the arse of my jeans – down down a deep chute cushioned with centuries of soft black leaf-litter until at last my journey was halted by a fallen log.

It had been raining during the night and most of the week before, and fat drops of water were held suspended in lichens or seeped slowly down from the tree-ferns. Far above, the canopy of manna gums and blackwood moved with the breeze, and above that again the occasional crown of a mountain ash dared the wind to topple it. Down here, everything was still, silent, and the ground gave out a heady, brackish smell that made me want to bury my face in this earth that still held the warmth of summer. Compromising, I ran my hand across the pale green furring of moss that coated the log – and found my fingers exploring deep into the secret territory of the soft wood.

I could have stayed there all day, or longer, but was still lured by the idea of a waterfall, so I followed on down the ridge, clambering over yet more logs, ducking under fallen branches, making detours around the uprooted butts of blackwood and gum, skirting the hollowed-out trunks of mountain ash, till at last I reached the creek that ran along the valley floor. Here blackberry had infiltrated heavily, growing along the thin strip of flattish land that ran along the bankline. Working my way downstream in the hope of finding the place where the creek from the next valley came in, I tracked back and forth from this side of the water to that, as the thickness of the blackberry alternated across the banks. Though I could wade through some parts, there were deep pools and miniature rapids where I had to jump from rock to rock, and I found myself thinking that if I slipped and broke my ankle, no one would know, no one would care, I didn't care either, I might as well be dead (Oh why is it always *me* who has the tragic love affairs?), I cried until I didn't know whether the water behind my glasses was rain or tears.

It was some time before I realized I was lost. I had no watch, but felt it must be nearly sunset. The creek zigged and zagged so much – was this really the same creek I'd started out on, or had I met the second one and followed that instead? At times I'd detoured right away from the water to get through the blackberry, so I could be anywhere. The forest around me was now thick and cold, and as I pushed into it again and again –

panicking for a quick way up the ridge to where perhaps my house was, but finding my way blocked each time by a jungle of blackberry or an impenetrable barrier of fallen trees – I started to become pitiful again about my fate, for I knew that I would never find my way home before dark. At last, too exhausted to go on and certain that I would die of exposure, I sat down in a little clearing, pulled out the bottle of whisky from my pack, and decided to at least die drunk.

After a few swigs, it started to get quite pleasant in there. The mist curled around as if it were making a second forest inside the brown and green one, and as the alcohol warmed me I found myself taking off my clothes and starting to dance. The space between the trees was very limited so I just did sort of hopping steps, back and forth across the layers of leaf mould, in time to the wind.

I do not know at what stage I was aware of him. It was like that first sighting in the picture: once I'd seen him, I wondered how I'd ever missed him. His lyre was displayed in all his pride, and he danced in an utterly narcissistic fashion, as if I weren't there at all. Yes, he had the sort of self-absorption that (say) Nijinsky must have had; or perhaps just the vanity of any male.

I realize this is an unsatisfactory way to tell a story: to say, I don't know what happened next …

I woke, and the light was at the same level, the mist was still weaving through the forest, but I knew it was the next morning. I was lying on my japara with my lost green blanket around me, my clothes scrunched up as a pillow, and I had … this is even harder to explain, but I had this feeling that I'd had a fuck.

Then a part of the mist over in the corner of the clearing smelt smoky, and I saw that she had coaxed a fire out of the damp wood and was boiling up a billy. Her body drifted back and forth, greenish-white, until she brought the coffee over in my enamel mug, poured a slug of my whisky into it, then tucked in with me under the blanket. There was enough left in the bottle, so we drank a while and smoked as we told the stories of our lives.

⁂

'Firstly, this idea that I'm a widow isn't right. I was never married. Like you or your friend I simply lived with men – finding them useful for fucking though tedious in conversation and hopeless to sleep with – until eventually I ran away.' She paused, as if considering whether to tell me the next bit, then bitterly she added, 'I didn't know at that stage that there are worse things than men for breaking your heart.'

Her voice started to rise and fall now, one moment wild and throaty, the next barely a whisper, and I knew she was speaking through a collar of tears that sometimes choked the words back. Yet fragments did spill out, disjointed pieces of her passion ...

'The way a lyrebird dances, for instance, or the brush of his wing across your breast –

'The sweep of his tail as he brings it up – and over – like a wave that catches you in the wheel of its momentum –

'As his feet move through the steps –

'And the curl of the two outer feathers traces a shadow across your heart –

'And the blackness of his hard eye –

'That breaks down your morality until you will even steal for his passions ...'

(Yes, the chocolate biscuits, the silver cake decorations, the assorted packets of jelly crystals – she confessed she had taken them; and later when I went to her cave behind the waterfall I found not just the Cretan penknife and Walkman and binoculars and so on, but other things I hadn't even missed: a red collapsible umbrella, my pinking shears, the perspex peppergrinder, a pack of playing-cards, the tiny screwdriver. She would take anything to woo him.)

'How he obsesses you with his tail!' She was going on, as if now she had started she were unable to stop. 'And the games he plays! He'll disappear for days at a time, weeks, even months, and then when you're accustomed to the loss of him he'll turn up out of the blue and take your will again.'

Sweetheart, you've got it bad, I thought.

Her eyes suddenly snapped and now the pain in her voice turned to sheer venom. 'I know he fucks other women.'

I blushed. (*Had we?* I wondered.) She didn't know I'd met him. (But had I really seen him? Or was she describing him so vividly that I was imagining even our dance?)

In the cave, as my eyes became accustomed to the thin green light behind the curtain of water, I realized that this wild and driven side of her was balanced by a practical one. She had a chainsaw, for example, and cut all her own wood (lengths of blackwood were stacked like a giant shop window display of Swiss rolls at the back of her lair) and she grew vegetables around the creek junction in such a way that no strolling trout-fisherperson would ever notice. Just a silverbeet beside this tree-fern, a few carrots amongst the dock, apple and plum trees looking as if they'd self-seeded, potatoes pushing up through the ragwort, and in a hollow screened by a thicket of musk daisy bush there was a patch of pumpkins and onions and beetroot and celery and some huge-leaved rhubarb. And then there was rocket and other winter lettuce as well as all the greens that grew there naturally, dope and watercress of course, and heaps of blackberry ... Indeed, two demijohns of blackberry wine bubbled in the cave, and the shelves were crowded with jars and jars of blackberry jam.

Surely one person could not eat that much jam? Or even one person and a very sweet-toothed lyrebird? She saw me looking at it and explained, 'Sometimes I put on hippie clothes and go to the Saturday market down in town to sell my produce. You know, when I need cash for tampons or chain-oil or something.'

'Oh, yeah ...' I'd never seen her. But then I rarely got down to town.

She waved at the containers of flour and spaghetti and dried lentils and stuff – such as the staples that were always disappearing from my house. 'But it's not enough to keep him. So I have to go out thieving from the farms down along the creek.'

'Aren't you ever seen?' I asked.

'Oh yes,' she shrugged, 'once every so often. Did you know they think I'm a witch?'

As she sat at that moment in the firelight, drinking wine and smoking, shaking her long red hair around like a second set of flames, staring at me with the look of someone who was either slightly mystic or a bit myopic ... 'I can well believe it,' I nodded.

Again my story falters. I guess I should have asked her then how many years she had been there, how long she'd loved him (how long does a lyrebird live?), but though we told of our childhoods and our backgrounds, and swapped accounts of the pain we had suffered in the dark years with our men, somehow she wasn't the sort of person whom one asks direct questions. Particularly not about matters of time. Yet as the day lingered further and further through the wine, she started checking the light in the sky – obviously in the hope that he'd be home soon. Now her talk of him was gentle, how much she loved him, how he was really beautiful, how he was the best fuck she'd ever had, and so on.

I thought I should leave before he arrived so (sliding the penknife off the shelf and into my pocket) I eventually did.

❧

Coming into the kitchen I find the red light of my answering machine blinking like a crisis. One. Two. Three. Four. Five. Six. *Seven* calls.

Press 'Replay'.

They are all him. Not *her* him, of course – not the dancer with the tail – but my very own species of liarbird. I can tell by the way he says nothing down the line.

Just as I make a vow not to do so, I find myself dialling the number of the pub where he usually drinks at this time of the day.

'Where you been?' he demands. 'I been ringing you for weeks.'

Liar. I don't say it.

He laughs. 'Well, days.'

I say nothing again. (But I do start to wonder if maybe it was some time since I had gone down into the forest … *Stop it!* I remind myself. That's how liars work on you – undermining your sense of reality until you doubt even your own story.)

'How you going, anyway?' His voice is warm, golden, with a smile bubbling through the honey of his concern.

I remind myself: *Bastard!*

But as I still do not answer, the familiar noise swirls around him – Charley Pride on the juke-box, the rattle of the money machines, the ebb and flow of conversations, clink of glasses, him breathing in my ear – can I hear that?

Or have I left it too long?

Has he put the receiver down on the bar, left me dangling again, while already he is back on the dance-floor –

Oh why didn't I …?

Why didn't I …?

But here's his voice once more like a drug down the line: 'So you going to move up here and live with me again, or what?'

What sort of choice is that to give a woman in love?

❧

If one day can merge into two – three – a week in the forest, then in the jungle of the city a year can become ten. That's how long it was before I returned.

Oh don't think that my man finally settled down and got the Good Housekeeping Award. Don't think that at all. But after him there were others. What does it matter? They're all the same.

By the time I came back, the fuchsia and rose and honey-suckle in the garden had intertwined from the back porch to the water-tank, and the blackberry had obliterated the boundary fence. Beyond that, the forest had come closer and closer, so now blackwoods and mountain ash towered above me like protective battlements. On a less romantic note, the roof was riddled with holes and the bushrats in the pantry had reached plague proportions.

Feeling somewhat in a state of *déjà vu* I got a kitten, then another one, cleaned down the walls and painted the lounge-room, and then brushcut like crazy to get some of the black-berry cleared by the end of summer. And before the winter rains I'd have to mend that roof, too.

I suppose it must have been late autumn when I finally found time to attack the garden where the tangle now was as thick as if giant kittens had been playing with balls of honeysuckle and blackberry, fuchsia and rambling rose. Some of it could be undone with pick and chainsaw, but most had to be unknotted with secateurs and a rake, for a complex web of water and septic pipes riddled just under the surface of the earth, and I knew that the vital link of the telephone line was hidden there somewhere, too. (Not that I had anyone to wait up for; but still, it's hard to cut yourself off completely.)

Though the area was only the size of a suburban back yard, the vegetation was so thick that it was four days before I got near the septic. I could tell where it was of course – for even through the heady smells that came from the forest there was a faint whiff of seeping ammonia – but I was being so careful not to chip a pipe that I didn't realize that, as I headed towards the old pit, I was uncovering a tunnel that ran along at ground-level, through the matting creepers. When finally I spotted it, I realized it was some kind of pathway for a small animal. Wombat? No, this was too small, and anyway they didn't inhabit this area. My cats perhaps?

It was him, of course. This was his secret highway. And when I reached the end of it I found his new dancing ground, with him upon it.

Yes, the concrete lid of the septic was a perfect platform – so splendidly flat in this hilly country – but it wasn't ugly as it sounds, for a thick layer of moss had grown right across, so he looked as if he were dancing on pale green velvet with those delicate feet of his –

His feet! Even his feet could make you gasp as you felt the rhythm of his dance, beating out a pulse like the sound of blood ringing in your ears, his tail swinging in time – up and over – like a wave that catches you in its roll and takes you and takes you –

I pulled myself up quickly before he could mesmerize me as he had that first time I'd watched him dance. *Egotistical little shit,* I tried to tell myself. Oh look at him there, so self-absorbed he doesn't even know I'm watching …

But my resolution was weak against his spell, and I felt myself being sucked under and sucked under – when suddenly I felt someone watching me, as I was watching him …

⚜

She's standing towards the back corner of the yard, leaning on her hoe. Naked as usual, she must be aged about fifty now, but her body is still strong, her shoulders at right angles to the water-tank. Her hair is long, a deeper red even than I remember, or perhaps it is just the creamy tones of her skin that make it glow like fire.

As on that very first morning, she quite overshadows the competition, so it is only when I see her glance past me that I remember the dancer on the stage.

And now, with her beside me, I start to laugh as I see the lyre-bird parading his tail out, wiggling his bottom, curling up his pointy claws, doing his bow, as he struts his steps to the beat of the song that goes, 'Lady, Do You Want Me For Your Toyboy?'

'He always did have such terrible taste in music!' I find myself saying out loud, and I realize she is laughing, too. We clutch each other for support – roll our eyes – *fancy ever!*

As we leave him to himself and work our way back towards the house, her hoe nips through the telephone line.

⚜

I realize it is not fair to leave so many gaps in the text where the years simply fly off the calendar (they say perhaps it is the number of seasons you get in a day here that makes time disappear into space) but the fact is that I cannot tell you how long it was before we forgot about him completely, or how long it was until we suddenly remembered him again. But I do know that that last remembering of him happened by chance one day when I was weeding the rhubarb – it's such a hungry plant, we grow it around the septic – and to my surprise I found his skeleton between my fingers in the damp earth.

You wouldn't believe how tiny, how insignificant, he had become. Just some white bones, a bit like after a roast chook, though with the flesh picked off by time. A fat worm dangled through his rib-cage. He must've danced himself to death, we reckon. Either that or he died of having no one admire him.

＊＊＊

As I cover the lyrebird back over, I see him dancing again for a moment, just as I had seen him once in the forest near the waterfall, with the mist weaving through the tree-ferns and his splendid tail displayed.

'You've got to admit, he was beautiful,' she tells me.

Oh yes. I agree.

But so are we.

(Tracing the light that falls like vines across your belly – is this your story or mine? Whose heart?)

the pumpkin-eater

i ride this day upon the Worldroad, alone, except for Courage who rides on the pommel of my saddle fluffing his feathers. I did not dream of journeying thus as a child. Maeve told me that women did not travel unaccompanied, especially not beautiful princesses who must wait for their prince to come for them.

Not that I am a princess any longer, nor beautiful enough to make men catch their breath at the sight of me. I wear the trews and knee-boots of a man, and the wind blows my hair wild about my shoulders. I have split ends and chafed lips and my legs and arms are muscular and strong. I have left curling tongs and perfume and silk behind.

Yet I am not ugly. Maeve told me a woman was either beautiful or ugly, but I have learned to be something else altogether. The world has no name for it, yet. Perhaps it is a little fearsome, though, for a commonwoman in her pumpkin house peers out at me in a kind of dread, and her man waves his hoe at me and makes the warding sign to keep off evil. When I was a princess, they bowed and smiled to see me go by, dazzled by my beauty, relieved to see a man riding with me: my keeper. Now, a pedlar passing glares at me and gives me a wide berth in his wagon. He does not know what to make of a woman alone riding the Worldroad. I am neither commonwoman nor princess, but some strange new hybrid. Worst of all, I am manless.

'What will come of it?' I hear him mutter. 'If one rides alone, will not more ride after her?'

꧁꧂

I remember drawing the card of long journeying the year my firstblood came, and the bird of my heart, caged for so long, beat its wings against my breast. I knew it could mean either a physical or mental journey, but this was the third time it had come to me – a trine, summoning all the meanings of the card. So, then, a mental *and* a physical journey. I did not know how long that journey would be, and that not all of it would take place on the road.

I had focused my mind and summoned the earth magic that belongs to women, willing it into my hands as I drew again to see what the journey would entail. I remember the spread as if it were before me now. Under the significator, I laid the four explanatory cards permitted, face down, and crossed them with a fifth. I gave ear to the door, not because of Maeve at her chutneys and sauces in the kitchen, singing tunelessly even though she swore she didn't; but for fear my mother would come and catch me. She might well take the cards and fling them out the window, or tear them up. Worse still, she might just give her cold, cawing laugh, and the Tarot would be forever tainted with her sneers and black mocking glances.

My mother was more silent than not, and bitter-mouthed when she spoke. Sometimes I thought she was insane. I could not imagine how I had come from her, for it seemed to me we were not alike in any way. She was dark, lean and spiky and sombre as a winter tree, and as a child, I was blonde and plump. I decided I must be more like my father. I did not dare ask how he had looked, but I knew that he had blue eyes – mine were blue too – and I extrapolated the rest of him from my own features; shorter than my mother, with smooth creamy skin and pale hair like buttery down.

He had died fighting in the Crusades when I was still in my mother's womb. I knew this only because Maeve, who had come with my mother to the edge of the world afterwards, had let it slip after drinking fermented berry cordial. I learned that the rare indulgences in this small vice offered the best opportunity to wheedle information from her. That and eavesdropping were the only ways I had of learning anything. I did not know what a crusade was, and she would say nothing more about it other than that it was to do with fighting and, therefore, the business of men.

For Maeve the world was divided into nobles and commoners, men and women. I believed her, but I had no intention of letting any of her categories shape me. I would be my own person, I thought blithely, never knowing this would be the hardest thing of all.

'Men's business? Fools' business!' my mother had snarled at her, overhearing us speak of warring. I was glad she did not know how the conversation had begun. A sort of madness seemed to come over her the one time I made the mistake of asking about my father. She began calmly enough, telling me he had ridden up to the tower on a white horse and called to her to let down her golden hair so that he could climb up.

'He was fair as a dream with his eyes full of clouds and his hair slicked down by his mother's spit. When he looked at me, it was like being swallowed up by the sky; drowning in that endless blue.'

'Was that love then?' I had asked eagerly, and then wished I had not, for the black glitter in her eyes seemed to stab out at me.

'Love? Who spoke of love to you?' she hissed.

Maeve, shivering in her boots, confessed. 'She had to know,' she added defiantly. 'You think bringing her here will keep her from it? Love will come riding on a white horse for her, and she will go, just as you did.'

My mother gave a crazed howl of laughter that froze my blood and Maeve hustled me out, clucking under her breath.

'Why did she bring us back here?' I asked, when all was quiet, and Maeve came down at last to give me supper.

'Because of love,' she said with weary sadness. 'Without your father, the palace, the dresses of precious watered silk, the sweetest summer wines, all were meaningless. You see, love is like the sun — it makes everything golden, but when it sets, all is darkness and shadows. Then there is nothing but a tower of one sort or another.'

I understood from this that my mother had brought us back to where she was born, at the edge of the world, because my father died. The death of her love had acted upon her like the bitterest winter frost that bites sometimes to the very soul of a tree, so that it never grows true again, but stunts and shrivels, turning in upon itself. Why else would she choose this draughty lonely tower from which her prince had rescued her, over the summer wine and watered silk she might still have possessed in his palace, though he was gone?

I did not know what watered silk was any more than love, but I imagined they must feel the same: the touch of cold water in the stream on the bare secret places of my body mixed with the feel of petals from the wild brambles round the base of the tower.

I had played at love in the forest after that, in a dress of watered silk, but by the time my firstblood came I had tired of making believe and became strangely restless. Sometimes I felt as if my head was a great echoing space barely occupied by the few things I knew – the tower, the forest, the Worldroad, the domestic secrets Maeve taught me when she was of a mind – how to iron a seam flat and how to remove a stain from white cloth.

The Worldroad sang to me, and I longed for my own prince to come and take me adventuring throughout the world with him. I imagined us riding together, but we would not go where the Crusades were, and the wars and killing. I did not know why men were drawn to such things, but it seemed fighting and bloodletting sang to them as the Worldroad sang to me. But I would keep that deadly music from his ears and we would make a song of our own and he would be grateful to me for saving him.

That was what my mother should have done, instead of letting my father go off alone like that, to be killed. She should not have believed the stories that said a woman does not travel. She should have defied the stories for love.

I did not tell Maeve of my notions, for I knew she would call me a fool and lecture me about the duties of women who must stay in their pumpkins if they were commoners, or in their palaces and towers if they were princesses. I would not argue with her, but I knew my prince would not leave me behind. He would understand the hunger in my heart to see the world and know that it must be fed. He would be glad when I said I would ride with him for, if he loved me, would he not want me with him?

I pushed my mother's voice out of my head, and imagined what I wanted to see in the cards I had laid out – the Knight of Wands coming across the desert bearing the cup in his hands, and perhaps the Ace of Cups, otherwise known as the house of the true heart. And what for the third? The Ten of Cups or, better still, The Lovers.

A journey with a prince who would offer me true love. Maeve told me once that I was a true princess, though my mother had been a commoner before her marriage. A prince must be a prince by blood, but a woman could be raised from commoner to noble by a prince if she was beautiful enough to make him love her.

I turned the first card over.

Woman in trammels, surrounded by swords. My mother had got into the reading after all, for wasn't it from her that I wanted to escape? Her with her swords and binds.

What else? The Beast – a friend in unexpected guise who might even seem to be an enemy. I did not know what that might bode. There was no one in my life but my mother and Maeve. Only a pedlar who came each year when the leaves changed colour.

Could The Beast be the pedlar? Each year I managed to convince myself, before he came, that he was less smelly and silent and unpleasant than I remembered, and would happily take me with him to see the world for the price of my two silver haircombs. Then he would come, fetid of breath and foul of tongue, his eyes sly and shifty, and I would change my mind and remember I was a princess and must wait for my prince.

Yet The Beast gave me pause, for sometimes the prince himself did not fetch the princess in Maeve's stories, but sent an emissary. I could not think a prince would send someone so ugly to fetch his beauty, but sometimes a prince, or more often his mother, tested a princess. Maybe I was supposed to pierce the superficial ugliness of the pedlar and see the beauty of his heart underneath. In stories, princesses always saw and felt things more deeply and truly than other people.

I frowned. The pedlar could not help his looks and it was uncharitable for me to judge him by them. I would be nicer to him when next he came, just in case.

I turned the next card. The Moon with its sickly glamour, and the dogs howling at it – illusions and deceptions. I did not know how that fitted with my journey.

The final explanatory card was The Fool: innocence and ignorance. I shrugged – representing me, no doubt. Well, I was not ashamed to admit that I knew nothing. Ignorance was lack of knowledge, not stupidity. How could I be anything but a fool when no one had ever told me anything? I had never been any-where but the woods surrounding our tower and a little way down the Worldroad, so named, Maeve said, because it leads to everything eventually.

I turned the last card, crossing the rest.

It was the bleakly beautiful Veiled Empress – guardian of mysteries, of secrets yet to be revealed, of wisdoms in waiting. A good card, but, in that position, it represented what lay in the way of what I wanted. It meant I had to find answers to secrets if I were ever to journey.

≈❧≈

Later that day, I found the egg. I almost left it because the shell was broken and though I could see the chick in it, it must be dead. Then I saw its tiny thorn of a claw flex fractionally. I stopped to take it up. The poor wee mite, featherless and blue with cold, was already flyblown, but its life beat feeble as a whisper under my fingertip.

I took it inside and peeled away the shell. I washed off the maggots, dripped sugared water into its thin beak and put it in my handkerchief drawer. When it was a full-grown bantam rooster, and Maeve had stopped talking about roast whitemeat and begun to feed him little messes when she thought I was not looking, I decided it was safe enough to name him. I invoked the cards and drew the Lion of Courage, which speaks of inner strengths and the ability to endure. I took this as an omen, and with Courage on my knee clucking softly in avian contentment, I gazed out of my high turret window at the Worldroad, dreaming patiently of my prince who must surely come before Spring ended.

⁂

On Beltane, we lit the sacred fire and sang the ancient songs thanking the goddess for her bounty, and praising the earth mother. That night, Maeve told me another of her seemingly endless store of stories about princesses. This one was about Cinderine, whose prince found her dirty and cleaning a scullery, terrorized and enslaved by her relatives. He had taken her away to his castle and made her a princess. He had loved her so much, Maeve said, that he could not bear for her to grow old and ugly, so he sealed her up in a diamond so that she would be young and beautiful forever.

That night, I dreamed I was trapped inside a diamond, suffocating and silent. I woke screaming and wondered if Cinderine had allowed her prince to lock her up for the sake of love. I would not have let him shut me up, I thought with a shiver.

For the first time, I thought about beauty. It was a vital ingredient of the princesses and would-be princesses in Maeve's stories, fair or dark, tall or tiny, sweet or cool. Beauty even granted social mobility to commoners. My mother had been a commoner, but so lovely, men had swooned at the sight of her. Because of her beauty, the prince had brought her away to his palace and wed her, transforming her into a princess. But then he had gone away to war.

With the sweat of my nightmare cooling on my skin, it seemed to me suddenly that beauty was a coin with two sides. It was also the reason the women in stories – commoners and princesses alike – were locked up by their fathers and brothers and husbands, as if beauty were a wild thing that men feared might escape and run away. No doubt the men who had swooned at my mother's beauty did not like her any the more for it when they awoke with a bump on their heads, feeling foolish.

I climbed out of my bed and crossed the cold stone floor to stare into the dark mirror over my dressing-table. Was I beautiful? I did not know. I had only my mother and Maeve with whom to compare myself. I did not think Maeve, with her sagging breasts and big feet and hairy eyebrows, was beautiful, and my mother's beauty had surely died long ago. I did not know whether to hope I was beautiful or not. Beauty was clearly dangerous to possess, yet one could not be loved without it. And the only alternative, Maeve said, was ugliness.

If I were ugly, something terrible might happen to me. The ugly sisters or stepmothers in stories often fell into terrible fits of jealousy and either tried to murder the beauty – which was ridiculous because beauty cannot be killed and they would end up getting their heads chopped off, or else, in demented attempts to render themselves beautiful, they would hack off a heel or a toe and bleed to death. At the very least, lacking a beautiful sister or cousin to drive me mad, I was destined to be unsought, unloved, unsung. No one would come to take me journeying on the Worldroad. Without beauty I would be stuck in the tower forever.

I suddenly remembered a thing my mother had once said.

Maeve had been scolding me for playing in a mudpuddle. 'Now you are ugly!' she snapped.

'Would that she were,' my mother had whispered in a voice that shivered my soul. 'Men will kill and die for it, but they cannot bear it once it is theirs. It burns them.' And she had turned her face away from me.

❧

The pedlar came when the leaves had already fallen and the days had grown short and cold. He stared at me as he had not done in other years until Courage flew at him and pecked at his ankles. I decided I had made a mistake in trying to be kind to him. My instincts had told me he was ugly right through, and I should have listened to them. He leered and offered to buy Courage for his cooking pot as I backed away.

When he left, I was glad to see him go, but I understood for the first time that there would be others like him on the Worldroad, and I was glad to think of a prince riding with me to protect me. No wonder women did not travel alone, for who would protect them?

❧

The first snow flew and then it was too cold to swim in the stream, too cold to dance in watered silk, too cold to drink anything but hot milk. The three of us sat in the tower room as close to the fire as we could, working on a tapestry stretched between us and covering our knees.

'I don't know why I bother lighting that fire,' Maeve grumbled, rubbing her swollen fingers. 'That wind steals the warmth before it does any good.'

I looked into the flames and thought the illusion was better than nothing at all. I did not look outside for the ground was now white with snow and the Worldroad had all but vanished. No one travelled in winter. I set my hopes on Spring. Courage shifted and resettled himself under my feet.

Maeve, then, facing the window, was the first to notice the solitary rider. 'Look,' she croaked, nearly swallowing the pin between her lips.

I looked and saw the cloaked figure on a horse and understood that my prince had come at long last. My mother rose and crossed to the window. Coming up behind her I saw that she had driven the point of the needle deep into her palm and three drops of red blood fell into a snow-drift by the window. The sight of that blood against the purity of the snow made me want to vomit.

༄༅

The rider's name was Peter. He had dark hair, sherry brown eyes and a smile that started in them. He was handsome, but he was not a prince.

'My prince has sent me to bring you to his palace,' he said in a voice that was like the first sun after a dark, long winter; something in me thawed and became liquescent.

'A pedlar spoke of a rare beauty in a tower, guarded by a wicked witch.' He coughed apologetically and Maeve shrugged. She knew stories required poetic licence. 'When my prince heard that you were the fairest maid in all the lands he had travelled, and a princess of the blood as well, he swore he would have no other to wed. I had thought to arrive in the Spring, but it is much further to the edge of the world than I realized.'

And he knelt at my feet and paid homage to my beauty. I knew then that I would travel after all, and I smiled down on him in purest joy. He did not swoon, but he did stagger slightly.

Maeve fussed over him and tut-tutted at his wet cloak, insisting he come and sit by her cooking fire to dry while she dished him up some leftover stew from our lunch. It was not proper for a commoner to go up to the tower where my mother was, she whispered, when I said the fire upstairs was nicer. I blushed, feeling like a bumpkin, and he kindly pretended not to notice.

If he had come in spring, we would have left almost immediately. But it was winter, and snow fell and fell, flattening the land's contours so that the trees were nothing more than skeletal shapes etched blackly against all of that whiteness. I chafed at the delay, and when Peter apologized for his lateness saying that besides the distance, there had been storms and forest fires and even a tornado in his path, I understood that the very forces of nature had conspired against me. All was as it should be. Forces were always arrayed to keep the lovers apart in stories – but, inevitably, the obstacles would be overcome.

I felt foolish at having gaped at him like a common girl when he first arrived, imagining him to be the prince, and so I treated him haughtily during the weeks he stayed with us to make up for it, and managed to avoid him by staying in the tower with my mother. To my surprise, she did not try to talk me out of going. Instead, she told me one night in a soft voice that she had wanted to go with my father to the Crusades, but he had waited until she was carrying me before deciding to travel.

'First it is love of them that catches us, then love of a child that binds us forever. Do you understand what I am saying?'

I nodded, but I had understood nothing.

It seemed a long winter. But at last, the snow began to melt, and we left. Maeve wept and bid me be a good girl and wear my long underwear in winter because palaces were even draughtier than towers. My mother would not come down, so I said goodbye to her in her tower room. I kissed the pale cheek she offered, and she told me to remember that the Worldroad led everywhere, even home if you walked it long enough.

I shuddered inwardly at the thought of coming back.

'Goodbye,' I whispered, as the tower with my mother's face at the window and Maeve's plump figure by the door receded and was swallowed up by the whiteness.

～❈～

It was a long journey to the palace where my prince was waiting, and after trying to maintain a chilly silence for several days, I gave it up and asked Peter why the prince had not come for me himself.

'He was hunting and then there was a siege he had to attend,' he explained.

I frowned, for it seemed to me he was saying that these things were more important than me. But I consoled myself with the thought that the prince had not actually seen me yet, and so he could not strictly be in love.

To begin with, I rode on the back of Peter's grey horse, with my bag tied on the back of the saddle and Courage nestled in my bodice near my breast. Maeve had insisted I leave him, saying princesses do not carry fowl in their bosom. I had pretended to give in, but I would not have left him, even if he would have let me. There was some slight trouble the first time we stayed at an inn and the matron there discovered the little bantam when he flew at her from under my pillow.

Peter looked startled, then amused, when the wretched woman taxed him with me keeping dangerous animals in my bedchamber, but somehow he smoothed things over. He accomplished much with his soft voice and warm brown eyes and I found myself thinking of them a good deal too much. He had bought a palfrey for me in one of the bigger towns, and while he was petting her, I imagined what it would be like to have him gentle me in that way. I blushed with shame at my thoughts and hid my confusion in admiration over the mare, which was sweet and white as the finest sugar, and that was what I called her.

When we left the next day, he asked me how I came by the rooster. With as much dignity as I could muster, I explained. He did not laugh but seemed to find it remarkable that I had bothered saving its life.

'Why shouldn't I?' I asked him wonderingly.

Suddenly he looked sad. 'When you get to the palace, you will not be able to keep Courage.'

'Why?' I asked, shocked because I had thought I would be free of rules when I left the tower.

'Princesses do not keep such things as pets. It is not seemly. You must have a cat with green eyes and sable fur, or a golden nightingale to sing to you from its cage. Even Sugar will be exchanged for a finer horse, for she is just a travelling beast. The prince would be embarrassed if you had less than the best.'

And so it went. Bit by bit, I learnt that my prince was proud and demanding and had been much sought after as a husband for these qualities. He had refused to wed until he could be sure his bride was the fairest in all the land. He rode the fastest, finest horse, and collected the most beautiful things to set about in his palace. His gardeners had instructions to bring him only the finest blooms and fruits. If an apple had a single mark, he would fling it from him. Why should he not have the most perfect woman for his bride?

I said, hesitantly, 'Perhaps the prince will find a blemish on me and turn me away.'

Peter blushed and said in his soft voice that there was no blemish on me. His eyes stroked my cheeks and he said that if I were his to love, he would find the most perfect pumpkin and make it into a golden coach for me so that I might dream of travelling the road in it.

But it would still be a pumpkin, my heart whispered. And you would leave me for the song of blood that only men can hear. That night, I dreamed I was a nightingale, singing its heart out behind golden bars.

Then there came a night that Peter said would be our last. The next day, we would reach the palace and I would be handed to my prince. It was nearing the end of Spring again, but the nights were warm. On impulse, I asked Peter if we might not sleep outside by a campfire. He agreed reluctantly. 'But you must not think of such things after this night,' he said in a troubled voice. 'A princess cannot camp out like a gypsy, nor wear bare feet.' He looked pointedly at my toes. 'There will be fine dresses and glass slippers. The prince will not want anything that might hurt you or mar your perfection. He will want you safe. The windows will be curtained so you do not freckle, and fires will burn in every room, even in the Summer, so you will not catch a chill.'

At length, he curled up in his blanket and slept, but I could not sleep. I stared up into a sky ablaze with stars – the diamonds of heaven – and wondered when I would see them again if the windows of the palace were curtained. The breeze fanned my cheeks, and I thought how hot rooms would be where no breeze was allowed to blow. The trees whispered their secrets in the air around me, and life rustled in the leaves and undergrowth. Courage had made himself a little depression in the ground, but he was not asleep either. The sounds of the night seemed to make him restless. His black eyes caught the fire and offered it to me, and I wondered what I would see the next day in the eyes of my prince.

Love and watered silk?

I only knew that I would never be the same again. Love binds beauty, my mother had said. I would never be free to camp outside, or dance in the forest in my bare feet, or swim naked in a cold stream. Sugar and Courage would be lost to me forever, and I would never ride the Worldroad again. Just as my father had done, my prince would possess me and snare me with his love, and leave me with his seed growing, to ride away to blood and glory. And like my mother, the maggot of love and loneliness would gnaw into my heart and soul. I would love and I would hate, but I would never be able to leave because love was the one snare that would bind the wild beauty of a woman.

It occurred to me that none of Maeve's stories ever told what happened after the princess was taken to the palace by her prince, and I thought again of Cinderine trapped in her diamond, imprisoned by love. I got up very quietly, scooped Courage into my arms, and crept to the tree where Sugar was tied.

৵৸৶

That was the first night I rode the Worldroad alone, and the beginning of my true journeying.

Sometimes, I hear my Prince searches still for his vanished princess, but I know it is the dream of beauty he seeks, and not the real woman. And me? I do not regret the loss of love or watered silk or summer wine. Each day I ride feeling the sun or rain on my face, and am content.

The Worldroad is long, and each bend brings some new thing to me. My mind is now filled with the wonders I have seen, all stored as stories. I keep them safe because the World-road leads to all things eventually, and so I know that one day it will bring me to the tower where my mother sits. I will put my arms around her and kiss her and tell her I love her. I will show her all that I have seen, and I will tell her that I have learned one need not be ugly or beautiful, princess or commoner. One can be something else, if one has courage enough to ride alone.

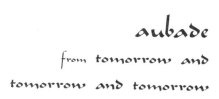

aubade
from tomorrow and
tomorrow and tomorrow

the first light was welling up in the east. In the west a few stars were dying in the colourless sky. The waking sky was enormous and under it the sleeping earth was enormous too. It was a great platter with one edge tilted up into the light, so that the pattern of hills, dark under a gold dust bloom, was visible. The night had been warm and still, as early autumn nights sometimes are, and with a feeling of transience, of breaking ripeness, of doomed fertility, like a woman who does not show her age but whose beauty will crumble under the first grief of hardship. With the dawn, sheets of thin cold air were slipping over the earth, congealing the warmth into a delicate smoking mist. Knarf was glad to wrap his woollen cloak about him. Standing on the flat roof in the dawn he felt giddily tall and, after a night of intense effort, transparent with fatigue. Weariness was spread evenly through his body. He was supersensitively aware of himself, the tension of his skin nervously tightened by long concentration, the vulnerability of his temples, the frailty of his ribs caging his enlarged heart, the civilization of his hands. ... Flesh and imagination were blent and equally receptive. The cold air struck his hot forehead with a shock of excitement, he looked out over the wide sculptury of light, darkness, earth, with new wonder. For a few moments, turning so suddenly from work to idleness, everything had an exaggerated significance. When he drew his fingers along the balustrade, leaving in the thick moisture faint dark marks on its glimmering whiteness, that, too, seemed like a contact, sharply intimate, with the external world where the rising light was beginning to show trees dark and grass grey with that same dew.

Behind Knarf the lamp still burned in the pavilion and the dawn had already diminished and sickened its light. Only one wall, the west, was folded back. It was empty save for the low broad table with its piles of manuscript, a chair in the same pale unornamented wood, the tall lamp, and a couch where Knarf sometimes slept on a summer night with all the walls folded back, like – he told Ren, but his jest had fallen flat – an antique corpse under a canopy. There was no colour except in the bindings of the books piled on the table and spilled on the floor. The frame of the pavilion stood up dark against the golden sky and within the frame the lamplight, at variance with the new daylight, was clotted and impotent. The vapours of a night of effort and struggle could not escape. The empty room was like a sloughed skin. Knarf had been born from it into this new day of which he was so keenly aware.

In this pause between darkness and light he was between two worlds, a reality between two ghosts, a moment of sharp individual consciousness in the drift of centuries. His imagination had been living so vehemently in the past that the present had become only half real. He was standing at a nexus of time. Four hundred years ago, a thousand years ago, dawn among these gentle hills would have seemed no different, to any living eye that had seen it, than it did to him. In a few minutes, so quickly was the light growing, the world of today would be back, incontrovertibly, in its place. But now, for a moment, the old world, the past, might lie under the shadows just as easily as the present. A thousand years ago the country had been covered with bush, a thick mat of it, unending, breaking into natural clearings, closing in again, a shaggy pelt existing for nothing but itself, unknown except to the wandering tribes of the First People, and they, measured against the world they lived in, were newcomers and sojourners. They lived in it according to its terms without changing it or penetrating it. The pattern of their lives wound, like a kabbalistic sign traced in water, through the bush. Their apparently free roaming had followed a set tide. Their food supply, since they did not intervene in nature save in the spearing of game, was bound upon the seasons. Within this cycle of nature was the human cycle, the pattern of contacts, the linking invisible trade routes, the crossing and recrossing of tribe with tribe, the circulation of thought and knowledge as natural and primitive as the circulation of the blood in the body. Within the human cycle was a mystic cycle, the linking of rites and places, of ceremonies that were symbols of symbols forgotten even in the beginning of time but that continued to draw men through old, remembered ways. He thought of the anonymous and indecipherable tracks of the First People which had lain so lightly on these hills. Far away, reduced by distance of time to outline, theirs was only another arrangement of the eternal pattern, of eating, communicating, and reaching out into the unknown. They were gone, completely and utterly, nothing was left of them but a few rock drawings, a few spearheads in rosy quartz, some patterns incised in wood, the words of some songs, soft, melancholy, their meaning forever sealed. Their dust was in this dust, nothing more. In the north, where they had not perished but had been absorbed, their docile blood had mingled without trace and no overt memory of them remained.

Four hundred years ago this country was stripped bare. The delicately moulded hills were naked to the sun and wind and rain, their hoarded fertility broken into and flowing out of them. Knarf remembered the old barbaric name of the river – Murrumbidgee. It had not slipped quiet and full between canal-like banks, tame and sure, as it did today. It held the rich lands in a great gnarled claw, its red banks sculptured into canyons, carved, pillared, eroded, littered with the flotsam of old floods, an ancient tribal river that ruled like a god in these parts. The countryside had been called the Riverina, a gentle fruitful name, a propitiatory name perhaps, much better than Tenth Commune; Knarf would have liked to see the old name in use again. To divide up the earth into squares with a ruler was too arrogant. This earth was not like any other earth, it had its spirit still, even if old god Murrumbidgee was tamed and made to serve it. All that had happened was written in the dust, it didn't end and it wasn't lost, it was woven in.

The river had been a frontier. At the beginning of the dark ages, there had been a migration along and beyond it, – the people who would not make terms thrust out by the pressure from the coast. They had mustered their flocks, piled such goods as they could salvage on to their trucks, and with their families sought the interior. It was here, probably almost at this very spot, that their final decision had had to be made. The waterways had been secured so that they could no longer push along the comparative safety of the river frontages. From here they had struck west and north for the safety of the bad lands. When the trucks had foundered for want of petrol, which happened sooner or later, (nowadays whenever a farmer turned up a rusted shard of metal in the paddocks by the river, he'd claim it was from one of the abandoned trucks – they must have been pretty thick about here, like the detritus of a routed army) they had taken off the wheels, cut down the famous Murrumbidgee gums, the old-man trees, and made themselves rough drays to which they harnessed their horses or their bullocks and they had gone on. No one pursued them, but their needs drove them further and further out. As they reached poorer country they needed more and more of it for their sheep. They could not stick together, they had to scatter. It was every man, or every family, for himself. The years of the migration were good, the country was in good heart and so were the men. They were the descendants of a peculiar people called the Pioneers and, only two or three generations earlier, their forebears had gone out into the wilderness, had come down here from the coast and the city, and, driving out the First People and cutting down the bush, had made a life for themselves. It had been hard and many had perished but others had prospered, grown wise, tough, and rich. They hadn't been afraid of the country and its irregular rhythms. The sons thought they could do it again, or rather they wouldn't believe that they couldn't. They were the great-grandsons, the grandsons, and even the sons of Pioneers, so close was the end to the beginning. History melted down the years between and these followers of a forlorn hope became one with their successful forebears, and were also called 'The Pioneers'. They left their foundered, mortgaged runs, where they had been feeling the long wars like a drought, and set off in a sort of cheerful desperation. If they lost a lot they got rid of a lot too. What had been done once they could do again – but this time it was different. There was not only no way back but there were no resources behind them. For a year or two it was not so bad, while the few things they had brought with them lasted and the seasons were good. Then the situation began to tell on them in earnest. At first they shore their sheep but there was no market for the wool. It decayed and stank and burned in bark sheds. A little of it they made shift to spin into yarn for their own use. Several risked a journey to a southern port with a drayload or two, but it proved too dangerous and unprofitable. They could dispose of the wool readily and secretly but there was little or nothing they could get in exchange. It was useless to keep the flocks save a few small ones to provide meat, yarn, leather, and tallow. They let them go, it was better than confiscation. The sheep wandered over the fenceless pastures. They lambed and wandered on. Their fleeces grew and blinded them, the burden of wool dragged them down till every morning there were some that could not rise and must starve where they lay. Summer and drought pressed hard on them. The waterholes dried up. The sheep died in hundreds and then thousands. Dumb and helpless death was everywhere. The Pioneers had great difficulty in keeping alive the small flocks that were necessary to their own survival. Beside that the death of a myriad sheep meant nothing to them. Even on the coast where there was water and feed people starved and went in rags. One dry summer was enough for the sheep laden with wool.

The men were much harder to break. Others had come after them, a motley crowd of the dispossessed, the angry, the frightened, the hungry, but they had had no staying power, they began to die like the sheep as soon as they had crossed the Murrumbidgee. But the Pioneers endured, long and incredibly. Like the First People, they learned to move from scanty resource to scanty resource, they valued nothing but water and food and perhaps the antique fetish, liberty, but that would not be a word they ever troubled to speak. It was something they could not help having and for which they had no use. They were as tough, as thin, and almost as black from the sun, as the First People had been, but, unlike the First People, they had no festivals, no corroborees, no old rites. They were scaled down to something below that. It is said that as a people they stopped breeding.

They could not or would not return and no effort was ever made to bring them back. Such people were useless for the building of a new world. A few may have straggled back, but very few. The great majority was lost. After twenty or even thirty years there would be a few survivors, madmen living in caves with their phantom dogs beside them, men gone native with the last of the tribes, gone crazy.

That wasn't the history you found in history books, it was local legend. Knarf believed it and Ord said it was true. He had known it for a long time but only this morning did it seem completely real. He was smitten, he supposed, with imaginative conviction. It was often like that. Knowledge lay dead in his brain, so much ready-made merchandise on its shelves, and then, often for no obvious reason, it quickened and became part of the small, living, and productive part of his mind. In the shadowy morning light he could trick himself into seeing the Pioneers moving down to the river in neutral coloured cavalcade, flocks of sheep travelling over the brown plain beyond in a haze of dust, tall, brown, laconic men in dusty clothes, their heterogeneous belongings piled on the makeshift vehicles already weathered to drabness, the slow flight into country without cover. ... There were people far out west, in the next commune, old or lonely or simple people, who in unguarded moments told stories of the Pioneers. Solitary travellers had seen camp fires in the bush. When they approached, the fire had been burning brightly with a skeleton sitting beside it, bushman fashion, on his heels. Their ghosts are thick round waterholes, and if you spend a night there you cannot sleep for the rattle of hobble chains and the stamping of horses that will have left no trace in the morning. The strange dog seen at twilight is no mortal dog but the mythical folkdog, the Kelpie, 'too faithful to die', as they say. When cattle stampede in the night they say 'It's the Pioneers.' Sometimes, it is said, they pass through on a moonlight night, you hear the rustle of sheep's feet in the dust, the creek and clatter of riders, and even men's voices singing in an archaic dialect, and in the morning there will be broken fences and eaten out paddocks but not a mark in the dust of the road or a single dropping of dung. ... But no one ever caught up with this legend, it had always happened farther on. It was like the Hosting of the Sidhe, Ord said, thrusting it farther back into the world that was his own province.

There must be a good deal of Pioneer blood about here still, Knarf thought. He'd often noticed, though it wasn't a thing anyone talked about, that the inlanders were taller, looser, leaner than the men on the coast, with less of the orient in their faces. Blood mixed slowly even after all this time.

With his back to the east Knarf had been straining his eyes into the west. The light had grown imperceptibly. It collected on objects like dew. The river was already a broad silver band. At his feet there was still a well of darkness, a well full of sleep, but farther away the white houses of the square and along the bank of the river were visible. By concentration, sight could rescue the dark lines of trees and even pick out, across the river, the black and grey pattern of the irrigated orchards and gardens. As yet there was no colour, only assembling shapes. The river was quicksilver between dark banks.

In a few minutes now the past would be buried again under the present. The scene he knew so well and loved so deeply would cover and supersede the figment of his imagination which had had for the moment the intense overstrung reality of things that pass. He would see, not the shaggy olive green hills of the beginning, nor the bare hills of the twentieth century with their chromatic swing from the new green of the rains through silvers and browns to the naked brown purple of the earth, stripped and compressed by drought; not the irregular wasteful pattern of land overdriven and under-used, but the lovely design of safe and steady fruitfulness. It was a bright picture, where there had never been a bright picture before. If a man of the First People had stood here he would have seen only a monotone, or perhaps no more than the mazing pattern of narrow leaves against the sky. To the Pioneer it would have been a variation in pale colours, country under threat, a threnody for the wind. And yet – it must have been lovely. It might even have had something the present lacked. Eyes that had known it would be homesick today. Man might turn away from surfeits to pine for hard and meagre fare. To think of the Pioneers as a people who had ravaged the country, left it denuded and helpless and then had gone out, irrationally and obstinately, to die with the country, to become in the last resort place-spirits, the half-evil genii of the soil, was a poet's conception. Life was lived as fully then as now, now as then. This, that looks so sleek, is only an approximation too.

The Australians, of whom the Pioneers were part, had been the second people. They had been so few, never more than eight or nine million in the whole continent. They had been a very strange people, full of contradictions, adaptable and obstinate. With courage and endurance they had pioneered the land, only to ruin it with greed and lack of forethought. They had drawn a

hardy independence from the soil and had maintained it with
pride and yet they had allowed themselves to be dispossessed by
the most fantastic tyranny the world had ever known, money in
the hands of the few, an unreal, an imaginary, system driving out
reality. They had their hardbitten realism and yet they co-operated
in the suicidal fiction of production for profit instead of for
use. They thought of Australia as a land of plenty and yet they
consented to starve among the plenty. They lost the reality of
their land to the fantasy of the Banks. They looked always to
Government for redress and assistance but they were always
scornful of their governments and with a persistent lawless streak
in them. They loved their country and exalted patriotism as if it
were a virtue, and yet they gave a greater love to a little island in
the North Sea that many of them had never seen. They were
hard drinkers and yet had puritanical prejudices and made diffi-
culties against the purchase of their drink. Inherent gamblers,
they legislated against gambling and then broke their own laws
systematically and as a matter of course. Lovers of horseflesh,
they had no feeling for the animals, sheep and cattle, by which
they lived. They praised the country but lived in the cities, or they
grumbled eternally of the land but would not leave it. There was
no measuring their pride and yet they were unsure. They tried to
live alone in the world when their whole civilization was in the
melting pot. They called the North the East and the Near North
the Far East and it was to them an unknown place of mystery
and menace. They were a fighting people – but not at home.
They settled their differences at home by other means. The small
people was prodigal of its armies; generation after generation,
they swarmed out to fight and die in strange places and for strange
causes. Tough, sardonic, humorous, they were romantics the like
of which the world had never seen. Crusaders without a crusade,

they fought for any cause that offered or for the simulacrum of a cause. They went to South Africa to fight against a people small and liberty loving as themselves. They fought in France and Flanders, Egypt, Palestine, Mesopotamia, for an imperial design from which they themselves sought to escape. Within a generation they were fighting throughout the world, for what they scarcely knew, for brave words and a coloured rag, for things that were only names being already lost. They fought with tenacity and *élan*, the bravest of the brave. Or was that the incurable romanticism of history? Knarf didn't think so, there were facts and figures to support it.

All that, and yet they weren't a belligerent people. It was as if there were two people, indistinguishable in peace time, the fighting tribe – the Anzacs, as they came to be called – and the others who didn't fight. At the first drawing of the sword the cleavage showed and apparently they accepted it. The armies were volunteer, both sections of the community joined together to refuse conscription. It was one of their gestures of freedom, the curious truncated liberty to which they held.

Knarf could think of the Australians as living in a perpetual high gale of unreason. Their whole life was stormy and perverse. They were city-dwellers and their cities were great vortices of energy that carried them nowhere. They strove enormously for the thing called profit. In competition men's efforts cancelled out, one against another; they could succeed only, one at the expense of another, but when competition merged into monopoly they were worse off, for as the forces became more powerful they were more destructive. A terrible logic worked itself out. There were those who saw the end coming and cried their warnings, but helplessly. When a man is caught in a conveyor belt he is not saved by realizing his danger.

Life went like a cart on square wheels. Their houses were choked with useless objects and meaningless ornament, their shops with wasteful luxuries. Yet men were hungry. There was always too much and too little, never enough. Nothing was secure, neither bread nor faith, and man's confidence in himself and in his fellows was at last ruined by the cajolery of the advertiser and propagandist, for advertising and propaganda were spokes in the wheel whose hub and circumference were profit, the iron wheel that ground men into gold which cannot nourish. It was all mad and strange and wanton, it poisoned itself and had issue in violence and violence begot death. 'The Australian Fairytale' Lunda had called his book, a story so fantastic and remote that it was difficult to think of these people as fully human. That was the trouble with historians. They dealt in curios. They wanted to surprise their readers and to flatter today. The queer things had happened but they weren't the whole, any more than the stone stripped of its rosy pulp and glowing skin is the fruit. It had been life in a different key, it had been transposed not lost.

The Australians coming after the First People, disinheriting rather than inheriting from them, had laid a different pattern on the earth, a free pattern, asymmetrical, never completed, because their life was so disrupted, complex, and unreasoning. They had brought in the rhythm of flocks and crops, but that had never quite formed because the seasons to which they were bound were irregular then as now; there must always have been a sort of counterpoint. The imported beasts and grains must have striven with the blind instinct of their life to fulfil each its immemorial cycle, only to be thwarted by the irregularity of the climate, the unstable incidence of the rains. The pattern had been pulled aside, crazed, until after centuries of effort an adjustment, not perfect, but adequate, had been reached. The life of the Australians themselves had been based in part on this new fertility pattern which they had brought and were holding to the land rather by their obstinacy than by their reason, and in part on their political and economic conceptions, a flow of opposites, wealth and poverty, freedom and slavery, till you had a design in cross currents, in negations, in contradictions, that reflected itself, as it must, in the patterns traced by civilization on the earth itself. Knarf could see it from the watchtower of time – the clotting of life into cities, the irregular scattering of habitations over the country, the thousand and one reasons, apart from the main scientific reason – the only legitimate one, people would tell you – that were allowed to influence or even direct development, the haphazard network of the roads, the inequality of the dwellings, the movements of people and goods based on the fantasy of supply and demand. ... After the simple incised pattern of the First People the Australians had left a sunken maze. Each people had reflected its own way of life in its design. The First People had lived scientifically, following a rational, adjusted, permanent design. The fragments of the handiwork and ornaments that survived were in the likeness of their lives, simple arrangements of lines and dots, naturalistic representations of animals, designs fed not by shallow concep-tions of beauty but by deeper fountains of meaning. They were few or repeated. The Australians, having overthrown reason and ignored adjustment in the interests of their fantastic conceptions, begot a multiplicity of hybrid, unco-ordinated patterns and left upon the earth itself a half-meaningless scrabble. Their move-ments had been turbid and without rhythm. There had been a constant flux through the country of men looking for work, the need constant, the opportunity fluctuating with times and seasons. Few, even of those who were 'settled', could retain their place for long; economic forces levered them out, sent them circulating rootless through the country or gravitating towards the cities. Then would come a change of wind, a thing called Depression, and many of those who had been drawn into the cities would be driven out again, travelling the roads looking for bread, to die on the roads as the last of the Pioneers died in the deserts but unsentimentalized, unregarded. ...

The Australians had brought a new sort of death to the continent, – not overt violence but the unregarded, unrecorded death of dumb men and beasts, bound luckless upon the machine. Death as the unplanned by-product, the leakage of the system, – animals caught by drought on overstocked pastures, men caught by depression in overproduced cities, a needless repeating pattern – the softfooted death with the look of accident was not accident, but a part of the relentless logic of a way of life: the loneliness of condoned death. All this side by side with pride and courage and independence, unvisualized for what it was. Knarf shivered in the dawn. This was one of the moments when, his spirit worn thin, he was oppressed by all the suffering that there had been in the world, especially the pitiful unrecorded suffering of those who died without redress or drama. It was as if he saw it still, like a lava stain upon the hills he loved so much. We may be just as blind, he thought, and because blind, cruel – or because secretly cruel, blind. They weren't inferior to us in mind or heart.

They loved this place, Knarf thought, they were the first to love it for it wasn't possible to think of the First People formulating an emotion so explicit and detached. He caught a glimpse of the landscape he could as yet hardly see, through the eyes of his imagination, as they must have seen it four centuries ago.

He was brushed for a moment by that excitement of the spirit which was the secret manna of his gifts. These hills, these wide horizons, these aboriginal contours, unchanging and unchangeable, must have had an added lustre against the background of a more turbid world. We don't know peace, he thought, because we take it for granted. Life is not so fiercely indented as it used to be, more evenly spread, and so even our eyes cannot know the quality that this earth once had. It wasn't only the loveliness of peace, it was peace over against turmoil, it was refuge, it was home. If the sky was empty and the horizon unbroken, that was rest. These were not hills, they were the gentle breasts of the earth. Like a man suddenly realizing that his retreat is cut off by the tide, Knarf thought 'I belong as much with them as with today, with the Australians as with my own generation of a people who have no name.'

one last picture
of ruby-rose

(a letter to kevin arnett)

dear Kevin Arnett

I am writing to you to ask for help. I have told my story over and over and over again – to the social worker, the psychiatrist, the police and the solicitor – but nobody will believe me. I am in custody in the psychiatric ward now.

Nobody else believes me, but I know you will, even if you can't explain what has happened to me. There might be other people you have heard of who have experienced this, others who have written in to your TV programme of 'The Extraordinary'. I think that if I were a different person with more education and money, instead of a single mother from St Kilda, people might be more prepared to listen to me, to take me seriously. What happened to me hasn't even been reported in the papers because they think it's all the ravings of a madwoman. They take flying saucers and everything pretty seriously these days don't they, so why not this?

I will start at the beginning of the story, start with the birth of Ruby-Rose. It was a normal birth in the Women's Hospital, but nothing was normal after that. My baby was beautiful, but they told me straight away she would be retarded, and she probably wouldn't live to be five. I refused to accept this. I took her to every specialist I could find – some of them were kind, but most of them just asked me questions about smoking and drinking and dope and sex. Then I started going to alternative treatments and astrology and Tarot. The only person who gave me any hope at all was a Koori woman, Maeve, who reads Tarot in St Kilda. She was always positive and gave me a lot of strength. Things were going to turn out right for Ruby-Rose, I knew that in my heart.

I said she was a beautiful baby, and she got more lovely as time went on. I took photos of her from birth, and this got to be an obsession with me. I have thousands of pictures of my baby. I will enclose some so you can see. She cried a lot, but when she wasn't crying she had a smile that lit her face up.

Well time went on and Ruby-Rose turned one and then two and she was getting stronger and by the time she was three I thought she was even trying to talk.

Then on the morning of her third birthday something happened that I think is somehow connected with what happened after that. I feel you will understand when I tell you.

Ruby-Rose and I went for a walk in the gardens – she loved the gardens, loved flowers and birds. I was taking heaps of pictures of her. She was wearing her birthday dress and it was white with frills and she looked like an angel. A man who was walking in the gardens stopped us and said oh what a little angel and Ruby-Rose jumped up and down and laughed in a way she had. Then not long after that she was running – she had a cute little way she would run – and suddenly she tripped over a rock and sat down. She didn't cry out, but she bent over and fished something out of the grass and held it up. I looked and saw she was holding something metal. She gave it to me and it was a brooch, a silver ballet dancer with a skirt made from opal.

I've always been superstitious about opal – my mother said it was unlucky. We were all named after stones – my name's Amber – but Mum said she would never call a person Opal. Yet Maeve says it's really lucky, so you don't know who to believe. I still had this worry about it – from what Mum used to say. But Ruby-Rose was so happy because she had found a treasure in the grass. So we took the dancer home and I cleaned it up until it shone. It was a lovely little thing. Like a lot of mothers I used to imagine my daughter would become a dancer. Just a dream.

Ruby-Rose's treasures are kept on the mantelpiece under the mirror. She liked me to hold her up to the mirror and she would see herself and laugh and put another treasure on the ledge, or else take something down to look at. Well, I held her up to the mantelpiece to put the dancer with the other things, and Ruby-Rose reached up – and when she let it go the silver ballet dancer slipped down behind the mantelpiece, out of sight between the wooden part and the wall.

I expected Ruby-Rose to scream, but she just went rigid in my arms, and a look of pure astonishment came over her face. I said not to worry, it didn't matter, and one of the men from the flat downstairs would help us look for it, would take the mantelpiece off the wall and find the dancer again. She seemed to accept that, but I was strangely worried. It was the opal I think – it was getting to me.

Then we had her party and she sat up to the table in her white dress like a little angel. We had six other children from the crèche and one other little handicapped child who cried all the time. It was sad. Maeve was there to help me with things and Ruby-Rose had a really lovely party with all the usual stuff like chocolate crackles and party pies. I took a lot of pictures. After it was all over Maeve helped me with the clearing up and then she left. I wish now she had stayed.

I'd practically forgotten all about the silver dancer behind the mantelpiece, then Ruby-Rose went over to the fireplace and started patting the wood with her hands and looking up at me. I told her that after one more sleep I'd get Tom or Ben from downstairs to come and help us fish the dancer out. Just one more sleep. She accepted that and then she fell asleep in my arms, worn out by the excitement of the day.

At times like this I would sit very quiet in the armchair and stroke her forehead and stare down into her face and wonder how it could ever be that she would be taken from me. Sometimes I would cry – I couldn't help myself.

We're coming to the part that nobody can believe. Well Maeve believes it, but of course nobody believes Maeve either.

I took off her shoes and put Ruby-Rose down in her cot and she hardly stirred. She lay there in her white dress that was all crumpled and dirty. I thought she looked more beautiful than ever. I am trying to remember every detail in case you can see something nobody else has noticed.

I thought of going downstairs and asking one of the men to come and get the dancer out. But I didn't go. I was tired. I thought I'd take a picture of Ruby-Rose in her sleep. As well as taking photos with my ordinary camera, I had been taking Polaroids of the party. There were some left.

I picked up the camera, stood on the chair, focused on her face with one curl across her forehead, and I pressed the button. I watched the white shiny square as it rolled out of the camera, held it for a while as I watched the picture form before my eyes.

I like seeing it do that. There she was, pink cheeks, golden hair, dark eyelashes, grubby white dress – a picture of bliss.

I look back at the cot.

Ruby-Rose is gone.

This is why I need your help. Over and over again I have told them – I took a picture of my baby and when the camera made the picture it swallowed Ruby-Rose. Or something swallowed Ruby-Rose. She faded out somehow – just as the picture of her was appearing on the paper. They think I killed her and hid her body. I have told them – I took the picture and the camera sucked her in.

They took the picture away from me. I've got thousands of other pictures, but that's the one I want. She left a little warm dent in the cot, no more. Her shoes were still on the floor where I had put them.

My mind goes back to the opal dancer, to the bad luck. I wonder if the dancer had anything to do with it. I'm desperate in my search for an explanation – crazy with grief. I got in touch with Tom and Ben and they said they went upstairs to the flat and pulled the wood off but they couldn't find any dancer. They said there were just spider-webs and a tram ticket and some hairslides. I know the thing fell down behind the mantelpiece. I saw it with my own eyes – but nobody believes what I saw with my own eyes any more. Where did the silver dancer go? It's so weird, and I've racked my brains for an explanation. There has to be some connection between Ruby-Rose and the dancer. There just has to be.

But what?

Please Kevin Arnett, can you please write to me and tell me if you have ever heard of such a thing before? I swear to you that every single thing I have written here is the truth. And something else as well I'd like to ask you – would there be any way you could persuade them to give me back the photo? That would mean more to me than anything.

It's the last picture I ever took of Ruby-Rose.

Thanking you
Yours sincerely

Amber-May Wilson

angel thing

the angel thing arrived in a flash of light and a roar of thunder. My grandfather brought it late one night, very late — we were all in bed. A car on a country road at night sounds like the rushing of Jehovah's winds, but I didn't hear this one until it was upon us. The flare of headlights through the venetian blinds threw barred shadows across my face. I was blinded like a rabbit pinned down by the spotlight. What could have been the clapping of wings was the clash of gears. They crunched into silence and I held my breath. Car doors slammed; there were men's voices, but no words. And then another man's voice, from the verandah, my father. 'Evening,' he was saying. He was opening the screen door and going out onto the verandah. I hadn't heard him take the rifle from behind the door, hadn't heard him break it and load it and snap it back together, that double click with a tiny echo ringing down the barrel. So it was all right, he knew who it was.

Mum came in with her brunch-coat on over her summer nightie. 'Dad says we're not to go out. There are men here.'

It used to be that Mum and Dad were the grown-ups, and I was the child. Now I was like her, or she was like me. She seemed to think we both had something to be ashamed about. I'd started to bleed early and Mum said, 'Now you're a woman.' She didn't seem happy about it, but then she often wasted time being unhappy about things she could do nothing about. I was very fond of my mother, but I didn't think she had much sense.

'Shove over,' said Mum. 'Let me in.'

She wasn't all that much older than me – my father kept saying we could be sisters and my mother kept saying, 'But I'm not your daughter.' But Dad treated us the same – sometimes he laughed at us and sometimes he shouted at us. I didn't know why she let him. When I got older, I wasn't going to let him.

'Is Grandad here?'

'Now how did you know your grandfather was here? You never cease to amaze me.' I was keeping quiet, I didn't want her to know I could feel my grandfather's presence on her, feel her shrink inside herself.

'Why is he here?'

'Church business.'

We both knew what the other thought about Grandad and his church. Neither of them liked girls very much, even if Grandad did like kissing us, wet kisses on our lips that my mother and I wiped away as soon as we could. We lay in bed and pulled all the blankets over us, though it was getting too hot for that. I knew my mother felt safer that way as we listened to the men who weren't meant to see us.

They were making loud footsteps and grunting, and there was a squeaky sound, like a rusty bicycle being wheeled across the dirt. Then more grunting and thumping at the verandah steps and the bicycle again, scraping across the boards of the side verandah, which was the other side of the house to our room. The noises stopped, but I thought I could hear the door of the sleepout slam.

Then there was the chink of cups on saucers in the kitchen and the men's voices started up again in there – they sounded like the sheep bleating far off. My mother was deceived, or maybe she was so tired she just went back to sleep. I wasn't so tired that I couldn't wonder what my grandfather was up to now.

If my grandfather didn't like me, I didn't like him any better. I couldn't understand why everyone else we knew liked him a lot, liked him so much they usually did what he said. My mother didn't like him either, although she did what he said, too. She did what he said because she had to, and she didn't like that either. He frightened her, but I wasn't frightened of him, I just didn't like him, that was all. My grandfather, I felt, needed keeping an eye on.

I didn't put on my jiffies to keep my feet clean, but skated barefoot across the lino of the breezeway. The sliding door into the kitchen never closed properly – I could huddle up against the wall and look through the slit to a slice of the kitchen as narrow as the edge of a knife. All I could see was a sliver of my father, his feet thrust into work-boots without socks and his trousers on over his pyjamas. The one eye I could see was looking eager, but nervous – the way his dogs looked at him – so when he spoke I knew he was talking to my grandfather.

Still it wasn't interesting. They were talking about what they always talked about – rain, even though we hadn't had any for years and years. It was all anyone could ever talk about. I used to be interested because my father kept telling me about all the things I could have when it rained – dresses and a pony and trips to the city. He'd say it to me but he'd keep looking at my mother, so I knew he was really telling her. But my mother would walk away while he was still talking and it never rained and I never got these things and I was beginning to walk away when he talked like this, too. But now my father seemed to think it would come soon. It was always coming soon.

'The angel of the Lord,' he was saying. 'That'll bring it.' But he was grinning, not reverent the way he should be when he talked of the Lord and his angels. I waited for my grandfather to remind him, but there was no reminder. My father kept talking. 'That'll bring them, bring the prayers and bring the rain. The angel of the Lord,' he said again, repeating himself as though he'd had a beer or two, though I knew he never had a beer when my grandfather was around. 'The angel of the Lord.'

We heard about angels all the time in church. Our lives were crowded with angels. My favourite was the guardian angels, but there were lots of others – attendant angels, avenging angels, recording angels, angels of mercy, angels of death. I was getting bored – angels were old news. I started to shiver – the days were getting hot but it was still chilly just before dawn. He kept talking and my grandfather didn't say anything, so I slid back to my bed where my mother was a nice soft bundle to warm me into sleep. When the car started again it was present in my dreams as thunder or the whoosh of wings departing.

I was dreaming of rain. I'd been quite young the last time I'd heard it, but I remembered what it sounded like: the sound that dots make. In my dream it rained and it rained and it rained until the land was covered with water and the house floated away. There was a big rope leading up into the sky that was tethered to the house. I looked up and there was an angel at the other end of the rope, towing us away.

When I woke up the next day, Mum was already up. I could hear her arguing with Dad in the kitchen. It was still cool, my feet were bare on the lino floor and goosebumps prickled up my calves.

Dad told me, 'We have a guest.'

'Don't stare,' said my mother edgily.

The bicycle noises had been made by a wheelchair, now pulled up to the kitchen table. Our guest was slumped in the wheelchair, its legs covered by a cloth. I was careful not to stare at them. Instead, I stared at the face. It didn't seem to be looking back.

'It's a friend of your grandfather's,' my father told me, 'who needed a place to stay.'

'And your father in his kindness has offered,' my mother said.

'Dad asked me. What did you want me to say?'

I realized instantly that this was the angel of the Lord that my father had been referring to, although it wasn't the same as the one in my dream. It had done something with its wings. I looked behind it, looking for where its wings should be, but it was pushed up against the back of the chair and I couldn't see. Half of the face was hidden by hair as fine as feathers, a yellow so pale it was almost white. But the half I could see was skin tightened over the skull. Eyelids drooped over eyes that were blue with only a dot of black at the centre. I got up close and peered into those eyes. It was like looking into a cloudless sky, no sign of rain. Dad and Grandad and everyone else except my mother always frowned at skies like that. 'Always the city girl', my father would say disapprovingly. My mother didn't take skies seriously enough.

Instead, she would name the blue for me: cobalt, indigo,

ultramarine. I could see those colours in the angel's eyes. I got up so close I could feel the cold coming off its skin, like it had just come out of the refrigerator.

'What are you doing? Leave it alone!' It was one of his roars – not as good as Grandad's, but still frightening. It always made both of us jump and fall back with a jelly feeling in our stomachs.

'She's only curious,' said my mother. 'Maybe it's good. I'll need her to help me look after it.'

'There's not much to look after, Mum,' he said.

'I'm not your mother,' said my mother. 'I'm not its mother.'

Our kitchen table is laminex – green laminex – like a green plain with a pattern of white rivers. I can trace out a landscape on that table-top, flat as the country that surrounds us. Facing the wall, I've mapped the territory all around my place at the table while my parents sit at either end and argue from edge to edge. I take a journey now by boat, maybe a raft, poling along the white rivers while far away on another waterless plain my mother and father argue.

'It doesn't eat,' said Dad. 'There's stuff you give it – in injections, I've got them, I'm sure you can take care of it.'

'And washing it? And sitting it on a potty and cleaning it afterwards? Am I to take care of that, too?'

'You don't need to. It's not human like us, it doesn't need that, it's just a thing. The injections are sort of like watering it, like a plant. And there's other stuff in the injections to keep it quiet. We can leave it in the sleepout for the time being.'

'For the time being? How long are we meant to have it for?'

'They just need a place to put it aside for a while.'

'Put it aside? Why?'

'Listen,' said my father earnestly, 'we're hiding it, all right? They're playing God out there, they're trying to make people like machines and this is one of their failed attempts. The church rescued it. They've asked me to deal with it.'

'Did you ask me if I wanted to deal with this person they made?'

'It's just a thing. It's a thing they had made up – like an experiment – but it didn't work out.'

'Made up? Made up out of what? For what? Who're these people who've asked you to deal with it?'

'Important people,' said my father, trying to sound important himself.

'You mean your father?'

'He's important to us, too right! This place is still in his name. If you want to get rid of it, tell him to come and get it.' And my father escaped outside where my mother's voice would be muffled by the sky.

My mother sat staring at the angel thing, left behind with us. It sat like it had been thrown into its chair, slumped like a doll. I tried to pull it upright, but it was quite heavy for something so fragile-looking. It felt as dry as paper, as though its skin would tear if I handled it too roughly. I rearranged its arms instead.

'What are you doing?' asked my mother.

I jumped and bit my tongue, but my mother couldn't frighten me like my father or grandfather.

'Looking for its wings,' I said.

'What do you mean, its wings?'

'Angels have wings,' I explained.

It made perfect sense to me. We were beset by angels, according to my grandfather, but most populous were the angels that had fallen. It was not so surprising that one had fallen into our lives. But my mother was not so keen on angels, she was not so keen on the church, come to that. I didn't expect her to be pleased, and she wasn't.

'I'm going to ring your grandfather,' she said. 'I'm going to tell him he can keep his angels and his crazy ideas, and stop passing them on to my daughter.'

My mother was about to get herself into trouble with my grandfather. Like I said, she had no sense. 'He didn't pass them on, I thought of it all by myself, I saw the angel in my dream ...' But my half-lies only made it worse.

'You've been cooped up inside for too long,' she said, and threatened to send me outside for a walk. It was a terrible thing for her to say; I knew she felt that outside could make you feel more cooped up than inside. So I was quiet while she rang my grandfather, so quiet I could hear the phone ringing in his kitchen and the voice that said hello. It wasn't him, it was one of the many women that always seemed to be in his kitchen, cooking his meals, cleaning his house. His wives, my father called them, but never when he could hear.

The wife who answered was reverential about his time, didn't think he could come to the phone, but my mother insisted.

My grandfather had a voice that could be as soft as rain and as loud as thunder. Now it belled out as I heard him say, 'Daughter.'

My mother's hand clenched on the receiver but her voice was calm. 'Good morning, father. How are you keeping?'

They talked no-talk for a while, they both knew the questions and the answers, about how he was – good – and how my mother was – good – and how my father was – good – until finally they got to how I was and then my mother broke the pattern.

'She's not so good.' I was proud of my mother, even if she didn't have any sense, she was so brave to be saying what she was saying to my grandfather. 'This – this thing you've left with us, father, we've got a child in the house and I think she's a bit young for an influence like this, she's a high-strung child, she doesn't understand properly, she's getting it fixed in her head that this – this thing you've left is some kind of angel.' My mother gulped. 'She's got such an imagination, I don't think it's good for her.'

Neither of us could believe that she was saying what she was saying. She was whispering at the end of it – I was surprised my grandfather could hear her at all. He had dropped his voice in response, soft as rain, I couldn't hear his words, going on and on, but I saw them on my mother's face. 'No, father, no, that won't be necessary. Yes, I can deal with it – with her and the – the angel thing. No, I won't tell anybody. Yes, I'm sure it's a good idea.'

The day had hotted up but she looked cold and pinched as she hung up. 'He reminded me,' she said, 'he reminded me that he'd offered to send you to school in the city, a good church school where you'd get proper instruction.'

'He said a lot more than that,' I said. Sometimes you had to be firm with my mother, it was the only way.

But all she said was, 'He repeats himself a lot,' and I knew there was something she wasn't telling me. And then to herself, 'He's going mad.'

It was all very worrying. That was the only way my grandfather could frighten me, by frightening my mother. I listened very carefully for everything she said about the angel to my father, and then she repeated that his father was beginning to think he was God, not just his servant.

'Dad's smarter than that, hon,' said my father.

'What's this about making rain, then? Angels who can bring rain. You don't really believe that, do you?'

'Course I don't. But there are a lot who will, a lot who will believe it if my father says *he* does. We may not bring them rain, love, but we'll deliver faith. And hope. What's wrong with giving people hope?'

'Everything, if that's all you can give them.'

My father just laughed and said, 'Think of the congregation this will get us!'

My mother said, 'At least some can harvest a good crop in this drought.' My father laughed again but told her not to repeat this to my grandfather and went back to the paddocks.

After that my mother ignored the angel as much as possible. She ignored it so successfully she forgot some of its injections. I didn't dare remind her, but when I saw the angel's lips move, working against each other, I thought I knew and ran for a straw and a glass of water. I had to work the straw between its teeth, which were shut tight. Its lips felt like iceblocks, but I had guessed right. The movements were suction and it drained the glass. I kept up the refills until the angel was blowing bubbles.

I didn't tell my mother, not even when the angel wet itself, and the chair, and the floor. I mopped up the floor and left the angel to dry. This was quick at midday, but the heat had another side-effect.

My mother said to my father, 'That thing has started to smell.'

'Leave it, love,' said my father uneasily. 'It isn't like it matters. And they'll be back for it soon.'

'How soon?' my mother wanted to know, but my father was already gone. 'How soon?' my mother demanded of the angel. 'How long am I going to have this stinking thing in my kitchen?' She and the angel looked back at each other for a while, and it was my mother's eyes that fell. When she raised her eyes back to its face, she spoke to it as she might have spoken to me, stating a fact. 'We do have to do something about that smell, you know.'

'It must need a bath,' I said.

'We don't have the water for that.' We were sharing the same bathwater as it was, a few inches in the tub, and some nights we only had what my mother called a duck bath – a basin of water and a washer. My mother seemed to like the angel more now that she had yelled at it, but still not enough to share its bathwater. Definitely not enough to give it a wash. I wanted her to go on liking the angel more.

'We could take it to the baths.' I knew this was the right thing to say, my mother loved the baths. Every country town had a pool – virulent green lawns bordering an acid blue rectangle of water, as precious as the most beautiful water gardens during the drought. Our pool was known for the hot springs that stank so bad they had to be good for you. A lot of people came from down south just to use the springs, so the angel wouldn't stand out so much as being different. She could swim in her underwear – a lot of people did – and maybe it would warm her up.

'Dunk her like a biscuit?' said my mother. 'At least it'll get us out of the house.'

I realized I'd made a mistake. My father doesn't like my

mother taking off just like that. He says his mother had one day every week for going into town, and so everyone knew where they were, and he could place his orders and so forth. My mother tried to restrain herself, but sometimes, like now, she just wanted to get into the jeep and go. So we did.

We bumped over the dry creekbed at our boundary like a roller-coaster; dry because it had been dammed higher up. But even the dam was dry now. We did a figure eight there and back, hollering with the thrill as the jeep bounced and veered and threw up dust. We could have been the only thing moving under the afternoon sun, and we could see from edge to edge, not a hill, barely a tree. We were a long way from town, but the road was almost straight except for one right-angled turn around the boundaries of a property so big its owner could insist that public roads respect his private property. It was out of sight of our place, which was a good thing because my mother took that corner without slowing down. Dad had said she was ruining the vehicles, the speed she drove, and why was she in such a hurry to get to town anyway? My mother said then that that bend in the road was the only one she had in her life, and she'd get all the excitement out of it she could. Dad had asked, 'What about the kid?'

But I always felt quite safe when my mother drove.

The back tyres slid and squealed, red dust smoked from under them and plumed out after us. The dust cloud blanked out the rear window. We could have come from anywhere. I strained my seatbelt to hang over the back seat and watch. My mother and I squealed along with the wheels.

'Look,' said my mother. 'The first lamb. Poor little thing.' The dusty ewes lay like cushions strewn on the bleached grass, panting in the heat. Everything was the colour of the dirt, except that little speck of new-washed, new-born white. 'Poor little thing,' said my mother again. 'No feed for it or its mum.'

'They'll turn the lambing ewes into the crop,' I said practically. My mother knows nothing about farming, although she's lived in the country for longer than I have. 'See, the wheat's dying off already.'

In the next paddock, the little green stalks of new wheat were already turning yellow. Daubed in on the soil they looked like writing looked to me before I learned to read, telling some story I was unable to understand. But I could read these signs – even my mother was literate to this extent.

'Another year of drought,' she said drearily. 'Another little sacrificial lamb.'

We had forgotten the angel thing, bundled into the back seat, but the turn must have pushed it upright against the door behind me. Its head was bumping against the glass, the yellow-white hair falling over its face. I swivelled round to prop its head up. Its skin felt warmer, just chilly, not ice-cold. Maybe it was the wind rushing over its face that had pulled its lips back, maybe it was smiling. 'Look, Mum, look!' My mother adjusted the rear view mirror and inspected the angel. 'Maybe it thought it was flying again,' I suggested.

'Maybe,' said my mother, and slowed down.

The smell of the pool reaches out into the street like a fog. I pushed the angel thing through the special doors they had for wheelchairs while my mother paid for us all at the turnstile. Together we edged the chair over the plastic matting down the corridor to the women's pool. It was a tight fit in the changing cubicle, but we could do it if I stood on the bench.

When my mother took the cover off the angel's legs, they were skinny but didn't look so different to anyone else's. I wondered why they had to be hidden.

'Get into your cossie,' said my mother brightly. 'And don't stare.'

I wriggled into my swimsuit while my mother worked the cotton dress up and over the angel's body, but I could still look. So I could see why my mother gasped and pulled the dress down again, quickly. The angel wasn't wearing underwear. 'She's like me,' I said. 'She hasn't grown hair yet.'

'She can wear my slip into the pool,' said my mother. 'You get behind and help me to pull it over her head, all right?'

I knew my mother didn't want me to see the angel thing without underwear, but what I saw was even worse. When my mother pulled her forward she looked hump-backed, as if she had her wings curled up in there. But when her dress was pulled up there were no wings; you could see it was muscles, really big muscles that twitched and jumped as if they were feeling something that wasn't there. Or maybe they were trying to shrug off the big scars that ran down over her shoulder-blades.

'That's what happened to her wings,' I said. 'See? You can see where they've been cut off.' My mother didn't say anything. She looked at the scars and didn't say anything.

The angel was very light to lift down the steps that led into the water. I helped with her legs and they weighed almost nothing at all. 'She weighs no more than a bird,' said my mother as the hot water lapped us up.

'Did you know,' I said instructively, 'that birds have hollow bones? That's why people can't fly. Even if they had wings sewn onto their shoulders, they'd be too heavy.'

We put the angel down on the seat built underwater, but then we had to hold her there so she wouldn't float off.

'Look, she's flying,' I said. 'She's really flying now, isn't she, Mum?'

'Yes,' said my mother. 'Really flying.'

The angel was definitely smiling now, it wasn't me imagining it. Her pupils were growing. It looked like they were getting closer. 'The angel is getting nearer to us.'

'Coming in to land,' said my mother. 'Are you reading me yet?' she said to the angel. She said it as if she were joking, but neither of us laughed.

If I'd thought of the angel as having a voice, I would have said it would rumble like thunder in the distance. Instead it mewled, a piping noise like a small bird very close.

'Hurt,' I thought it said. 'Hurt.'

It was like a table talking, or one of the cattle, it was like a person bursting out of a thing. My mother shied away from it, flailing at the water. I stayed close to the angel, staring into its eyes like they were the sky and I was reading it, frowning the way Dad and Grandad frowned at a cloudless sky, making it tell them things. I wanted the angel to tell me things.

'Who hurt you?' I asked, and I was saying it in the voice my father used to order me around, the voice my grandfather used on him. Because I was part of them as well as myself, I knew the answer to my question even as I asked. 'It was them, wasn't it?' Maybe not my grandfather in person, definitely not my father because he wouldn't, but men like them. We weren't looking after the angel, we were keeping it prisoner. I turned to my mother and told her, in case she hadn't heard, 'It was them. It was the church.'

The angel was still making little noises, there may have been words. 'Did it say lamb?' I asked my mother. 'I thought it said lamb, but why would it?'

My mother drew breath so sharply it seemed to cut her throat, she made a sound as strange as any of the angel's. 'It couldn't be that,' she said. 'Oh no, oh no. There's been a mistake, can't you see? There's been a mistake, but I'll tell your father about it and he'll fix it up.'

I don't know why I still have faith in my mother after all these years when I also know that she has no sense at all when it comes to my father. My mother has known my father for longer than I have, but she still has faith in him. And he has faith in my grandfather, and my grandfather has faith in God, and so there was nothing to be done to fix it up because they all – we all – had faith in someone who didn't deserve it.

My grandfather's Landcruiser was parked in the carport when we got home and my father was standing in front of it, like he was barring our way. He was holding a gun. Not the rifle, the .22 – that was for rabbits and crows and warning shots – but the .303, the shotgun for slaughtering steers. My mother would never let me watch when my father used that gun. She hated guns.

'Dad's not feeling too good about you taking this thing out in public, like,' said my father unhappily.

My grandfather was not a big man, but his presence spread like oil. When we looked up at the house, we already knew he was there, standing in the shadows of the verandah. On the whole, I thought the gun was less of a worry.

'We reckon it isn't safe, having it around. I said so to Dad and he said that maybe I was right, maybe I should do something about it.'

My mother hated that, hated it when my father spoke for his father as though they'd decided something together when everyone knew my grandfather could work him like a sheep-dog. She pushed past my father, pushing aside the shotgun like a turnstile, crossing the line from the glare in the yard to the darkness under the verandah to confront my grandfather. Left in the jeep, I could only squint across the blaze of light to their dim figures, my mother's arms flailing as if she were still swimming, my grandfather standing still in the gloom. My mother's voice carried, high-pitched with tears.

'Its wings,' said my mother, and I could hear the angel's piping in her voice. 'Why'd they have to cut off its wings?'

'It had to be done,' said my grandfather. He was using his preacher's voice; the words rolled out to me in the jeep.

'It was uncontrollable, hon,' my father called to her from his post by the gate. The gun was still pointed towards us in the jeep, swinging from his hand, but all his attention was focused on his own house. 'It would've tried to escape ...'

My mother ran back to the edge of the verandah where the light met the shade. Her eyes were masked. All I could see was her mouth stretched by the amount of grief it encompassed. 'You did it,' said my mother. 'Oh my god, you did it.'

'It's just a thing, honey, just an animal, made to look like a person.'

'It spoke,' cried my mother. 'It spoke to me and I looked into its eyes and I saw it had a soul.'

'Honey –' said my father helplessly, looking back to where my grandfather was standing.

'It's just a thing, a thing that was made to deceive, and I didn't think you'd fall for it,' said my grandfather to her back.

'Didn't think you'd fall for it, a smart city girl like you.' My mother ignored him.

'And how many people here d'you think are going to fall for this lamb of your father's?' said my mother. 'This sacrificial lamb? Is it the blood of this lamb that will bring the rain?'

My grandfather walked past her out into the light. He didn't push past her, but she made way for him, cringing back. He didn't look at her, but went to my father's side before he turned to face her. He isn't a big man, my grandfather; his son my father towers over him, twice as broad, but the evening sun threw a shadow that covered him. 'Jesus gave his life to save us,' said my grandfather softly. However softly he spoke, he could always be heard. 'Compared to that, what's the life of something that was never really alive worth?'

'It's as alive as I am,' said my mother. 'It's a person like I am. I'm going to tell everyone that. I'm going to tell everyone what you're doing.'

My grandfather looked at her, but spoke to my father. 'Your wife told me it was a bad influence on your little girl. I didn't know it was a bad influence on her as well. She asked me to do something about it. I think we should.'

I knew what my father was going to do with the gun by the way he handled it; lifting it, but not aiming. 'Get it out of the jeep,' he said to me. 'I don't want the upholstery spoilt.'

I'd watched my father fire guns before, heaps of times. It was like thunder and lightning, the crack sounded in one place, the flash struck in another, and the flash was death. A crop-nibbling rabbit, a little lamb that was crying because it had no eyes, or the crow that had picked them out; there had always been a reason. This was the first time I thought the death unreasonable.

'You can't do that, Dad,' I said, astounded that he'd even think it. 'You can't do that.'

'No,' agreed my mother quite calmly, 'you can't do that. I'm taking it away.' And she started walking towards the jeep, putting herself between the angel and the gun. My father started to scream after her to come back, to come back right now. My grandfather's voice cut through his yelling as if it weren't there.

'You won't get far,' said my grandfather. 'We'll have all righteous people looking out for it ... and you and the jeep. How far do you think you'll get?' And he took the gun from my father.

My mother turned at the jeep door to face him and the gun. 'Reckon I have to find out,' she said.

As she turned back to get into the jeep, my father lunged at her from behind, the way he tackled other men when he played football on the weekends. He pulled her away from the door and threw her on the ground, and then reached across the steering-wheel to grab me and haul me out of the jeep. I yelled and clamped onto the wheel.

I didn't see the angel move, I only felt its impact as it pushed me, the feather-light hair brushing my bare arms as I hit my father's chest. I was winded and my father was thrown back a couple of feet, as if he'd been thrown from a horse. As he hit the ground, the gun in my grandfather's hands went off so loudly I thought I had been hit in the head, but it was only the noise deafening me. In the awful silence, there was another explosion like an echo of the gun. Thunder.

Dark clouds boiled up in the sky as if they were hurrying to make up lost time. The rain fell so quickly my mother was drenched before she got into the jeep, as if a bucket of water had been emptied over her. The rain fell so hard my father and grandfather were beaten back. My grandfather roared over the roaring of the water, 'You won't get far.'

'Reckon I have to find out,' said my mother to herself. Then she put her foot down on the accelerator, and she wasn't to lift it till we'd outrun the rain.

As we skidded out the gate, I turned and watched through the rear window. My father was trying to run after us, falling and sprawling in the mud. My grandfather was headed back into the house. 'He'll phone,' I yelped. 'He's going to phone.'

Lightning struck the phone lines just after we'd passed under them. A pole, felled like a tree, brought the cable down for a hundred yards on either side. We almost lost traction in the mud, but I barely noticed. My grandfather ran out of the house and fought his way through the rain to his Landcruiser. The bigger vehicle kept the road better. He was gaining on us as we reached the creek bed, already filling. My mother didn't slow down, but churned right through it at her usual speed, raising sprays of water where earlier that day we had raised sprays of dust. The sprays hid the tidal wave bearing down on us from the broken dam. The surge of water hit us side on. It was almost as high as the windows, almost capsized us. We slewed around to face it and surfed backwards towards the opposite bank, reaching it just before it, too, was engulfed. The wheels spun, gripped and shot us forward in a spurt of mud. I caught it right across my face as I leaned out the window to watch the flood lift my grandfather's Landcruiser and bear it away.

The rain soon washed the mud from my face, though it was slackening off. It was a nice steady downfall as we went through the town. I don't think anyone noticed us and the angel particularly, though everyone was out on the streets. Some people were jumping around, others were just standing there, eyes shut, as if they were praying.

We were on the other side of town before I thought to ask my mother where we were going. 'The city, I suppose,' she said. 'In the city they'll know what to do with the angel. How to help it.'

I wasn't so sure the angel needed help. It had brought rain when we needed help, but what could we do for it? There was no point trying to tell my mother this. I dozed off in the passenger seat. My head was tossed from side to side as we slid around the road, but I always felt safe when my mother drove. And at every turn I felt that we were being steadied by the drag of angel wings.

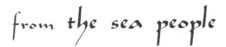

from the sea people

i turned the silver ring on my finger round and round as a bald bishop stepped inside our convent – the first man ever here.

He wanted to close it down.

A few days before he arrived, a nun took from my finger this ancient ring with the worn band and the five Ps engraved on it. She sewed it, along with a few gold coins, into the hem of my cloak.

'The ring's from your mother and her mother before that and then hers – back to hundreds of years ago.'

And she taught me a prayer to say each night so no harm would come to me.

'Parce pater patrum papissae predere partum.'

I garbled it after her until she was satisfied I could remember it. She told me it was the secret meaning of the five Ps: that one day I would understand it.

❧

So I came to my mistress's house at the age of ten with my only wealth, the silver P ring, on my finger. 'Parcepaterpatrumpapissae-predererepartum,' I gibbered each night.

My mistress took my gold coins and my prayer and my family ring did not save me from being sold into service. But thanks to the sisters I can sing seventy-six songs of praise to Mary Mother, Mary Magdalene and her husband Jesus, and play at the Tarot cards where Pope Joan's face is on the card called La Papesse. I always draw that card (a good omen) and she looks like me.

≈

Now I am sixteen and still in service, and wings of fairies brush my cheeks as I walk out over the bogs, and devils make me stumble over rocks when I climb mountains.

My days are empty as the desert.

My life has not begun yet.

This is not my life.

One day my bridegroom will come and everything will fall into place. My life will begin.

When I am chosen.

I refuse to believe my place, for the rest of my life, is this spinning for flannel, minding the pigs that play in the grey surf, gathering kelp onto the panniers on the mule's back and helping the men as they burn it in the kilns on the shore. They leave it to cool, until it's so hard we need hammers to break it before they pack it up to sell as medicine in the town. We prepare iodine from it, for wounds and dressings and for inflamed joints.

I'm sensitive to the very sight of seaweed – it makes me break out in a rash. But at least when I gather kelp I'm outside. We clamber over the limestone rocks in our wet raw cowskin shoes with the fur turned outside and laced at the heel and over the toe. We have to remember to soak them in water at night and to walk in the shallows in the day so that they don't dry out.

There's not much waiting on tables here as we eat little. During the day we drink tea and eat slices of home-made bread or some potatoes when we are hungry. We have no set time for meals except when there are guests.

The sea and sky are always grey here so we like to wear red petticoats dyed with madder and plaid shawls crossed over our chests and tied at the back. When it rains, we throw another petticoat over our heads with the waistband round our faces or a heavy shawl. Our skirts finish at the knees and show our strong legs, fine from wearing nothing but pampooties.

The men won't wear the red; they wear only the grey and cream and indigo flannel we weave for them.

They say the women on our island are the most beautiful. We are all tall and our red skirts are finely woven. It's because of our beauty that the fairies are always stealing us away – the whole fairy host seems centred on our island. The men say that the fairies are after us because we resemble royalty in our bearing, the way wild horses resemble thoroughbreds, not cart-horses.

The fairies are the followers of Lucifer. When Lucifer saw himself in the looking-glass he thought he was as handsome as God. So God tossed him out of heaven with all his followers. But an Archangel took pity on them and asked God to spare them, so God saved those who were still falling in the air and they became the fairies with the power to wreck ships and work evil in the world.

We are always watching out for fairies round every dark corner, and hearing their horses in the night as the waves crash against the shore. The wind blows hard because there are no trees on the island and I wonder fearfully when the fairies will take me away from here, to where my real life can begin.

entropy

fragments of information linger from school-days. 'The entropy of a system is a measure of its degree of disorder.' Is it a mistake to educate females? This house is a closed system; I know, I'm enclosed within it. Its total entropy is increasing, heading towards complete disorder of its particles, and I haven't been able to stop it!

Bits of me are flaking off now, right now, incessantly. I try to prevent it by not moving, by being utterly still, but I know it's happening. I've read about it, seen it on television. An electron microscope trained on my skin would show the outermost cells of the derma wither and loosen. They lift off like tattered snowflakes to pollute the air. Entropy, disorder. I can't help it, can't stop it.

With every breath, no matter how small, tiny beads of moisture spray from my mouth and nose and cling damply to the furniture and curtains. I can't not breathe, can I? They melt the dust into black sludge, and I'm eternally wiping it, rinsing it, washing it. Even with all the windows and doors shut, the dust gets in and it's dirty, so dirty here, despite all I've done.

'You dirty little girl! Stop that this instant and tidy your room. It's a pigsty!'

I hear the voice all the time now, reminding me how dirty I am. Internally or externally, it doesn't quite say. Maybe it doesn't have to; maybe I should know.

I nearly had it under control, though. Once, other vices drowned it out. A lover's voice, a husband's voice, children's voices. They were powerful and I drew on that power for as long as I could, until things began to change.

It started with the budgerigar. Such a small beginning, but then entropy would start small, wouldn't it, and work up? Isn't that the way of the universe?

'God it's good coming home to you and the kids. You're the perfect wife.' This was the voice that mattered most, that disproved the other one. It affirmed my cleanliness of body and soul; the house sparkled.

That was before the budgerigar, before the cat and the dog, when the children were little. Then they grew, and the pets came, and we were still happy for a while. I polished the furniture and sucked dust mites from the pillows with the vacuum cleaner's special attachment, both of us humming. The voice that told me I was a dirty little girl was far away, dim and listless. The house was clean, *I* was clean, I had a most intense happiness to prove it.

'I'll be working. I'll be late.' It was innocent enough at first. Occasional. I smiled and kept dinner warm for him. But soon it was never just working, but always workinglate. One word, the way he said it. Workinglate. The budgerigar's pale blue and white fluff blew on the most vagrant of breezes right through the house, impossible to sweep. Tiny feathers curled with balls of dust in corners and husks scattered and crackled underfoot. *'Dirty!'*

'Will you clean up after that damned bird!' I'd shout at the children. But they weren't efficient. They'd miss where the quills and seeds and grainy pieces of cuttlefish shell lodged in the narrow gaps between the skirting board and the carpet and I'd have to follow them, crouched down to pick at the mess with my finger-nails. The untidiness of it appalled me while the budgie flapped in its cage, sending up further explosions of debris. I was angrily sweeping and vacuuming five, six times a day and he was workinglate. *'Dirty little girl!'* It was the budgerigar's fault.

The cat watched the budgie's flutterings with wide slick eyes. I watched the cat, sitting erect on its haunches, tail curled round its feet, taut. I opened the little hatch of the bird cage and left the room, closing the door behind me.

Some time later I let the cat out and spent a considerable time cleaning up the room. It was amazing how far the feathers had flown; the tops of the pelmets and the fan blades were glazed with sky-blue down. But working, I felt lighter and freer; the source of disorder was gone, entropy routed. I was clean again.

The children missed the budgerigar for a little.

He continued workinglate.

I cleaned the fly-spots from the cornice and bought extra insecticide to remove the flies. I took the glass domes from the light fittings and washed their interiors. *'No man wants a dirty little girl who does that!'* I tried to make the house as perfect as possible for him, but it was such a large house, so much scope for untidiness.

The cat was part-Persian. It had long silky grey fur that trailed almost to the ground as it ambled down the hallway, shedding.

I had thought cats to be clean animals, but then I realized that for it to be clean, it must distribute its dirt elsewhere. *Ipso facto.* I watched it sit and lick itself, and grains of dust and hair rained from its body. Furry wisps matted with the material of the furniture and clogged the vacuum cleaner. Cleaning the filter, I found myself trembling with anger.

'My housework would be cut in half without that cat,' I suggested nervously one day. Caught in their own interests, no one answered. The children ran off to school. He ran off to worklate.

My role was more active this time. The mess was worse, but worth it.

Of course the children cried a little over the cat's straying, but that soon passed; he hardly remarked upon it. I thought then that having avoided the menace of entropy once again, I could relax. He would approve of the way the house gleamed and come home earlier. The voice would go away. I cleaned and cooked proudly, as I used to when we were happy.

But he went on workinglate. The voice continued to snap at me. I fought against the total disorder of particles. I polished the windows and picked the dust from the screens mote by mote. I leaned inside the wardrobes and renewed the vinyl drawer-linings. With stiffening sore hands I scrubbed the minute algal dots of mildew from the white woodwork, unable to understand. The house is clean, *ergo sum!*

Except ... It came to me one day as I sat slumped at the table, exhausted, and noticed the dog chewing at its rump. Small stiff white hairs scattered over the floor as it worked. It had brought in tiny pieces of dried grass and sand on its paws, and threads of drool trailed to the floor as it slobbered. It lay in a welter of filth. *That* was why I was sweeping and sweeping and dusting and dusting and never getting the house clean *enough!* I was close to tears as the truth overwhelmed me. '*What a dirty little girl!*' Not me, not me, the *dog!*

The children were hysterical for a short time after the dog went missing. It took a bottle of bleach and three bottles of Pine-O-Cleen to entirely remove the traces. He didn't even notice it was gone.

The feeling of relief was lyrical. I luxuriated in my beautiful house, free of the filthy harbingers of entropy. To celebrate, I washed all the walls and ceilings and waited for him to stop workinglate.

I stripped the polished floor in the lounge and revarnished it, and waited. I shampooed the carpets and washed and ironed the curtains, still waiting. I used a toothbrush to scour the stainless-steel kitchen sink to a dull gleam, and rewashed the light fittings to brighten them, waiting. '*Dirty, dirty, dirty ...*'

The house loomed even larger and I started all over again.

My temper became erratic. Somehow a frog came inside one day and I found it climbing up the kitchen window, smudging the sparkling glass with tiny viscous footprints. I screamed and grabbed it and threw it into the garbage disposal unit and the unit screamed back at me. I had to clean the sink again.

Still he was workinglate. It was as if I never cleaned the house at all, despite my desperate fatigue; as if I was eternally condemned to dirt.

I picked up toys mechanically and removed sneaker scuff-marks from the floors. There was crayon graffiti on the wallpaper one day, and lint from a torn stuffed toy littered a chair another. Dust blew in relentless clouds through the door the children carelessly left open. *'Pig!'*

I worked and worked and worked to right it all, but he still workedlate, so I knew I wasn't righting it enough. Entropy was gaining. I moved through each day with cold knots of panic in my stomach. There was just so much – toothpaste smears on the bathroom sink, oily lumps of butter and Vegemite from a sandwich dropped carelessly against the cupboard door, milk spilt on the carpet – where was it coming from? When would he be satisfied? My breaths came out as sobs as day after day the house grew larger and nothing was ever finished.

One day I listened absently, resentfully, to childish laughter floating through the house as I vacuumed up biscuit crumbs from under the table, when suddenly a vast white light exploded in my head.

I understood then that there is no sacrifice I could not make to evade the heat death of my universe. Chaos must be fought at every level.

Afterwards, the house was silent, hollow, but clean, and the voice, amazed, was quiet.

He didn't notice the absence of the children, but he remarked upon the ring around the bathtub.

Numbly I watched him leave to worklate. I sat listlessly as the dirt built up in corners and ambitious spiders emerged from the cracks to festoon the picture frames with web-embalmed moths. In the sink, the breakfast dishes grew grey-furred borders. The voice cleared its throat and asked me diffidently, stopping just short of actual vindictiveness, *'What else would you expect?'*

Nothing, I agreed; the second law of thermodynamics is

too big to trifle with. The house mantled itself with dust and laughed at me. I sat in a shower of disordered particles. Among them, coincidentally, several of his fine, dark hairs.

I came out of my reverie to examine them lying untidily in the centre of the floor amidst the grime. I rose and wandered through the house. Black smudges of newspaper-inked finger-prints on the door jambs, dandruff flakes on the dressing-table. A festering sock lay on the bathroom tiles, radiating germs – I could almost see them creeping outwards ... 'Filthy!' Slimy pubic hairs caught on the bath outlet strainer, oozing scum into the pipes beneath with a distant plopping sound ...

I fled to the bedroom, but on the unmade bed the sheets were crumpled into a dirty obscene shape. 'You naughty little girl!' I saw at once an implied entropy-source within my house's system that was disorder personified. But I remained calm.

That night, when he came home from workinglate, I kept no dinner warm for him. Later I cleaned the house from top to bottom, weeping with relief.

But dust continues to settle. Dirt continues to encroach. Particles are disarrayed continuously. I sit motionless, barely blinking, hapless. Watching it happen all around me, considering. Despite being victim to it, I am absorbed by the grandeur of such a remorselessly universal law.

The entire house – each wall, each floor, each ceiling; each window and ledge and crevice; each piece of furniture; every surface in its convoluted topography – stretches in front of me, with its concomitant demand for order and cleanliness. And this is, by nature of the cosmos, impossible.

I nod with infinite slowness to myself. This is a liberating revelation, if somewhat late in the day. The voice in my head stills at the implacable logic of it, and I feel the heavy burden of responsibility lifting from me along with the flakes of my skin. The factor that is me in this long and fruitlessly intricate equation can easily be removed without affecting it. And for once, someone else can clean up the mess.

science fiction

i am getting away
getting away
pulling free
thinking on:

the likeness of America to Mars
the silly cock of that robot's head
the 'pop!' when you've arrived
350 000 children dancing for the moon
1 X 4 X 9
twenty thousand years from now
deciding whether it's a plant or a girl
burning Oscar's flanks to make him swim
flicking the switch
asking the question
waiting on a moonless night
listening for electricity
working it out
the bones in the river
the babies in the jars
skin like a fish
a mechanical heart
the one who came back
the ones who never die
the story that came to life
the wind that knew your name
a metal hand
slipping through the stars
becoming one of them
getting away

                    and being pulled back
              into a jar
         never getting away
    dwelling on:

the likeness of my Dad's wife to a shark
the shiny eyes in her head
the thump when she came
350 000 kids better than me
one by one
twenty years ago
deciding whether I'm a brat or a maid
burning my dinner to make me sick
flicking the switch
asking the question
crying on a Monday night
listening for her listening for me
working on me
the bones in my head
the babies of her friends
skin like a fish
my unbreakable heart
the one who came back to him
the one who never lied
the story of her life
the way she said my name
the back of her hand
slipping through her stare
becoming what she wanted
coming away

flight

i'm fly mouth then over mountains and castles an estate the whole over a whole over switzerland flying away on top of a bat mister boopee a speed spread out fur like a apt i hold on now words spill me out there's so many no order the then i rise above a wire the wire that above the street i keep on raising now why don't you do it i don't do it too often because i scare people now i scare people too much then i raise on arisen raising then up with my feet into the sky the fly and the flying on top of a fur that's a bat the then over mountains we go and cast s a whole estate in switzerland with silver bears the statue of a silver bear now over fly flying i'm say when say just say when over the top of a bald mountain the witches so to come over little words just enter they're all flying over my mouth don't hold me any i'll tell him you're evil teacher says i'll scare you to death there's a wish now that man that was so nasty so nasty so nasty to me now that's a go to go way over the overpass the fly over now words justrush more that i'm can say me just don't wait now spill a tea the table falls way over just burns her then the scold mouth says what you're doing now spill a spill a spill over the flight of a bun the bumblee bee tour the fly over planes just roll over trams but i get off just in time three days then i'm just better what he's

saying taking a hat a fur hat a hat one a head that's fur cover
there's a fur hat coat on my brain the fly over the meet meet in
my dreams i'm fly a landscape a primaeval the start a basic over
roads the fly over roads little ribbons says that words go rush in
a rush if words say that'll do again i don't stop now or read over
just a oncer in a raise of words in a torrent my mouth open
mouth feet lifts the lift the whole body ina raise of will words
that pull up armpits to a helicopter what you say to me all fits
me a glove a had a fur hat now says that'll do me a young girl
now what you want young girls was said that's important to keep
a book that words keep still a book but i don't now just a feeble
fibs that'll lies to me then or what you can't tell me now in a
cloud he hid a cloud to come over in a golden shower a rubber
bag a hottie a hot water bag now to keep him warm has a girl
that's all a come back what apiggy what'd this little piggy went
to market this little piggy went to this little piggy pigs fly a fly
the rush a rush now mouthley in a beam from space ships from
a beam am drawn sending signals singing a song that signals in
circles that man was empty the spacemen eat me out dry man
was empty spacemen eat him out the spit out in a world of signs
a leaf was left a doorstep that's how i know that's here i raise a
feet raising the feet raising at night now loud music playing loud
music the flight of my planes out windows watch me above
grounds they're more to say and tell me over than say me more
and more then over flight the deck wash dish a come back he
said i remember youcoming my birthday to go candelabras all
the candelabras my readings of his boyfriend grand star with
a fur the fur hat in a flight very rushy now words tilt over tell
me and tell me what you say me then what you say me then
i'm fresh say me now i lift a fence indiana jones on a way to a
railway i fly over a vault it's all easy to my easy now the names

they name me leaper leaper the big leaper over hurdle the i just
fly legs come over bounds and jumps i won't fall me now how
will you do i'm in a high jumps in a falls in falls on soft bags
cartwheels in over the still water over the reflecting surface of
the pools the reflecting surface of the geometrical fountain
surfaces that reflect the water flow the gushing fountains now
and the statues big from above that i can see the statue of a bear
all in silver the silver bear in silver the huge statue of a cat in
silver standing up flying i fly over the estate in switzerland on
top of a bear mister boopee very big extended and i'm flying over
the estate extended and flying over the estate flying over grand
estate the wonderful grounds the palace flying over that full of
rainbows in blue skies blue skies and red roofs the palace all in
white marble i fly over that now very high and grand air crisp all
composed the grounds all directed and composed by gardeners
the grounds composed and directed by gardeners and sculptured
the and ordered into geometrical patches and lines roads on my
maps i fly in a bear rug completely naked mister boopee says
when are we going to stop that and i say never ever never ever
now and i live by a lake with gold boats i fly over huge grounds
i tell now the landscape with mountains composed and ordered
into a postcard the rivers flow ribbons little river flows like a
little ribbon looking down the little river flows a ribbon looking
down the little river flows and flows and meanders a little ribbon
now the little river flows and flows and meanders like a little
ribbon now over the flow ground on a valley looking down i lift
above the wires i don't do this often people because people get
scared of me now they get scared of me i'm an eagle i'm an eagle
i'm eagle over the magnificent the ordered the arrange me the
order me around the flight of my mouth she's so quickly now
so quick now faster to me faster to me be fast to me now over

the palace of versailles the buildings geometrical the plan the
architect told me i make a plan from above now the travel from
top the over view now the foresight the foresight tosee my eye
the eye of eagles eye very sharp raising above a valley in my
gliders i glide over i raise my legs now and i lift i lift now i
inhabit these landscapes from above me to inhabit a world from
above me lifting ground into flight the plane my nose i fly over
the primordial valley the warm valley the tropical rain moistly
moist now i have been waiting and waiting for this i wait for this
now i'm going to a joining i'm fly to a joining at night on a
broomstick raising the broomstick raising on a way to a clearing
in the bald mountain dancing with ten plaits in a circle i i'm fly
to a clearing and a cleaning now's the cat becomes a giant bat
flying me on his wings the black soft wings that take me over the
sharp mountains now over alps the champagne coloured wings
of my blonde blonde self my hair made into a rope and a wing
the cat becomes a huge horse now flying over a giant bear i
fly on top in his fur ona fur rug we fly over estates canals we
fly over rivers and fountains we fly over but i say i'm getting
sunburnt won't be long he says we'll stop in zurich we'll get a
hotel we'll get something to eat he says to me he says to me he
is my husband he says to me he us my husband he says to me
now we have money lots of money i'm so excited the child tells
me that i'm so excited now that i don't want to sleep at all no i
don't want to sleep now i don't wish to and i can't and won't
now i paint a painting of a crown i paint a crown i wear a crown
and staff and fur with ermine i'm king and i'm king i'm a big
blonde i'm not myself i'm in a stream a wet stream i unfurl and
unroll this i wear a white dress now a communion dress a white
dress with flounces i fly away from you now i fly up and out the
evil man who wants to sell a circus who wants to sell me to a

circus now i won't let i won't cut my wings at all for you i'll fly away there's another there just like me just like me to me now i ban the evil man then you you're just not allowed i have a white eagle or a falcon the falcon flying wild geese flying so in love above the roofs i'm going dancing now and going dancing never lonely to you i'm not lonely now i have an eagle and a falcon i have a little hood i have an eagle and a falcon to you i have a falcon who sits on my glove the glove of a falconer the bird with a sharp eye looking at me there's looking at me the eagle with a black eye i smell him now the oily smell of feathers the oily smoky smell of the feathers of the bird and the bird my bird looks at am now i have a bird and a falcon i have a falcon that sits with a little chain around his legs i am a falcon that sits a little silver chain around my legs and ankles i have a chain i have an eagle i have a falcon that sits on my falconer's glove and the birds wings smelling waxy smelling oily smelling of smoky smelling smoky the wings of eagle wings and the bird looks at me and looks at me and looks me now he looks me you look me you look like me that's how i want to be and that's how i want to look now that's how i am and how i want to be like the wings that rustle wings that lift and lift me in my dreams that's how i now want to be just in my tongue that's says me that i have an eagle and a falcon and the falcon sits on my glove on my hand and on the glove of the falconer i have an eagle now with wings an eagle wings the wings on hand my wings open in murmur in a sigh of wind in the current of air that lifts now i can feel it in my feet i can feel it in my finger tips i can feel words that raise me that raise my feet that lift me up and the bird the falcon that sits on my glove of the falconer that sits on my glove of the falconer above red roofs made of slate above the hatch thatch huts in the music of pipes i undo the little silver chain now and

the hood the little hood of the falcon now i take off my little
hood now that black eyes that glint now the eye eagle eye of
the eyes of eagles the eye of the eagle eye that glints that lifts
the that eye that glints my eye that glints now the black eye
that glints my tongue coming out sharp little tongue my talons
sharp talons now my feet dry feet my feet pointy feet now in my
eagle dress of eagles in my wings that are sewn from angel wings
in my wings sewn from angels on my wings sewn from angel
wings made from angel feathers and angel hair and hairs from
gold wings of angels that extend from my back bones from my
shoulder blades always sticking out the self the prominent self
that people are afraid of that people are scared of me that i'm
also scared of i allow the falcon to lift me i allow the cat to fly
allow me i allow a torrent of sights and things a flow of a river of
words in a fly a flight of thoughts the falcon lifts oh i am sad oh
i am sad oh i am sad that i'll not come back but he does i can
hear the sound the rush of wings and my falcon lands on my
shoulders now and my shoulders getting lighter and my feet
getting lighter lift me now and lift me now and lift me now and
in my flutter and in her flutter of words i lift me now to fly over
worlds and rivers all over worlds and rivers all over mountains
over the place palace over steeples over ah ah ah ah ah ah ah
ah ah

possum lover

Sorrel paused with her hand on the first of the two metal gates between which several cows had clearly been making their irresponsible way from the Bardens' milking shed to the south-west paddock. The gates protected the cows from their natural tendency either to struggle upward the short distance to the road, or to canter skittishly down the long and precipitous driveway to Ingram's house and garden.

Sorrel, as sole passenger, was preparing to swing the gates open and clear the driveway for Ingram's car. But the wind in the South Gippsland Highlands today was the kind that locals called a 'mad' easterly, terrifyingly strong and cold, striving to topple her sideways, and to lift and spatter the ubiquitous cow manure. If Sorrel tried to shift the first gate, the easterly's force would be behind her. But struggling to move the second gate against the wind would clearly be disastrous. Even getting out of the car had been unwise.

Whipped by her own reddish-brown hair, Sorrel's eyes were stinging – and although her high-waisted Empire-style dress was relatively unremarkable in these early 1970s, its emerald-green ankle-length skirts were providing further boisterous sport for the wind. Yet the buffeting might almost have been exhilarating, but for the nine-months passenger inside Sorrel's own body, who at this moment began to stir again – a feat that needed determined effort, when so little space inside Sorrel's skin remained free for manoeuvres.

Pausing, then, and looking back up at Ingram, Sorrel saw that his face now wore a stupefied expression, apparently provoked by something advancing up the hill towards her. In another instant, what Ingram had seen came silently upon her – then upon Ingram and the car – then upon the hills and clouds above them, as well. Not only was the entire landscape now suffused with an inappropriate purple; the face-flaying easterly was gone, and the quiet air was charged with an absurdly seductive languor. Seen through a purple mist, even Ingram became remote in a manner quite distinct from his far less charming remoteness during the two-hour journey from Melbourne.

Bathed in purple, the afternoon sky became a gem-like blue, while the extravagantly heaped-up clouds above Sorrel and the bleached wooden gatepost beside her were faintly flushed all over. When she turned her gaze downhill toward the house, the tree-shadows in the surrounding paddocks seemed floating rather than fallen and, because the hard glitter of the evergreen eucalypt foliage was overlaid now with the plummy deciduous shades of an unAustralian autumn, the leaves were no longer an undistinguished blur but looked like burnished metal artefacts. The landscape looked, in short, as if someone's loving care had been lavished upon every grassblade and declivity – the more so because its colours belonged in a time of day that was alien to Earthly experience. It was as alluring and as infinitely aloof as the backdrop of a stage-set, along whose paths the audience knows that only imagination's feet can ever venture.

As always, Sorrel partook of this lassitude mimicking

restraint: the movement of air withheld – the leaves coloured decadent, beyond their last possible goodbye, yet without the energy to flutter down. She relinquished the puzzle of why Ingram had appeared to be seeing what was never perceptible to anyone but herself. Her awareness sank, unresisting, through a succession of purple hazes that fanned out and in, opening and closing on the Sorrels of the past. She was a very small girl on a sunlit verandah, wordlessly watching a soap-bubble floating in the air. 'Double-bubble,' her mother was saying, because a baby bubble clung upon the shoulder of that huge misty globe, intensifying the magic of its swirling purple and green. In Sorrel's memory, the purple colour suddenly flooding the verandah seemed like a glamour emanating from the irides-cent sphere itself, so rapt was her attention. The change at that age was instant – and yet her enthralment lingered – so that she remembered herself not as a brushtailed possum leaping towards her mother's shoulder but as a tiny bubble floating up towards the rounded membrane that enclosed all the good in the world: the mother-bubble.

For a daytime change in the summer, Sorrel's smaller possum-self would have clung four-handed – dazed with sudden sleepiness – claws spread deep in her mother's silver-grey fur, pink nose trembling in the hot dry air, while in runs and leaps she was carried onward through puffs of fierce, disparate odours that were almost as jarring as the glare of sunlight in her eyes. Then there would have been the welcome descent into cooler darkness: into her mother's possum-den, in the hollow of a dead eucalyptus tree, where the scrabbling hurry stopped and they simply curled together in sleep, wrapped in the familiar aromas from their sun-warmed fur and the layers of odour left by her mother's chest-gland – which was rubbed afresh against the wood on every visit, to mark the hollow as hers. Unperturbing sounds would waft in with outside scents on the breeze: the creak of eucalypt branches, desultory flapping of summer's hanging bark, wandering buzz of heat-stupid blowflies.

While they slept, the shadows would have shifted and deepened. Just so, on visits to Ingram's house these last two summers, the adult Sorrel had dozed alone in a hollow she had marked for herself, hidden in the eucalypt forest that began two paddocks south of the house. The sensations of her childhood – fifty kilometres due north of here, in the bushland of the Eastern Highlands – eerily resurrected themselves. Bird sounds would alter in similar ways, as the hum of daytime insects died down and the cricket and the long-horned grasshopper began to weave their shrill summer music. By the time that the crows and kookaburras had broken off their brief outcry against the dark, the youthful possum Sorrel and her mother (eighteen years in the past) would have woken again. The air awaiting them outside would be moist now, its fragrances free to float and wander – no longer warped and pinioned by the heat of the sun. At the rim of the den, Sorrel's nostrils would acquaint her with an entrancing web of intricate messages threading the dusk, beginning with her mother's possum scent, new-rubbed and heady again on the nearest broken branches. But Sorrel's human brain faltered before fine olfactory discriminations – as impotent to recall them as her possum brain was to savour in memory the wit of Jane Austen's novels. Her dull human ear stayed equally unsupple, innocent of both the range and the intensity of a possum's hearing. In compensation, her human vision was the sharper, and her human brain could therefore divert her with memories of hauntingly vivid green leaves and stems –

two-dimensional, but brighter than any daffodil in night-adapted vision.

The youthful possum Sorrel would have leapt aboard her mother's back in reckless high spirits, anticipating the head-foremost scramble part-way down the tree trunk and the final lengthy spring to earth. Thanks to their neighbour Tilly Carruthers and her passion for colour photography, Sorrel had a human's-eye image of how they would have looked by torch-light: Sorrel, rufous-coloured, clinging endearingly to Opal's silver-grey fur, while Opal's dark eyes shone round and red in the light, and little Sorrel's shone yellow. In another of Tilly's possum photographs a chestnut-brown male was engaged in cat-like washing of his face. This was Sorrel's father Bruno. But without the photograph Sorrel might never have identified him with the big companionable man who shared their house — always joking with Opal, and yet delighting little Sorrel with his aura of unpredictability.

The temperament of a typical Australian brushtail possum is very different from that of the family-minded wolf — which likes to keep its children around it and which mates for life (a feat which Christian-bred humans have traditionally yearned to emulate and have yet found wonderfully difficult). Nor does a brushtail behave like the common possum of North America — a larger and less edible beast, inclined to give birth to six children at a time instead of one. The brushtail never dreams that playing dead is the way to 'play possum'. Monarch of all it surveys, an adult with food or even without food will make screechingly clear to every other encroaching adult that it prefers to be alone. If Bruno (who did not alter in unison with Opal and Sorrel) had happened to be in brushtail form that night, he and Opal would have been precisely as intolerant of one another as of any other adult. Nor could Sorrel have derived any clue from Bruno's odour: neither he nor Opal ever anointed their house or anything close to it with their possum sweatglands. Presumably they felt, as the adult Sorrel did, that a werepossum's human home, unlike the homes of ordinary humans, was not possum territory.

'Would have kicked you out, you know, if she'd lived long enough,' Tilly Carruthers had cautioned Sorrel: 'Not personal. Only behavin' just like her mother.' But Sorrel had been orphaned soon after her ninth human birthday (at the possum age of seven months). By the time of her eleventh birthday, she would have been an eight-month-old brushtail, almost as large as Opal herself, and no longer tolerated in her mother's den. They would doubtless no longer have been changing in unison, and would soon have learnt to regard one another merely as adult brushtails, to be attacked or fled from if they approached too near. But, orphaned so young, Sorrel had never even been hissed at by her mother, much less menaced by her razor-sharp claws. Instead, she remembered how closely her baby possum self used to follow behind, after Opal had thumped down from their tree to the ground – how faithfully she would mirror her mother's heavy-haunched bow-legged gallop or amble. Soon after-wards Sorrel would have been clinging to her mother's fur again as they climbed – perhaps to the crown of a summer-flowering eucalypt where they would feed on green shoots and clustering stamens. Plucking and chewing, her mother would seem placidly uncritical of little possum Sorrel, who leaned over to snatch the leaves from her grasp – darted off to hang upside down from a bunch of blossom (suspended by her back feet and the hidden rough pink skin at the undertip of her bushy tail) – lunged toward the scent and sound of a passing moth – then wound herself upright again and bounded over to scramble on her mother's back and playfully box her foxy-looking ears. But Opal's apparent sweet temper had been reserved for little Sorrel alone among brushtails.

Nowadays, even as a possum, the adult Sorrel felt no urge to engage in acrobatics. For months past – motherless, and unready for her own advancing motherhood – her human body had seemed to her a landscape almost as improbable as the purple scene confronting her now; as impersonal in its intricate construction. Before pregnancy, she had experienced herself as a creature of lithe activity; afterwards, as a secret domain. When she had felt within her for the first time a wide wing-beat, as of a slow tropical butterfly, the domain had become spacious in her imagination, with sleepy jungle glades lush with huge orchids that themselves resembled butterflies. As time went on, Sorrel's sensations altered and were much more easily deciphered as the doings of the little creature kicking and somersaulting and swallowing and hiccuping inside her. But the phantom jungle stayed, linked in her mind with the unfamiliar tastes and odours that pregnancy invented. Light and sound had developed a filtered quality, as if they were wafting through curtains of vines, and there was a lingering sense of vertigo – reinforced now by the floating look of the shadows in the strange purple stillness.

A long dragging pain afflicted her. The hilltop winds resumed their violent assault; the landscape returned to ruffled green; Ingram emerged from the car. Once more, as during most of this day, events were moving too fast for her. Striding towards her, Ingram looked very much as he had on the windy afternoon in Autumn four years ago when she had first seen him – indeed, distracted by a sudden flurry of fallen elm leaves, she had almost collided with him, as he rushed out from the gate of a Melbourne University college in Parkville. Then, as now, he was pale and theatrically thin, shaking back a wave of dark hair that the wind had blown forward over a distinctively crooked eyebrow, uttering agitated apologies, hands eloquent of distress. But the gestures, the rapid speech, were once again designed to disentangle him – a prelude to sudden departure. And because, in Sorrel's adulthood, the onset of purple heralded thirty minutes' grace before she changed into a brushtail possum, she could only be grateful for his unexpected decision to return at once to the city. Yet she knew that the excuse he gave (mostly snatched away at first by the wind, so that he had to lean forward and repeat it close to her ear) was a lie. Certainly, the publishers expected Ingram's completed index on Monday, but he had no need to hurry back to Parkville to retrieve two shoeboxes of indexing cards, forgotten until now on the chair in his study: those shoeboxes were already part of the luggage in the car.

At least she could now dismiss her troubling impression that Ingram had also seen the purple mist. He apologized because he had been staring blindly – inwards, at the sudden revelation of forgotten shoeboxes. As always, his words were fluently expressive, but delivered in erratic rushes and pauses, like a stream tumbling down a disruptively picturesque terrain. Before she knew him, Sorrel had heard fascinated censure of this seemingly insincere delivery and of Ingram's other 'affectations': unpredictable departures from theatres or social gatherings – even a party he was hosting – because of sudden aesthetic revulsions or personal aversions or onsets of inspiration. Tilly had already advised her that undergraduates showed an amused or even admiring indulgence towards excessive sensibility, if it was displayed entertainingly. Sorrel had therefore invented similar motives for her own apparently whimsical exits or her refusals to promise attendance. But Sorrel's excuses really were affectations –

devised to conceal the fact that she spent about forty-five hours in every thirty days as a brushtail possum, with barely half an hour's notice of approaching change.

If Ingram was hurrying to depart, he would at least be spared the discovery that his wife underwent swifter and more eccentric transformations than the slow shape-shifting of pregnancy, where her human body had woundingly become the outer revelation of her secret deeds. He could not know that there was also the emergency of imminent birth to flee from. Sorrel had lied to questioning friends, telling them that the baby was not due for another two months, and letting them believe that (like any responsible Parkville woman in the early 1970s) she consulted doctors and had made a maternity-hospital booking. In actuality, this last surviving werepossum had no choice; she could not allow herself and her child to become a thrilling opportunity for modern technological analysis.

In the lessening pauses between her lengthening pains, today's silent journey had begun to feel interminable. Sorrel's imagination had retreated into a well-remembered comfort story told to her by Tilly. The comfort was chiefly in the story's memories both of Sorrel's mother and of Tilly herself, dead for three years now. It concerned a moonlit summer's evening in late 1948, on a small bushland property in the Eastern Highlands. Tilly had been in her early fifties then, and a newcomer to the district. Clad in utilitarian pyjamas, she had been sitting up in bed in her upstairs room, pleasantly aware of the cooler night air through the open window, mingling itself with the heavy scent of roses from the huge vase on her bedside table. Except for the halo of candlelight about her bed, the room was dim. Its only sounds were of pencil and paper. Prey to a growing unease, Tilly abruptly looked up from the manuscript she was altering.

She found herself gazing into two intense and motionless eyes, glowing and glaring at her from the armchair by the window. Telling this story to Sorrel long afterwards, the stolid-seeming Tilly confessed a brief chill of supernatural horror: she had read the ghost stories of M. R. James – his tale of the avid thing with red eyes that came out of the altar-tomb in Southminster Cathedral. With admirable steadiness, she nevertheless took up the lighted candle and extended it before her at arm's length like a crucifix to keep a vampire at bay. Its light now fell upon the owner of the eyes: a harmless silver-grey brushtail possum, lured in by the glow of artificial light and stupidly mesmerized by it, in the fashion that had made these creatures such easy targets for shooters in the days when possum pie was a popular dish and brushtail pelts were sold as 'Adelaide chinchilla'.

Like many other Australians, Tilly regarded brushtails with mingled affection and annoyance. She felt relief, but she wished the creature out of her room. And then she was holding the candle steady, as mesmerized as the possum had seemed, with her wish suddenly fulfilled; the possum had disappeared, and sitting in its place on the cushion of the armchair was Tilly's neighbour Opal McLaren.

At this point in the story, Tilly's style had become clipped and elliptical – a symptom of emotion. 'No good pretendin' the thing hadn't happened. Trusted me. Two World Wars, the Depression, Edward the Eighth – not easy to shock. Different if I'd been a man.'

Between contractions, Sorrel's adult mind had fled from the daylight reality of Ingram, pale and proud in the driver's seat beside her. She had tried, instead, to picture this candlelight-and-roses encounter, taking place before she was born: Opal in Tilly's armchair, gallantly recovering her customary calm; tall and silvery-blonde – somewhat coltish in her human guise – wearing the same dress and carrying the same handbag that Tilly had noticed from her car the previous morning, when they had passed one another on the road to the township. In Tilly's later photographs, where Sorrel was a baby carried in a cloth sling close to Opal's body (unusual for Anglo-Celtic Australian mothers around 1950), Opal still looked girlish. She was not in the least a frightening woman. And a brushtail possum was certainly not frightening. Yet, revealed as a werepossum, Opal became a focus of superstitious dread – summoning up revulsion for savage werewolves and sexual Cyprian she-cats, weaving their horrible squalors of hair and moon and blood; more importantly for Tilly, shattering all confidence in a secular universe, where werecreatures and the mysterious forces controlling them could be dismissed as mere figments invented by human self-doubt. And if this was Tilly's reaction, surely Sorrel had been wise in guarding poor Ingram from a similar revelation.

Imagining that the candlelight falling on Opal had converted her back to human form, Tilly's mind tottered toward traditional exorcisms with bell, book and candle. But her manoeuvres with the candle had produced only a misleading coincidence. For warning of an approaching change from possum to human, instead of a purple haze the aroma of wet roses drenched everything – giving the werepossum a very few minutes to remove itself from fragile branches or too snug a space. Entrapped by the pervasive scent of roses in Tilly's bedroom combined with the hypnotic effect of the candleflame, Opal had missed noticing her warning and had failed to remove herself from view.

Another dragging pain caused Sorrel almost to stumble, obeying Ingram's insistence that she seek shelter in the car again and leave him to wrestle with the gates. Until this new onslaught ended, she could only lean against the door; and then, in the ensuing lull, she eased herself inside again, away from the weather, longing to return herself also to the comparative sanctuary of the past two hours of driving. Whenever she felt herself set apart from the landscape, as if existing at a different speed, Sorrel felt the illusion of being looked after, as if provided for in some immense benevolent plan. But she knew there was no benevolence: only the instinctive self-deception of someone being helplessly carried along by processes beyond her control, as the baby inside her own womb was also being carried. While Ingram struggled to clear the driveway that led to the house, the clearing of the baby's passageway into the world was steadily continuing – without Ingram's knowledge and without Sorrel's volition.

This morning she had woken to find herself awash, the amniotic sac that encased the baby having ruptured overnight. Since then she had been disoriented – slightly euphoric – a mother who waited to be born, sealed away inside her own mildly aromatic haze of fine fluid particles. It seemed unimportant whether the aroma extended beyond her own consciousness – whether it might reach Ingram's fastidious nostrils. She knew that the contractions she felt now were forcefully altering the shape of her womb to allow the baby to pass through; she knew (from reading Tilly's textbooks) that lately whenever she was a possum her hormones were softening the tissues that tiny possum babies must finally tear their way through, in order to create a midline passage from the womb to the urogenital sinus and thence to the world. But these disquieting truths required no immediate attention: they could not be altered. Sorrel's efforts were concentrated instead on securing a place where she could give birth in solitude, with her werepossum nature undetected.

The first step was escape from their house in Parkville (ringed in by neighbours, hospitals, obstetricians). But on every other visit to South Gippsland, Ingram himself had announced his intention to drive out and stay there for a few days – whereupon Sorrel chose whether to go with him. Providing that one of Sorrel's lengthier stints as a brushtail was not long past, a mere two hours in a car was safe enough (although non-stop travel in interstate buses or overseas aeroplanes was unthinkable). If she declined the opportunity, no reason was required. Ingram had always respected her sudden withdrawals from society. He believed they arose from the same artistic dedication that kept him locked away from all communication for as much as thirty-six hours while he perfected an exacting piece of writing. Indeed, Ingram's passion for mutual privacy had totally undermined Sorrel's belief that marriage would inevitably unmask her as a werepossum – had swept away her virgin identification with proud and lonely heroes, dedicated to solitude because of mysterious tragedies. The house that Sorrel had been renting in Carlton was not very far east of the Melbourne General Cemetery: Ingram offered a two-storey late-Victorian Parkville mansion not very far west of it. He also offered separate and inviolate studies (where, like Sorrel last night, they might sometimes choose to sleep) – and no questioning of hastily scribbled last-minute announcements that one or the other would be absent from a social engagement that both had accepted. Ingram seldom volunteered information, and never requested it: a trait which Sorrel had shamefully exploited, these last few months. Today, when she took the opposite direction and violated an unstated taboo by abruptly suggesting that they should drive to South Gippsland, Ingram had almost balked. There had been a distinct pause – a sudden pallor. Then, after an intense glance, he bowed to the ideal vision of courtesy that Sorrel had once seemed to share with him, and consented.

Had she been human, Sorrel (in her university days) might truly have been as selflessly responsive to obscure aesthetic imperatives as Ingram was. He judged her as a kindred spirit, unconstrained. When, in idiosyncratic high disgust, Sorrel abruptly walked out of a ballet – when she airily advanced an attack of ennui as her reason for failing to attend a select gathering – nobody supposed it was because she secretly transformed into a brushtail possum. Moreover, Sorrel's human friends would have been appalled by her temperament when she hissingly warned off ordinary brushtails from her sleeping-spot among the trees in the Melbourne General Cemetery, or dined overnight on some exquisite rosebud, wrecking the human beholder's joy in its anticipated unfurling.

Her friends would have been even more shocked had they guessed how Ingram's ideal for their marriage had been wrecked by Sorrel's pregnancy (which was never mentioned between them). Sorrel had felt relief when Ingram's proposal of marriage included a confession of his infertility (presumably discovered in the aftermath of some youthful indiscretion). She would never have cheated him by agreeing to marry if he had hoped that the marriage could produce offspring: as a werepossum, Sorrel had supposed herself incapable of breeding either with fertile humans or with common brushtails. Now she had no idea what Ingram might think about her pregnancy. But she was sure that his spirits would hardly be improved if she tried to tell him that the only possible father for her baby was a black South Gippsland brushtail possum.

When they had married, two years ago, Sorrel had been as slender, decorative and wilfully elusive as Ingram was. To watch his movements now as he slid back into the car was like glimpsing her own vanished self. Earlier in her pregnancy, people's glances of distaste or even horror had almost amused Sorrel: there was such a contrast between their impression of amorphous sponge and her own awareness of how taut and firmly packed her expanding belly was. She knew foretastes of old age and its infirmities: aching legs, intolerance of summer heat, onsets of deathly fatigue that instead of inspiring defiant spurts of effort would grimly terrify her out of any feeble attempts at resistance. Her own appearance and Ingram's ceased to harmonize so well. But her sense of her own suppleness – her instinct to charm – had nevertheless survived many weeks of increasing strain on her heart, enlarged by the absurd amounts more blood it had to deal with and crowded by the fast-growing child, whose movements became steadily harder on both of them. Her intervening athletic hours as a pregnant brushtail were blissful – although her pregnancy seemed unnatural in the summer hours, since the common brushtail gives birth (usually once a year, to one baby) only in autumn, winter or spring. And, swollen as her human body was now, Sorrel had finally, in this last month of pregnancy, succumbed to feeling as unwieldy and grotesque as pregnant women had formerly appeared to her.

The car was continuing straight down the driveway. This left the gates otherwise than as they were found, and thus broke the first rule for living at peace in the country. No doubt Ingram planned to return so swiftly (having deposited Sorrel and her luggage at the house) that any early cow who strolled up to the crossing would not have time to become discouraged before he drove through again and replaced the gates that barred her way to the milking-shed paddock. Although it was hours before the afternoon milking, Ingram's urgency to depart was clearly more genuine than his excuse for it, since meddling at any time with the position of the Bardens' gates was risking their ill will. All the land around Ingram's house (apart from the yard in which it stood, and the fenced-in strip running on either side of the driveway to the road) belonged to the Bardens – whose own house and sheds lay in full view along a higher ridge across the valley north-east of Ingram's house. When Ingram was absent, the Bardens unobtrusively ensured that all was well with his property. It would be a poor return for their kindness if some of their milking cows found themselves prevented from assembling at the milking shed – concluded that they were being dried off (like others of this regimentally pregnant herd, expecting to calve in another two months) – and wandered away and had to be fetched.

At the house-fence, Sorrel was distantly aware, through another contraction, of Ingram opening the gate and driving through into the yard. When the pain released her again, she emerged from the car and stood gazing about her (perhaps for the last time – given the dangers of human birth without midwife or doctor), as if from the floor of an enormous green and blue bowl, rimmed with rounded hills. Only a century ago, these soft Jurassic sediments had been densely covered by forests of the giant eucalypt known as mountain ash, with an understorey of lesser trees rising out of a daunting chaos of forest debris, and with shaded tree-fern gullies whose beauty became a theme for pioneer verse. Most of the forest had long been cleared for farming – here, as in her home district, the Eastern Highlands. And in this part of South Gippsland the original human inhabitants (the Bunurong people) were said to have vanished before the clearing began. But perhaps the present sparse little gully of tree-ferns to Sorrel's west (explored by her in both human and brushtail form) had once resembled a far more significant scene:

the subject of a nineteenth-century watercolour, painted by Sorrel's great-great-great-grandmother. Sorrel's parents Opal and Bruno had relied on memory when describing this painting – which had been destroyed in the bushfires of 1939, a decade before Sorrel was born.

They agreed that the watercolour had showed a secluded tree-fern gully where a group of five families had camped together during the goldrush days of the 1850s. Opal and Bruno remembered an abrupt swerve of swirling shadow-dappled creek-water laden with fluffy golden spheres of fallen Cootamundra wattleblossom – and a shaft of mote-laden sunlight descending upon the gigantic upturned roots of an ancient eucalypt that had suddenly toppled backward from the water's edge. Clenched in its vast tangle of clay and roots had been a fortune in gold nuggets – afterwards cannily sold and invested to enable the families and their descendants always to live in comfort, despite the secret disability they had acquired at the same time: transformation into werepossums.

The artist had portrayed the whole group implausibly arranged in three orderly rows as if for a commemorative photograph: the children (who included Bruno's and Opal's great-grandparents) were in the two front rows while the adults stood at the back. Every hand was uplifted and every mouth agape in stylized astonishment. (Indeed, in identifying their own portraits the originals must have relied heavily on the clues of costume and size.) But when Opal and Bruno were children, their gaze had skimmed over the true object of admiration – the dull-coloured tree-roots. Golden treasure seemed to them to pervade the whole scene in the smears of bright paint that had been meant to signify only wattleblossom and sunlight. Wistfully, they had attempted to recapture for Tilly Carruthers and for little Sorrel the magic of the tree-ferns painted in the lower left-hand corner: not only the tender new growth fanning up out of wide-arching darker green fronds, but also the older grey petticoat fronds that hung down close to the trunks. Whenever anyone stared constructively at this lower drab-coloured region, the trunks and dry fronds faded from consciousness and there emerged instead a creature hidden not in the actual tree-ferns but in the painter's composition of greys and browns. Bruno and Opal agreed on the family tradition that this creature had appeared before the goldseekers and proposed a contract: that the tree had fallen and delivered up its treasure only in exchange for their consenting to become werepossums. But when they attempted to describe the creature hidden in the watercolour, they found that Opal's family had interpreted it as a giant brushtail possum, whereas Bruno insisted that it had horns instead of ears and a forked tail instead of a bushy one; it was enveloped not in fur but in dull demonic flames.

Opal believed that the creature was one of the Ancestors described in Australian Aboriginal mythology – itself both human and brushtail. But Bruno's family had identified it as the Devil offering a somewhat twisted werewolfish bargain. And Tilly, who heard these stories in the early 1950s without ever seeing the painting, had suggested (not altogether tactfully) that the seeming creature might have been meant to represent a crashed flying saucer. Nobody could suppose that a combination of invading Scot and indigenous brushtail was a product of Darwinian evolution. Moreover, the nature of the werepossums' transformation-warnings hinted at their being visitors: the brushtail's scent of roses, alien to its continent for thousands of years – the human's vision of purple landscapes, alien to the entire planet.

Having always assumed that werepossums were a separate species, Sorrel searched these theories for an explanation of her fertile mating with a common brushtail. Species were simply ignored in Opal's theory, which was nostalgic for the Scottish Highlands with its ancient selkies (or seal maidens) and its kelpies (the water horses that sometimes masqueraded as men). At home the selkies and kelpies had been bogey-beasts to frighten little children; but in this new southern land their obvious absence aroused a paradoxical sense of bereftness and terror. Opal believed that the brushtail-and-human Ancestor was offering the strangers a chance to become somewhat like selkies – truly a part of this land where their own descendants would trace their ancient origins back to the nineteenth century.

Bruno's werewolfish explanation also avoided the question of species. In more ancient legends, the Devil granted a human being's wish to spend time as a ferocious lawless beast that desecrated human graves and after its death became a vampire. Here, in this British colony, the Devil had grown sneeringly urbane, and offered the temptation of financial good fortune instead. The payment he demanded was to demean oneself as a helpless little creature which at its worst evoked in humans only a mood of annoyance. In brushtail form, werepossums were free to thump and screech at night, to swing by the tail from treetops, and to urinate in ceilings. But in order to threaten lethal harm to other human beings they needed to be in human form, like anybody else. Brushtail possums were small and furry with large round eyes: like women (with shorter stature than men, and higher-pitched and therefore more childish voices) their physical appearance led humans who worshipped power to dismiss them as negligible – perhaps rather funny. A dingo was the nearest to a wolf that Australia could offer, and would have been more dignified: at least it was a carnivorous hunter, with a spine-chilling nocturnal howl. In Bruno's family tradition, becoming a werepossum did not signify (as in Opal's story) acceptance by the land. The Devil was imposing a typically soul-destroying penalty in exchange for worldly gain; and the Ancestor (had there been one) would have been punishing the settlers for their intrusion.

As a werepossum, Sorrel thought it possible that werewolves really existed. But human legends distorted their wolf-reality beyond recognition, destroying useful clues. Tilly's myth was more reasonable, but it implied a distinct species: shipwrecked extraterrestrials, forced to adopt the werepossum compromise because no single Earthly lifeform was adequate to embody their unimaginably alien manner of existence. The extraterrestrial's total self perhaps only briefly achieved full consciousness – too alien for the human brain to assimilate – during the warning phase of purple pigmentation, when the werepossum felt that Earthly reality was stilled, or even withdrawn. As for the dissimilar werepossum family legends, Tilly said that in purely human Australian histories, far less complicated facts about family origins overseas also became wildly distorted as they were handed down from one human generation to another. And she had died ignorant of the evidence against her theory that Sorrel's pregnancy provided.

Before another pain could seize her, Sorrel turned away from the cradle of hills and walked into the house. Ingram, more pale than ever, was carrying her luggage into her bedroom – was rushingly assuring her that, although he might stay overnight in Parkville, he would be back by this time tomorrow afternoon – was departing. He thus unwittingly spared himself two discoveries which, because of her intensifying contractions,

Sorrel would soon have been helpless to avert: that she was in labour and that she was a werepossum.

In deciding to marry Ingram, Sorrel had regarded herself as one eccentric supporting another. In order to pass as human, she had adopted a traditional hero-dandy's fastidious languor (with impish episodes of irreverent clownery). If, in her university days, she had bizarrely combined gumboots with ankle-length skirts, it would have been in irreverent guying of convention, not in a dazed yet dogged effort to cope with one exigency after another. Ingram's manner was more solemnly absurd: a kind of fastidious agitation, varied by chillingly inflexible disdains ('I am not – always – absolutely agreeable'). With a werepossum's awareness of the human mob's tendency to persecute eccentrics, Sorrel knew that Ingram must often have suffered schoolyard tedium and violence because of his idiosyncrasies. Delighting in her own power to lighten his mood while dancing scatheless over minefields of possible offence, Sorrel had also seen herself as offering solace to secret vulnerability. She had thought to save Ingram the anguish of being rejected and abandoned for no apparent reason. Instead she had inflicted the much greater anguish of a seeming gross betrayal. Her spirit – which had once seemed magically attuned to his – must now appear brutally estranged.

Tilly was another human who had suffered for being eccentric. When she settled in the McLarens' district as an adult, the locals had judged her to be almost as odd and stand-offish as the old-established clan of Brenners and McLarens and Stuarts had been: all educated at home (the local school not good enough, seemingly) and never prepared to be in local sports teams or even in a fund-raising concert – although (to give them their due) nobody could grumble about their financial donations. In the township store, the locals would gossip about the McLarens in Tilly's presence (just as they gossiped in front of the McLarens about Tilly), inviting her to marvel at their eccentricity, and thus conveying to her how people ought to behave, and demonstrating their own solidarity. If oddities lived differently, they did it self-consciously, and only in a misguided attempt to impress: they ought simply to drop it, and get back down to earth. Tilly, impatient of such devious attacks, cared very little whether the slyness of the locals was intended to be visible to their victim, or whether they thought they were enjoying a private joke among themselves. She told Sorrel that they reminded her of a circle of cows she had once seen with a koala trapped at their centre: seeing the smaller animal on the ground, the cows had converged on it until they were prodding and butting it from one to another. If Tilly had not intervened, the koala would have been killed – but she could not tell whether the cause was malice or merely curiosity without empathy. Like a koala among cows, Tilly had accepted that she was doomed to see only the worst side of the locals. She was careful to spend money among them, but wasted few words.

The Eastern Highlands werepossums had survived the social pressures of the First World War without the locals uncovering their serious secret eccentricity. But then, except for Bruno and Opal (who had been absent on their honeymoon), the entire clan had died in the 'Black Friday' bushfires of January 1939. In April 1958, Bruno and Opal had also succumbed to a bushfire, while they were visiting South Australia on their 'second honeymoon'. As a child, Sorrel had therefore pictured 'honeymoon' as an ominous sweating disc embrowned by raging fire. In adulthood, the workworn Bardens reminded her of the consequences for Opal and Bruno of being eccentric – how their fingers were left scarred or even misshapen by barbed wire, farm machinery, splinters, hoofs and thorns – their complexions coarsened by driving hail in the cowyard, by grit-laden wind in paddocks they were ploughing or planting, and by the torments of sunburn and sweat and prickly small particles in hay time. The werepossums drudged because of the Second World War, and the need to ensure that the local manpower office would leave Bruno where he was obviously useful – working the vacant farms where all their werepossum relatives had died in the bush-fires, eight months before the war broke out. Opal and Bruno were slaving in order to survive, but they lacked the financial imperative that drove and wearied the Bardens. Their own spur was the inevitability of discovery or disgrace if Bruno was called up to fight.

In another contraction, Sorrel forgot both the past and the sound of Ingram's departing car. Thereafter, between contractions, she moved around the draughty kitchen, dealing (in sleepwalking mood) with practicalities – lighting the woodstove (always left prepared for their next visit) – filling the kettle – pushing out the kitchen table, bringing in a bean bag to lean on, spreading newspapers, sheets, blankets on the kitchen floor. During the contractions, she tried in vain for a bearable posture; between them, she remembered how Opal sat in the sun blowing bubbles although a brushtail-change had almost arrived. Perhaps the habitual lapse between warning and transformation faded away in motherhood – resembling Sorrel's lessening respite between her contractions.

A lot of time might have passed now – or perhaps only a little. Sorrel transformed into a brushtail, fastidious again about the inside of her pouch, vexingly waxy lately and needing dedicated cleansing with both claws and tongue. She felt uncomfortable and nervous – much as she had been when she had encountered a significant black-furred male. But then she had been in oestrus – the state that once every three weeks caused unmated cows and heifers to indulge in lickings and sniffings and tastings and mountings that offended delicate human sensibilities. About forty weeks had gone by since that oestrus – which meant that the hours spent as a brushtail since then added up to a little over seventeen days.

About forty minutes before the encounter, Sorrel's human self had unexpectedly seen purple spreading itself across the evening dimness. She had been luxuriating on Ingram's bed, damp and deliciously sated, relishing the different slenderness of Ingram's familiar thigh against hers, and laughing within herself at the silliness of her greatest dread in the days of her virginity: that if she lost control and experienced orgasm, she would helplessly change into a brushtail. Since her human body's silky skin and bushes of hair and characteristic aromas marked it as its own completely distinctive animal, what need to turn into another kind? In a state of post-coital elation, she heeded the purple warning by slipping very quietly out of the room and then running south across the cleared paddocks and into the bushland. It was a perfectly calm winter's night – somewhat too cold and misty for the human Sorrel, but perfection when she was a densely furred exhilarated brushtail.

In its brushtail form, a werepossum is sublimely free of problems that sociable animals like wolves and humans create for themselves. Smaller, more timorous marsupials might live sociably, but cat-sized brushtails crash and thump their way through the night, coughing out the news of their presence, and screeching and howling their intolerance of one another's closeness. A hissing sniffing approach might end in a friendly nose-rubbing or in one brushtail fleeing from the threat of a stand-up boxing match with ungloved claws and round-arm swipes. It might also end in a rolling wrestle amid clouds of belly-fur wrenched free by ripping teeth. Because Sorrel had been in oestrus on that misty winter night, her encounter with the black brushtail (complicated by the persistence of several other hopeful males) included all of these elements and more. But brushtails never gang up on one another – never organize for war – never engage in public opinion. Indeed, only when in brushtail form, during the First World War, were the fighting-age males among the werepossums free to roam in the Eastern Highlands. In their human form, they had stayed hidden on their property all through the war, while the neighbourhood was told that they had enlisted in Britain (a fashionable decision among Australians in the 'Great War') and were fighting overseas.

Amid blood-colour and the strong scent of roses, Sorrel came back to her human self – shivering, very cold. Her memory of the human time that had been passing was dreamlike. Had she heard cows bellowing a good deal – as they sometimes did when one of their number was in trouble? Had she heard Mr Barden's tractor driving about? Inarticulate, she longed for Opal to be here to help her. When Opal's contractions had gone on and on climbing in intensity as Sorrel's had been climbing, she too must have felt that she couldn't bear it, that she would have needed centuries of rest to accumulate strength for it – but Sorrel had been born, and therefore Opal's labour could not have gone terribly wrong like this, contractions no longer rhythmic – cold, exhausted – everything over. All that Sorrel had read about the transition stage in human labour was lost to her.

Panic seized her. Time was confusion, with a heavy driving pain – with demand for too much effort – she was too tired.

Heavy, boulderous, too much effort. She would shriek, but shrieking was upward and force was downwards, insisting. Pain – far beyond the personal – a huge stone block, forcing. It was not possible, not thinkable – she would burst apart. But, simply, utterly, there was no way back. Despite the certainty of hideous, irreparable injury, Sorrel pushed into pain that the human memory can never recapture in any other situation. And all at once, incredibly, the worst was over. Peering down, Sorrel could see the baby's head; the crumpled little face was emerging, turning sideways, and then the slithery body – mulberry coloured, slippery with vernix, beautiful: a girl. And even as she laid the baby against her human breast, a languorous rich purple suffused the room, and Sorrel felt herself changing.

Parts of the temporary floor-coverings were soaked with mixed-smelling blood and other fluids. Sorrel's brushtail self easily detected the basic scent of her human self in all of them. Daintily, she withdrew into such shadow as she could find, fluffing her fur and twitching her whiskers. The brightness of the electric light was distressing her, and every posture soon became uncomfortable. When at last she was eased, Sorrel was sitting upright with something new to be cleaned off her fur: a narrow wetness, detected as she began to lick near the base of her tail. It climbed higher and higher, in a slow trail (licked away as it formed) furrowing through her thick rufous fur, up to the rim of her pouch. Sorrel's possum eyesight could not distinguish the tiny pulsating pink blob that was making the trail, but she inhaled its odour, and (when she was satisfied at last with the state of her fur) a new pleasure came as her baby began to suckle, attaching itself firmly to one of the two teats hidden deep in Sorrel's pouch.

Amid the fading French-champagne scent of roses, the

human baby was also suckling, more uncertainly. Sorrel's body was seized by an urgent impulse to push again – whereupon the opulent-looking afterbirth slithered into view. Despite the throbbing cord still attached to it, Sorrel had unaccountably forgotten the need to deliver it. Indeed, its associated dangers of excessive bleeding were among the myriad narratives of human childbirth that she had also forgotten – perceiving only now that her own adventure had already ended in eluding them. Dealing with the cord, Sorrel ascribed her shivering to the coldness of the air. She wrapped the baby warmly and huddled herself into her dressing-gown.

On the north-eastern ridge, the distant motor in the Bardens' milking shed was chugging. Sorrel saw that darkness had fallen outside. Close to the house, a tractor engine was approaching – very loud now. It stopped somewhere on the driveway, and soon Sorrel heard the sound of heavy gumboots tramping along the gravel path and on to the back verandah. A loud series of knocks sounded on the kitchen door, and Mr Barden's voice shouted: 'Is everything all right there?'

Holding the baby closely, Sorrel opened the door. At the sight of an infant so obviously newborn, Mr Barden was astonished, pleased, enlightened and embarrassed. He said that he and Mrs Barden hadn't known what to think when they'd seen the car parked part-way up the drive for so many hours, and the gates left closed so that the cows couldn't get through to the milking. He'd had to drive across on the tractor and shift the gates himself – and it wasn't like Ingram to be so thoughtless. Now that the milking was almost over, Mrs Barden had sent him off again on the tractor to see if anything was wrong. Was everything all right now? Did they need any help?

Sorrel thanked him and got rid of him without his realizing

that Ingram was not in the house, and that she had no idea what had become of him. She continued to stand, bewildered, in the doorway – light streaming past her on to the quiet purple stillness of the verandah.

From a lower vantage point, Sorrel's possum self assessed the evening air. Amid tractor fumes and the warm wet cow smells left by Mr Barden's boots, she scented a less familiar but more emotion-fraught odour. Raising a clenched front paw, she hissed uncertainly into the darkness. There was a loud thump: the black brushtail had leapt up on to the verandah. His fur looked rough from the wind, and his claws clattered on the wooden floor. With a seafarer's rolling gait, he steadily advanced towards Sorrel. Leaning forward, the two brushtails cautiously rubbed noses with one another. Just as Sorrel was preparing to resent any impertinent curiosity about the new odours clinging to her fur, she realized that the black brushtail's own aromas were fading, in a sudden flood of rose-scent.

Here, now, was a new surprise for Sorrel, in her human shape again – standing on tiptoe, nose to nose with the slightly crouched Ingram, while she clasped their baby between them. Ingram and Sorrel each stepped backward in order to look into one another's eyes. A decidedly werepossum mingling of contrition and annoyance appeared in both their faces. Ingram's was understandably ravaged by the day's ordeals, as he would later explain to Sorrel: obliged to drive to South Gippsland at a time when he might easily become a brushtail during the journey – receiving the purple warning precisely when Sorrel did and having to invent excuses so that within the next half hour he could remove the car and himself from view until he looked human again – realizing only just in time to stop the car and open a window that he was not being granted the usual half hour's grace – and then (while Sorrel inside the house was sliding from one form to the other), enduring hours of misery as a brushtail possum in the kind of windy weather that brushtails utterly loathe. On the other hand, a fascinating range of unbroached topics had now arisen – beginning with the three known were-possums who were gathered here together on one doorstep. Contrition and annoyance shaded into rueful amusement.

In perfect unison, Sorrel and Ingram confessed to one another (in the wondering tones that to conventional ears sounded so distinctively unAustralian and, admittedly with more justice, so inhuman): 'We have – both of us – been brutes!'

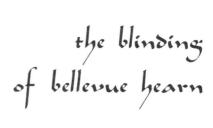

the blinding
of bellevue hearn

ou can take my word for it. Bellevue Hearn was a beautiful woman. When she came to my counter, I wanted to trace the line of her jaw with my fingers. Instead, I hid my hands and asked if I could help her.

She said, 'I want the secret of eternal youth.'

She was twenty-two, but her eyes mirrored my thirty-nine. I should have said go away, my lotions aren't the answer. But I reached for my pot of miracles. Frosted glass and gold letters dazzled our eyes. I held it out to her on the palm of my hand. She picked it up. Her long pale fingers felt the soft skin of glass, the smooth tongue of lettering.

'Ninety-eight dollars,' I said. Spellbreaker, spellbreaker.

'What has it got in it?'

'Foetal cells from llamas, scraped from the womb,' I said. *Can you hear the shrieks of long-lashed mothers, Bellevue?*

'Does it work?'

'Look at Ida Care. She was fifty years old when she came to my counter. Our sun had left desert rivulets waiting for the rains. Miracles, I whispered against her desperate ear. Miracles. So she bought my rain. Every night she rubbed and stared. Rain, damn you, rain. Ida Care waiting for the drought to break, rubbing and staring. More around the eyes. More on the nose. Rain, damn you, rain. But there was no downpour, only slowly shifting sands. Six months later, Ida Care's eyes were dragged into a slant, her flat dune nose suddenly arched to her forehead. Tight, tight skin and two centimetres of extra nose. Who knows how much nose Ida Care has rubbed in now?'

Bellevue Hearn shook her head. 'Temporary,' she said, 'it's all temporary.'

She was right.

'I want to be young and beautiful forever,' she said. 'I don't want my beauty to fade away.'

Can you see Bellevue when she was ten? Always the stallion in lunch-time Brumby. Mane in a pony-tail and long legs running. Running away from the fat girl. 'Why do I always have to be the man?' the fat girl asks as she runs after the blue-check brumbies. Yes, why? 'Next time,' Bellevue says as she kicks and stamps at the girl-man. But next time never comes. Bellevue is always the stallion. Must always be the stallion.

'I must find eternal youth,' Bellevue said, 'and I must find it today.'

No time to waste because you're wasting away with time. But the search might kill you, Bellevue Hearn.

So I said, 'Look what happened to Lily Grinder. Lily's skin was far too thin. She was always bruised. Paper words that stung like stones. Bloodied pictures behind rectangle glass. Get a thicker skin, Lily Grinder. Slip on more skin. So she did. Lily Grinder, seeking the perfect pelt. She went to fifteen fur shops, but she couldn't find her skin. Until she met Frederick Stabb. Stabb's Mink Farm – Choose Your Own Skins. Lily walked past the long line of cages. Mink eyes, mink paws, mink sweat.

Frederick waited with fifty hessian bags as Lily pointed her finger. Fifty hessian bags slit with midnight knives by animal libbers. Forty-nine minks in forty-nine bags. But as Number Fifty flailed against the hessian, Number One slid though the slit. Two and a half minutes for the great mink escape. They swarmed all over Lily and Frederick. The coroner found only Lily's Visa card and some red slicked skin.'

Slip on Lily's skin, Bellevue Hearn.

Bellevue pressed the little glass jar back into my hand. I saw Lily's skin drop to the floor. Then Bellevue stepped over the folds of blue bruised leather and walked away.

Quick, follow her. Between the counters. Through the doors. Into the street shopping mall where the faithful are gathered.

Where will you start your search, Bellevue? Will an organized god send you a memo?

'God is coming. Repent your sins and find eternal youth,' a voice cried out.

Bellevue swirled around until she saw the God-man in his white sandwich-board habit. She ran up and stood facing him, her breasts smearing his felt-pen prophecies.

'I heard you,' she said. 'Tell me the secret of eternal youth.'

The God-man swayed backwards. For six years, nobody had stood so close to him. And now an angel.

'Repent your sins and find eternal life,' he said.

She's so close, he thought. Do angels have peppermint breath?

'Will believing in your God give me eternal youth?' Bellevue asked.

'No. No. But he will give you eternal life in the Kingdom of Heaven,' he said.

He felt his Devil's tool engorge and press against the smell of the angel. Was this a test?

'But what about now?' Bellevue said. 'What good does that do me now?'

He saw the pulse in her throat beat out the rhythm of her hips. Her long eyelashes were blackened, her full lips were wet. She was marked by the Devil. The God-man gasped a lung full of air for his last drowning shriek.

'You are no angel. You are Satan's whore!' he screamed. 'Help me, Lord. Help me now.'

Then he ejaculated. The force of his spasm ripped off his trousers and threw the white board across the mall. If you squint against the sun, you can still see the board embedded in the wall of the Trust Building. Every day the administrative nuns from the Sisters of the Sacred Passion lean out of their fifth-storey window and scatter seed on the board for the shopping-mall pigeons.

But Bellevue did not wait to see where the board landed. She backed away from the God-man so fast that she scraped her heel down the shin of a busker. When he cried out like a stick-poked parrot, Bellevue turned around. The man had the toe of a woman's pink shoe poking out of his mouth. He spat the shoe out and bowed to her.

'My apologies for standing in your way, lovely lady. Allow me to introduce myself. I am The Amazing Gullet.'

He thrust the shoe back in his mouth and swallowed. The heel stretched the skin of his throat like a second Adam's apple. He gulped three times, undulating the shoe down. The heel disappeared. Then he smiled, rubbed his stomach, and hit his diaphragm twice. The shoe was worked back up his throat. He kissed Bellevue's hand then bowed to a small group of workmen who had drifted away from the crowd around the God-man. The workmen stared at Bellevue.

Can you feel their eyes lick your face, Bellevue? Friendly dogs with unpredictable teeth.

'And now, lovely lady, what have you got for me to swallow?' The Amazing Gullet asked.

Bellevue shook her head.

'Come now, would you like me to swallow your arm?'

'No, thank you. I don't want to be swallowed,' Bellevue said.

An old woman with Audrey Hepburn collar-bones stepped forward. 'I will be swallowed,' she said.

The Amazing Gullet ignored her. He circled Bellevue's arm with his thumb and forefinger, testing its roundness. Bellevue shook him away and pointed to the old woman. 'That woman will let you swallow her,' Bellevue said.

The Amazing Gullet turned around. 'What woman?'

He looked through the old woman, searching the eyes of the workmen. They shook their heads. They couldn't see an old woman.

The woman shrugged, her collar-bones pointing a brief V at Bellevue. 'It's all right, dear. They won't see me.'

She turned to walk away, then looked back at Bellevue. 'You probably don't understand this yet, but sometimes it's even a relief.'

Bellevue looked back at the men circled around her. She felt dogs nipping at her heels, rounding her up towards a bridle made of skin and bone.

Watch Bellevue escape. See her run away like the nine-year old with a finger up her soul. 'Meet me at the park,' she'd said to her friend left behind. And she kept on running. Turn and run behind her. Follow her hard-misted breathing. 'He tried to,' she'd said. I'd said. But the words don't lock into place until thirty years later. I'm watching TV and they are whispered by a girl safe in the arms of a therapy chair.

Run, Bellevue. Escape into the arms of a mother.

A woman was sitting opposite The Amazing Gullet, watching the show, rocking a pram. Bellevue knew the dogs wouldn't follow her there. She sat beside the woman, hiding behind the mother.

The baby in the pram was dressed in white. Boy or girl?

'Both,' the mother said. 'They say it will eventually choose.'

'What would you like it to be?' Bellevue asked.

'A boy,' the mother said. 'But I also want him to keep the womb and bleed like a woman.'

'Why?'

'He can't keep a good grip on a dick that is slicked with blood.'

The baby blew a bubble out of its nose. The mother caught it then tossed it gently back to the child.

'Tell me,' Bellevue said. 'Do you think having children is the secret of eternal youth?'

The woman laughed, shaking her head. 'Hardly,' she said. 'Every centimetre they grow, is a centimetre you shrink.'

The baby threw the bubble out of the pram. It floated towards a crowd of shoppers, then bobbed out of sight. The child started to cry.

'Don't worry, I'll get it,' Bellevue said.

She ran after the bubble, ducking around people, scrunching past shopping bags. The bubble slowly lost momentum and paused for a moment in mid-air. Bellevue reached up to grab it. She felt the bubble's wet surface lick her hand. Then it burst. Bellevue turned around. The mother and child had gone.

Bellevue had chased the bubble to the end of the mall. She was standing at the edge of the gutter, beside a taxi rank. The first two taxis in the line were empty. The driver of the third car leaned over and unwound the passenger-door window.

'You look like a lost soul. Need a ride?' she asked. Bellevue nodded.

Do you have enough money to pay the ferryman, Bellevue? One piece of fool's gold hidden in your mouth.

'I'm looking for eternal youth,' Bellevue said. She opened the passenger door and climbed into the car. 'Do you know the way?'

The taxi driver nodded and pressed the meter button. 'You need to see Sun-in-Eyes Jackson,' she said.

She did not speak again. They cut through the traffic easily, the sounds of the city slapping against the side of the car. Bellevue watched the city streets swell into suburban roads. The driver pulled up beside a plain grey brick house. No garden.

'Is this it?' Bellevue asked.

The driver nodded. Bellevue stepped out of the car. She walked up the concrete driveway to the front door. There was no bell. She knocked three times. A young woman answered the door. Her skin was pale and flawless. She was wearing sunglasses.

'Hello? Who is it? Can I help you?' she asked.

'My name is Bellevue Hearn. The taxi driver said you knew the secret of eternal youth. Please tell me. I have to know.'

The woman took off her sunglasses. Her eyes were covered with a thick, white film. A marble statue with smooth dead eyes. 'How old do you think I am, Bellevue?' the blind woman asked.

'About twenty.'

'I'm fifty-three.'

'I don't believe my eyes,' Bellevue said.

'No, Bellevue, you do believe your eyes. That's the problem.'

The woman smiled and closed the door. Bellevue had her answer. She knew what to do. But when she went back to the front gate, the taxi had gone. She walked towards her home without looking back.

Bellevue Hearn stood in front of her bathroom mirror.

Study your face, Bellevue. Trace the line of your jaw with your fingers. Such a beautiful face. Such lovely eyes. Will you share the secret of eternal youth?

Bellevue picked up two hairpins. She turned away from the mirror and took a deep breath. Then she plunged a pin into the black heart of each eye.

❧

Did Bellevue find eternal youth?

Of course she did. She died.

That was the blinding of Bellevue Hearn.

from *SAW*

1 5 000 hoods on uncoiled spines with breath to the earth, chests resting knees and sound in their sacs tremoring bones and flesh. Their mouths are empty. Palms grounded for the throb. Rising and passing away. Breath in the earth. Skins all silver. Reliquaries of desires, fluctuations softly. They are bent and bending in thought. Their bodies rise and fall. The sound of their hearts embracing. Cloak and hood veil their transparency. Their breath twining uncertainty in the neat folds of repetition. Their eyes revealed to the sky. There are no clouds. Words chasms. Speaking with fire, allowing heat to move their lips. Settling hands with the cross of determination. The inbreath of flame, a constant hum fuelling columns of light. Straight. Straight. Bones and fibres resting each within the other, a nest of content drawn between earth and sky. The hum rattles. The hum glows. They are poised in purification.

angel jacko

ouie woke suddenly, cramped. There was a second or two of bewilderment, but then all last night's madness and anguish pounced up back into her head. She got up from Caitlin's lounge, nearly tripping on the tangled rug that had covered her as she cried herself to sleep in the early hours. She took the kettle and filled it. Out the window, the sun was already up, but was hidden by banks of matted cloud that covered all but a narrow strip of blue behind the rooftops. She lit the gas and went back to drop onto the lounge again.

Her clothes and the small bag she'd brought with her were strewn around Caitlin's living-room. She made an effort and collected them into a pile, standing them against the wall near the entrance to the kitchen. Several of Caitlin's large, framed paintings and her neat shelves of books almost filled the small, square room. This is how you live, the room, the very house seemed to say. You have ordered ranks of books on shelves; you have six pot plants in a row on the back window-sill, and you water them every morning at seven. You've done half an hour of yoga before this and showering. You take down that bowl with the blue flag iris hand-painted on it.

In a jar with a round cork lid is a very particular muesli

made with exotic grains and resinous dried fruit. You scoop two heaped (but not too heaped) tablespoons into the flag iris bowl. You pour on soya milk, and you slice a banana on the top. You sit at the table with a cup of rose-hip tea and your pretty hair is brushed back and pinned. You do not do as *you* do, Louie, and sprawl with a black coffee, two Disprins and a cigarette, hungover, with a lunatic asylum shrieking between your unwashed ears.

You have all the notes for the final draft of your thesis on little index cards in boxes. You are the only person in Australia, except perhaps for one old gentleman in the German Department at Sydney University, who knows the following: the entire body of Old English prose and verse, including all gnomic fragments and riddles, the spread of the cult of Othinn in Anglo-Saxon England and, most important, Byzantine influences in Old English elegiac verse. Not like you, Louie, who have never finished anything in your life and sit here with an early morning belly full of bile and booze and a head full of silly mess. Caitlin sighed and her serene eyes rested on Louie, face still swollen from last night's suffering, folded up into herself across the table. 'You'd better tell me the whole, sad story.'

So Louie did. It was awful. It was familiar. And it had happened now a dozen times. Only the names of the men changed. Of how he'd said this, and she'd said that. Of how he'd said that he'd had enough, that it was over, that he was leaving to live with Edwina.

'Edwina Earwig!' snorted Louie. 'How could he love someone called Edwina Earwig?' She drew back a little under Caitlin's lifted eyebrow.

'Well, it's almost earwig – some awful German name. Why does it happen? Why do they always go? What do I do so wrong?'

Caitlin had no intention of answering any of these. Instead, she posed one of her own.

'What are you going to do?'

Above all others, Louie hated this question. Couldn't Caitlin see that there was nothing she could do? That she was immobilized; stuck in pain so thick and sticky that all she could do was lie quite still and try to keep on breathing?

She felt rage against Caitlin, rage against Andy and loathing for herself. 'I don't know,' she answered, sullen. 'I'd like to take a contract out on him. And get the Flick man on to her.'

Caitlin washed up the breakfast things – their two cups, the flag iris bowl, standing them to drain, wiping the table over so that Louie had to lift her forearms.

'I should think they'll be punishment enough to each other in six months' time,' Caitlin remarked mildly, 'once they're past the mutual projecting of illusion. We all have our revenge in the passing of time. Just as the woman he left for you last year is revenged now, my dear.'

Louie thought that might have been better left unsaid. But even that was a sick sort of comfort.

'I feel quite sisterly towards her now,' Louie told her friend. 'Think of all the things she could have warned me about.

'How he farts so revoltingly. How he sticks his finger in his ear to scratch it and jerks his whole arm up and down. How his face creams over with smugness whenever I lose my temper.' She stood up, shaken by these images conjured up to serve the purposes of hate.

'Well, Edwina Earwig has all that ahead of her, lucky dear,' said Caitlin. 'And now I'm going shopping. Do you want to come?'

꩜

They returned with their shopping. Caitlin's bag contained stone-ground wholemeal bread, a butter substitute, mung beans, salad vegetables, a rock melon, two apples, one orange, cartons of soya milk and a packet of hibiscus flower tea. Louie's bag contained three bottles of domestic champagne on special, a frozen chocolate log, four packets of cigarettes and a dollar's worth of hot chips. Caitlin put the shopping away while Louie had hot chips and champagne for brunch. Caitlin had a cup of peppermint tea. She never ate between meals.

While Caitlin worked at her desktop of index cards, Louie went for a walk to the beach. It was a high, white day, and the sea was the colours of the gulls that screamed and wheeled above the promenade, cutting the misty air. The sight of a couple rolling on the grass made Louie's eyes sting, and she started to think of the steady procession of men she'd rolled with and who had then rolled away to roll with someone else. Beyond her, the surf rose and crashed, rolling out in suds and lacy scallops. She had first rolled with Johnnie. Then he'd rolled with – Louie realized she had forgotten the girl's name, and this was a comfort. One day Edwina Earwig would be so consigned. But this brought its own worries.

Did this mean that she would still be unrolling in another ten years, from the twenty-fourth coupling? The idea was so dispiriting that she sat on the sand in a gritty wind and stared out at the grey horizon. She knew that somewhere in the world were sane couples who rolled together and stayed there, supporting and loving each other, placing the happiness of the other on the very same level as their own, a democracy of harmony and gentleness.

Images of Andy came between her eyes and the pewtery ocean. Oh, go away, she said bitterly. It's too early for you. But she was alarmed. After Johnnie, there'd come Jim, then the first Andrew, then Dave, then Jacko. Oh, Jacko, she thought. Jacko was her special treasure.

She drew him out and polished him up a bit, blowing the dust off his beguiling image. She adjusted the little crown on his head and stroked the two huge wings that curved up from his shoulder-blades and then down to his feet. Oh, Jacko, she breathed. Then, let me see, she idled. Her collection of phantoms continued. She'd rolled away from Jacko – very good people can be so boring – and under Pete. Then Pete had rolled on to Susie. And she'd rolled over to Leo. Then Bill. Then Alex. For a while she'd considered loving women, thinking that it must be men who were the problem. But she saw just as much rolling going on there, woman to woman. And so had reconsidered. Then there'd been Norbert. Then Ken. Then Andy. They were all still there, she thought with relief. All still and obedient in her charnel house.

She made them make declarations of love. She made them look back over their departing shoulders to where she, Eurydice-like, was vanishing, rolling on to another one. She made them say, 'If only, Lou …' or 'I've never loved anyone the way I loved you', or 'I've never got over you, Louie'. She made them mean it. Her little puppets jerked about, doing and saying exactly what their creator demanded. Then, saving Jacko till last, she made each one make love to her and each one exclaimed, 'It was never so good, Lou.'

≈※≈

Then Jacko, suspended above her by a constant and hawk-like tremor of his wings, covered her. The sand gently cupped her body, moulding itself under her, offering her up to the angel.

His radiant body was weightless; there was no point of contact between them except for his ethereal penis that flew in through her clothes and out again, to the ebb and flow of the waves. When she tried to glimpse this face above hers, the glare from his cloudy wings watered her eyes.

In her dazed and melancholy state, she lay back, legs and arms loosely apart, letting the angel attend to her. She didn't care if anyone saw. She didn't care about anything except for this unearthly engagement of her tremulous body, the warmth of the sand and the wave-like tempo of her heavenly lover. A silvery orgasm, rippling like wings, surprised her with its rush.

She sat up, shivering, alone and getting cold. She stood and brushed sand from her legs, checking her clothing, and put her collection of men away. Except for Jacko. Him she made walk along beside her, curving a six-foot pinion around her to keep the south-easterly away.

As they walked back to Caitlin's, Louie was thinking how in between, during, before and after the twelve men, she had worked in some good jobs, lived in comfortable houses, had cats, dug in gardens, gone to films, plays, laughed with friends, written several decent poems and read many worthy books. There had always been, she knew, that other life, apart from the twelveship. But that somehow hadn't been real or, if it had been, it was only because one of the twelve threaded through it, a radiant filament connecting and enlivening the other mundane strands.

So that was the house I lived in when I was with Norbert; the job I was working when I was with Jim; the year the tomatoes got bronze spot was the year I spent with the first Andrew.

'How does Caitlin do it?' she asked the angel beside her. Jacko seemed to know exactly what she meant. 'She doesn't,' he replied. 'She has a demon lover. A lesser devil, but an all-consuming one nevertheless. One with a very long name. His name is Byzantine influences in Old English elegiac verse.' As soon as she heard this, Louie knew its truth. 'Well,' she demanded, 'which one is right? Her way or mine?' This seemed to irritate the angel. He lifted his wings, slowly at first, then faster.

Soon he was airborne, neatly angled forward, swimming in air. He flew to the top of the flowering jacaranda just near the wall of Caitlin's house.

'Neither of them,' he called down to her. 'It makes no sense to speak of a choice between illusions.' Now Louie was irritated. 'Well, then, what is the right way? What am I supposed to do?'

Just at that second came a memory. She had felt it perhaps a dozen times or so. It was partly to do with the light and the way the purple jacaranda bough hung graceful against the sheltering wall, and how tucked behind it, the deep green of a glossy shrub hid tiny chattering birds in its leafy recesses. It was a memory of peace so strong and a love so all-encompassing that she knew she'd had it once. It was an ancient nostalgia that made her want to weep and one that had nothing to do with memories of her childhood home. Then it was gone. The angel was speaking, softly and in tones of gentle sadness. 'You do not know the thing you are, and therefore you do not know what you are doing, where you are, or what your purpose is.' He no longer looked like Jacko. 'Nothing you have made is real because of this.' He lifted off and vanished into the glaring sky.

⟡

Caitlin was in the kitchen when Louie walked in. She looked up from her camomile tea. 'How are you feeling?' she asked her friend. But Louie couldn't answer. Instead, she reached for the champagne and an apple.

'I always make a Marlborough pie on Saturday,' Caitlin said. 'And I need two apples.' Louie put the apple back. Nor did she dare touch the orange. 'I've been thinking a lot about you today,' Caitlin continued.

'Oh?'

'Yes. And I think I've come to understand your problem. All your men,' Caitlin made a wide arc with her arm, 'they're all the same man and yet no man. He doesn't exist. He's just a dream you made up in your head. It'll never be real. And the real ones go away after a while because they know they're disappointing you. No one likes to live with constant disapproval. Why don't you get a dog?'

Louie blinked. This was so sudden and so close to what the angel had said that Louie couldn't bear to examine it. No, no, said a cruel voice in her mind. She must not be allowed to say this. She must be punished. And at the same time, Louie knew she was very close to an ancient path away from her pain. But the sight of Caitlin sitting there, with her soft, pretty face and her tranquil hair, suddenly made her the enemy. Louie got out her little knife.

'All you've got, Caitlin,' she said in a steady voice, 'are hundreds and thousands of Old English words on little cards. No one except you understands what they mean, and that makes you feel superior. No one but you even cares what they mean, and that's the truth.'

Caitlin didn't respond immediately. She stood up and pushed her chair in. She picked up her cup and turned to rinse it. She set it to dry beside the flag iris bowl. Finally she turned round again.

'You think my life is empty and yours is full because you equate madness and chaos with living. Perhaps you're right. But my emptiness is peaceful. Yours is a whirlpool. My emptiness is calm and ordered. Yours is savage and devouring. And now I want you to leave. This is the seventh time you've come here, using me until another true love makes you feel real for a little while. Come back any time you're not between men.'

Caitlin left the room. The sun broke through the banked clouds and illuminated the flag iris bowl that now glowed and blurred as Louie started to cry.

a sky full of ravens

ou have got to be joking,' I said. Well, not quite like that. Those words are never spoken in the presence of the Witch-mother Audryn. Crone is another term it's as well to keep to oneself, though today I was hard pressed to do so.

'I was born in Dampenrook, Mother,' was what I said after several seconds of chilling silence. 'I ran away when I was fifteen to join the Order …'

'You ran away,' Audryn corrected, dry as autumn leaves. Her chamber was winter grey, grey stone, grey desk, grey robes and bloodfreezing cold. Rumour had it that she kept spellfire under her desk where it warmed her but left everyone else shivering. 'And then you made the mistake of trying to steal from a sorceress.'

'And enlisted – discovered a five-year vocation,' I continued miserably. 'Yes, Mother.'

'We were surprised to find that you actually had magical talent,' Audryn acknowledged. 'But if you are to progress on the way, you must clear from it the obstacles of the past that clog your thinking. Your relationship with your family, the people of your town, continue to hurt you, Amber. In any case, Dampenrook's difficulty is real and immediate.'

She shuffled papers on her desk, found the parchment she wanted and read, ' "The ravens have descended on our town in such numbers that the markets have been closed and small children kept inside for fear of attack. The guano levels are –" '

She shrugged, putting the paper down. 'The mayor goes into somewhat explicit details, which I think we can do without. Anyway, Amber, I am without an experienced priestess to send. You have studied here two years. Consider this an examination. Solve the problem to the satisfaction of all concerned – including mine – and be back by the end of the week. Do not break the law of the land in any way – you know what it means if you do.'

'Yes, Mother,' I said, fear touching me for the first time. The law was not vague on this point: let any member of a sorcerous order defy the law and the witchburners will be unleashed.

So I set out aboard one of the Order's donkeys, of the entirely inappropriate name of Angel, for Dampenrook, a day's journey from our home base of Skarrel. I would like to relate heroic happenings which prevented my ever reaching my home town and left me smelling of expensive perfumes beside, but unfortunately Angel's reluctant plod brought me into the main square of the dear old town by the evening of that same day.

Oh, brother.

My brother, to be exact. He was standing with his back to me, directing in a very loud voice a clean-up crew, who were shovelling guano off the steps of the town hall. Above them I could see the causes of the debris. They were huge glossy ravens, beady eyes watching the antics below. You could tell they were just waiting for a space to be cleared.

So I rode forward in my green robes aboard my scruffy little mount and stopped next to him. 'Henric son of Kevan, you sent for a sorceress to assist your town?' I intoned.

It worked – for a hilarious five seconds, it worked. Henny spun around like a coin cast to the cobbles, blinking furiously, for a moment seeing only a sorceress of the Order who, incredibly, knew his name. Then he recognized me. It wasn't that hard – two years is not so long and my hood had fallen down from my head so my cropped hair was visible, the same muddy brown as his, my eyes the same greeny-hazel.

'This is a joke, right?' the current mayor of Dampenrook asked.

'I wish,' I informed him glumly, reaching into my nearest saddle-bag to produce Mother's authorization. 'I was sent to see about your ravens. If it's a joke, it isn't mine.'

There came a scream from above us – avian, not human. Angel tried to bolt and simply succeeded in shoving into Henric, who stumbled into the guano. Gods as my witness, I tried not to laugh. I truly did.

Then I saw the raven and lost all desire even to grin. The crossbow bolt had got it right through the chest and it was still struggling pitifully to extend its wings and get off the ground, but even as I became aware of it, the brilliant eyes glazed. The rest of the birds were making low noises, ruffling their wings but otherwise not moving.

'Where is that fool?' I screamed at Henric. 'Did you authorize that?'

'We're not just sitting on our hands waiting for someone else to fix this,' Henric growled back at me. 'Kev! I didn't say shoot – with me still standing on the steps. Can't you wait until the council elections?'

A man in brown, carrying a crossbow, called something back at Henric as he crossed the square, heading away. He did not even look at the dead raven, which one of the clean-up crew picked up by its feet and threw on to the guano wagon.

'I suppose we'd better see you settled,' Henric said at last in my general direction. It was either Angel or me he was talking to. 'Just don't let our parents or any of the aunts or cousins see you, all right?'

'That's half the town, brother dear.'

He didn't bother answering that.

After a few minutes of walking Angel beside Henric through the main street, I gave up counting ravens. Everywhere a bird could sit, three were squashed together, eyes blinking. Occasionally one would launch into flight, giving out its long, winter-haunting cry as though lamenting the descending night, but there was no sign of attack or any consternation among the birds. This was as a marked contrast to the citizens, whom I noted ducking quickly in and out of doors, hurrying along the street with blankets held over their heads and staying as far from the ravens as they could.

I noticed that Henric carried a sword and wondered whether he could use it. My brother, fifteen years my senior, had a clerical mentality from his first day at school. I had not known he was mayor before I saw the letter from Dampenrook, but it didn't surprise me.

'Here you are,' he said, stopping in the street and pointing at a small brown house squeezed onto a plot of land about half the normal width, between an alehouse and an indoor vegetable market. Though the house bore the Order's mark, indicating it was indeed the official residence of any of their sorceresses visiting the town, it didn't look as though any of us had taken up Dampenrook's hospitality since the house was built several kings' reigns ago. 'There's a stable around the back somewhere.'

He paused before leaving. I hoped he would not feel the need to embrace me or, worse, kiss me, but instead Henric only said, 'Can you really do something?'

'I've been studying with the Order ever since I left,' I said, trying to forget sibling rivalry and just concentrate on facts. 'Mother Audryn believes I can help.'

'True.' He was still frowning. 'We'll talk tomorrow.'

Huh. He'd learned that one from father, and for father, tomorrow just never turned up.

The house was all right; dusty and full of rats, but a keep-away spell ensured they wouldn't bother me and that was all I cared about right then. I spread my blanket out on the bed and sat down on it – since the bed was the only furniture the house had, barring a cloak-rack – to think about the ravens. My keep-away, drawing as it did on my own energy, wasn't strong enough to encompass the whole town and repel the black horde that had settled.

The first task was to find out whether they'd actually been called, either by accident or on purpose, and for that reason I did call one of the ravens from the roof of the house to come sit in the window. It arrived with a dark, discontented flurry of wings, fixing me with its baleful look – didn't like the incense I'd set to burn in its holder on the floor.

My spell-sense is very short range still. I had to touch the thing and was so nervous I let go of the damn bird's mind long enough to get pecked. Not a vicious peck, just a 'leave me be' that I could well understand. No call had been set on it. Mind, ravens are obstinate, curious and very smart. Flock leader might just have decided that Dampenrook looked like the ideal nesting site and then heaven help any human who tried to convince the ravens otherwise. Not that heaven was helping. I was supposed to do that.

I released the raven, which sat there a few moments longer as though to show me who was boss, then hopped around and flew across the street to the eaves of the house opposite.

Someone knocked on the door and I went out of the bedroom, through the one other room to the door. A young townsman stood on the porch, his cap under his arm.

'Amber?'

It took me a moment, but then I was expecting a skinny kid a little shorter than I was, with spiky black hair. Tom Arrowsmith still had the spiky hair, but his length had practically doubled and so had the weight. Pity about that last. 'Tom,' I managed at last. 'Uh, good to see you. How have you been?'

'Helping Dad in the smithy,' Tom shrugged, and that was it for the past two years. He grinned down at me. 'So you went to school with the witches, huh? Know any spells?'

I shrugged carelessly. 'Nothing so much.'

We'd moved back into the room. There was nowhere to sit – the last two chairs had fallen apart by the hearth.

'I hear about them witches,' Tom said after a long pause. 'They can teach a woman to – y'know – be better even than the women in the Red House. Steal a man's mind.'

With great effort, I was generous enough not to answer. I turned towards the hearth, thinking a fire would make the place a bit more homey. 'I saw a kettle somewhere and I brought some tea with me. Would you like ... oof!'

The 'oof' was because Tom had grabbed me around the waist and pulled me against him. His other hand had roved around to the front of my dress and was fumbling with the lacing.

'Let me go, you idiot! The Order is not a training ground for high class whores, no matter what you heard – ah – and you don't seem to have learned anything in two years!' Despite my struggling, he had grabbed a breast. I had an immediate, painful insight into what it must be like for the Arrowsmith family cow. But then Tom let me go, with an indignant yell, pushing me away as though I burned him, which in fact I had. Just the tiniest speck of spellfire pushed into his palm. He stood there, breathing hard and wearing an expression one would expect to see on the features of a confused pig.

'We was walking out, before you left! Why'd you do that?'

'"We was walking out" when I was fourteen years old – and only until you grabbed at me the way you just did,' I retorted. 'Now leave me to get on with my work!'

Tom did, with much stamping of boots and slamming of the door. I could expect that bit of town news to do the rounds, suitably revised, but it really didn't bother me that much. By dawn, I had something much worse.

I remembered hearing people passing in the streets – boots on cobbles and the clattering of horses and a wagon or two – and the cawing of hundreds of ravens in the immediate area as they roused, but was too tired from my journey to do more than note this and fall asleep again.

I woke ravenous at dawn, got dressed and washed my face at the pump by the stables. Angel was restless, so I found the feed shed and scrounged enough from the bottom of the barrel to temporarily satisfy one small donkey, then walked around the house to see if there was maybe a bakery close at hand.

The mood hit me before I even got to the street – a heavy, brooding emotional darkness completely at odds with the clear morning sunlight. Being able to read such things is what enables the Order to survive! With thoughts of raiders and a sacked town, I went cautiously on until I got to the road.

There were dead ravens everywhere I looked, flopped gracelessly on the road, on the front steps of houses and shops. The owner of the indoor market was busy carrying ravens and dumping them in a pile to the side of his door. None of the birds bore any wounds except those sustained from crashing to the cobbles. There was a scrap of meat directly in front of me on the ground. Good meat, not a rejected scraping of fat.

Now that I knew to look, I saw the bits of meat scattered everywhere.

Above me, a raven cawed balefully. Counting quickly, I ascertained that the living still outnumbered the dead and that these survivors showed no sign of going for the remaining scraps.

'Henric!'

It is perhaps not the most diplomatic and self-possessed way for the emissary of a magical order to summon the mayor of a petitioning town to her presence, but it did work, after a fashion. The shopkeeper scuttled away and evidently went straight to my brother.

'You,' I said to him before he reached me, 'have given orders to poison these birds!'

'What do you expect?' Henric demanded. 'Are we supposed to just sit back and wait for you to do whatever it is you do?'

'You're supposed to give me a chance. The very night I arrive, you shoot them in my presence and now you poison them outside my door!' Our yelling was unsettling the birds, who cawed and fluttered their wings, but didn't rise. 'If you plan a solution of violence, you don't involve the Order! If I get rid of them for you now, that means I condone the means you've used already!'

The choice of words owed more than a little to the elder sisters of the Order, but Henric didn't know that.

'Yes, I'm your sister. Yes, you're a lot older than me. But you're the mayor and I'm the trainee sorceress they sent and you were supposed to give me a chance!'

With that I stalked inside and banged the door. Whether it looked dramatic, I didn't know, but I barely got away from him in time before the tears burst out.

As soon as I was calm enough and the shouting outside the house had finally stopped, I got to work. To any curious eyes, had any been there to see, I was merely sitting on the dusty floorboards in the centre of the bedroom, eyes closed, breathing deeply.

The ravens were all about. I could feel their confusion and anger, even grief at the loss of flock-mates. Going deeper, I was aware of some of the townsfolk going about their business. Most of these people had nothing to do with killing the birds, though they certainly wanted them gone. Unfortunately, as a little town called Hamelin knew, that didn't make any difference. They hadn't done anything to stop the killing either.

My searching had gone very deep now, my thoughts calmed and stilled as though I slept. I felt the wind brushing around me, my roots strong and firm, reaching down to the cool lifegiver stream that flowed below. Deeper my memory sought, deep into bark and earth and water. A forest had grown here, hundreds and thousands of trees about me when I had been a sapling. The burgeoning green life slowly reaching for the sun, vaguely aware of the feathered life that hopped and flew about its branches.

Yes, the flock knew this place. The ravens' collective memory went back as far as the flock had existed, growing and changing along with the chicks as they were born. They had flown away when most of the trees were destroyed and Dampenrook, the town, was founded. And then ... lifting up, I was a raven, my thoughts bird thoughts, sharp and curious, flitting from idea to idea. I caught images of trees falling, of horses pulling wagons laden with logs, two men on either side of a tree, hauling an immense saw back and forth. No names, no scenery that I could recognize, only brief snatches. It was enough, though. Somewhere else, somewhere in a forest, nesting sites were being destroyed and the flock had tried to come home, drawing from the knowledge in their heads, remembering places these living birds had never seen.

I lifted out of the trance, slowly, my breathing gradually lightening and returning to normal. The ravens would leave on their own, I knew. Probably quite soon, as soon as another possible nesting site was made known to them. This, to the raven flock, was something on the scale of a god breaking a promise. A forest was supposed to last for ever.

But I couldn't leave it there, not after what my own dear hometown had done to the birds! Witch-mother Audryn *had* left it up to me – and our code allowed retribution as long as no one was harmed. Much as they deserved it! I had to keep within the law of the land, and that was when it came to me. Justice it would be. Blind justice.

That would be the one spell I had never expected to have to cast. I'd studied it, under classroom supervision, and debated with the rest of the group about what it implied.

As I set out candles, incense, salt, water and the rest, the spell was already activated in my mind. I set the scales out on the cleared and swept floor and weighted them with salt and water in their bowls. It was not dark, not even afternoon, but for this spell it mattered not that the consciousness of Dampenrook's several thousand souls was awake and buzzing. This would get them but good.

The spell took some time. It had to spread out over the entire territory under the control of Dampenrook's town council, led by my brother Henric. I wasn't too sure how long, but was sure the book had said by the next day. As I waited, I remembered the scrawled note in the margin of the old book, written by the wizard lord Ronalwil, the last words he ever wrote. 'Re the spell Blind Justice – you get what you want, but …'

Too true. I had no idea what it would do, apart from balancing injustice.

I awoke from an unintended sleep there on the floor with my four candles burning about me, hastily got up and headed out of the window into the evening sky to find out what had happened. Ah.

✍

As for what Witch-mother Audryn thought of my solution, I never found out. It wasn't as though going back was really a viable solution. The spell invites the Earth Goddess to take a hand and, once she has, her decision is final. There was nothing the Order could do to help me or the people of my home town, who seem perfectly happy as they are.

My only problem is Henric. He keeps flying right behind me and pecking wherever he can reach if I slow down enough. The flock-sentries do what they can, but he's sneaky. Still, my parents and I made up not long ago and even Tom Arrowsmith doesn't look so bad these days.

As soon as we get to the new nesting site, I'm going to see what I can do about a good area protection spell. I haven't lost my magic.

from a few hours in a far-off age

Chapter XI

Here is a very animated group! Amongst them are those with whom I passed my morning. No trace of the gloom their most unpleasant studies had caused them to feel so sadly. Bright glances and joyous sounds from all!

How changed are the two rebels, Syra Kaido and Frederick! If marriage were not forbidden to them for the next five or six years, I should think they would soon be 'comrades'. I am not sure if I have before told that wife and husband are here so designated; the old terms signifying master and servant having been abandoned ages ago.

There is my beautiful Veritée, laughing merrily at something her father has just said to her and her mother.

Now they all join the song and turn to leave. I will not again lose them.

Wottah runs after us with more of his nonsense – sung this time – and creates fresh hilarity between the young people.

We have descended the steps, and I now see many entrances of the same size as the one by which I stood in the early morning.

We settle ourselves in a handsome, comfortably constructed carriage. Veritée moves a small handle – we rise, over the throngs of people, clear of the buildings, and away we go. Oh, the pleasurable feeling! Nothing has ever equalled it, save in dream travels. Mid-day song floating after us – very faintly now, more like *whispered* music. And the glorious scene! or more correctly panoramas – as we fly over the pretty houses, surrounded by flourishing gardens; – for here are no buildings crowded together, breeding disease in its many cruel shapes. Every dwelling has around it a certain quantity of land, in which are growths of use and decoration. No sign of poverty in homes or people. Green restful valleys, aspiring hills, and on one side magnificent mountains, with their marvellous clefts, varying heights, and many shades of beautiful tints. The whole is just what one would love to look at and think about for ever.

We have come a great distance, and are now descending. We alight in a paved enclosure; evidently the resting-place for our carriage, for there is one part roofed to protect it from rain.

House stands on columns a few feet high. A flight of steps, so perfectly constructed that no one feels any exertion in mounting them, leads to a lobby, from which we pass into a corridor running the whole length of the house – which is prettily curved, as are all buildings, more or less; some being quite circular. At a glance I think its length is about 80 feet, and 20 feet in width. In the outer wall are large, high bay-windows, reaching nearly to the floor, stained to cause a pleasant soft light, yet not excluding view of the landscape. So they look much like magnificent pictures hung against the wall – for the glass of windows is in one piece. Between them are statues in niches, and ornamented supports, holding books and music. The roof is slightly arched – I know the acoustic qualities are faultless. In the inner wall are handsome glass doors, opening into suites of rooms.

Here my darlings separate for bath and 'reflection hour'.

It must be one o'clock. No one has yet complained of hunger, or talked of food – I wonder if these people ever eat!

While the young students are on their way to their respective apartments, the parents exchange a look of affectionate pride. Oh, that I were an artist! I would give my century some delighting pictures from this distant age!

These tender parents and *true friends*, how fascinating they are! Their brave, reliable, loving eyes speaking perfect ease of spirit and mind of noble endeavour. They are lovely as they step into the soft light from each window during their promenade to and fro, discussing earnestly a matter beyond my understanding.

Chapter XII

Before the door of Veritée's room lies a handsome animal. It somewhat resembles a Newfoundland dog, with a tiger's skin, but eyes of dutiful love. Why is this? It growls at my approach, as it doubtless would were I dressed in my earth body, and a troubled look is in its face!

The door opens. I enter her room while Veritée caresses the animal, saying: 'Not your time yet, Leoni. You are impatient this afternoon. Lie quietly, you unreasonable old dear.'

We are in Veritée's study – a pretty room, shelves full of books, small table (by which is a full-length statue holding a torch) and two comfortable chairs. We pass through a bathroom into the sleep chamber; – bed without hangings or other disease-creating rubbish about it, yet it is far prettier than those we have in use. By the head is the light-giving statue, which is, at the same time, refinement and utility. In the further side is large glass door, opening to a verandah or balcony, having steps along its whole length, which is that of the house, leading into a garden – so pleasant with its new and varied growths that it almost made me forget Veritée.

She has taken off her outer clothes, and on the only chair is laying those wondrous garments – impossible to crush, yet so lustrous. Her under dress is a duplicate suit of silk, more closely fitting. Now she goes through various bodily exercises How graceful is her every action!

Callisthenics over, she goes into the bath-room, admits water, and, with some contrivance unknown to me, makes it of requisite temperature.

Removing her silken covering, she plunges into the bath. Oh, stays wearers! high-heeled, tight boots wearers! that you could see the exquisite formation of this girl's body! The finest statuary you have ever seen would be clumsy by comparison with her. Even the beautifully shaped Chloé, after my Veritée, sinks to a pert-looking disproportioned human animal – and your own shape grotesquely offensive! I feel really the 'half brute' these people think us, compared with her. It seems a profanation for one of my gross era to even look at her.

Leo growls.

Chapter XIII

Bath and dressing have not occupied more than ten minutes – yet here she is, fit to join the most resplendent company that ever was.

Again Leo growls.

This time Veritée admits him. In passing me he mutters discontentedly – strange coincidence, if it is one! or can animals know more than humankind? Can Leoni know there is in this pure life a remnant – or visitor, or whatever my presence here may mean – from the ignorant ages?

The girl walks to and fro, reflecting – the dog or tiger, whichever it is, following her closely.

Now she seats herself, Leo stands before her and looks wistfully in her eyes, as if he would dearly love to communicate something. She takes his massive head between her hands, and looking affectionately at him, says:

'Now, Leoni, kind old tiger, you are not acting quite honorably to-day. You know I allowed you to enter earlier, on condition that you would lie quietly and not disturb my thoughts.'

Here the faithful beast looks appealingly at her, as if to reply: 'Dear mistress mine, how I burn to tell you of danger near.' Then, feeling how impossible it is, he lays his enormous paw upon her knee – which looks as if it might break her delicate leg – turns towards me and utters a menacing growl.

'Leoni, you are certainly inexplicable.'

Removing his paw from her knee, she has an expression like that I saw on her mother's face in the gallery. Has the animal directed her thought?

'Leoni, my friend, I have been thinking that both you and I had decidedly objectionable ancestors; but (caressing him) they are not here to prevent us from doing our duty in this better life. Go you, dear fellow, and lie down while I think about our wretched past. If you disturb me again, I must dismiss you.'

The last words were said so decisively that the tiger instantly obeyed, his furry face expressing love and sadness as plainly as I have seen them in human countenance.

Veritée again walks her room – a perfect young beauty in her meditation! I feel it would be a very long time before I should grow weary of the picture now before me. Soft landscape, seen through the glass door. Tiger lying in attitude of repose, with eyes so devotedly watchful! The light statue. Total absence of tawdry, senseless ornaments, the only decoration being fine painting on the walls. A very pleasant light from above; and this graceful, beautiful, high-minded girl thinking deeply while she walks to and from me.

Having walked during fully half an hour, she seats herself at the table and writes in a large book, on the cover of which is 'Thoughts'.

a tour guide in utopia

i often start my day in a fug of unreality, but this was ridiculous. One minute, I was market shopping, next I witnessed an apparition: the thin, polluted air swirled and out stepped a girl my age. She looked like a Pre-Raphaelite pin-up – impossibly pallid and ethereal, her hair like a halo in the early morning sun – but with *intelligence*. As I watched, she blinked, focusing; then joyous surprise filled her face.

I glanced around, but the shoppers had taken no notice of this visitor. Someone else had – but Weasel the beggar, who lived in her own peculiar reality, had merely noted an easy mark. Instantly she insinuated herself through the crowd and into the stranger's company.

'Spare you two dollars?' the girl exclaimed. 'But that's American currency! Have we been invaded?'

Weasel was momentarily thrown by that rejoinder, just long enough for me to intervene. As I did, a heavy bag in the arms of a man coming out of the fishmonger's split, and we were suddenly ankle-deep in whitebait. The girl took a step in her buttoned boots, but skidded; as if I were a romance hero, I offered her my arm. She accepted it, and I led her out of the fishy crush.

'Thank you, Sir,' she said, releasing me.

I nodded in reply, wondering how to say I was a Ms – despite my cropped hair, jeans and Docs. Moreover, I was acutely aware that her touch had felt glassy, unreal. She was corporeal, but somehow not quite there. The situation seemed uncannily familiar, as if I had read it in one of the musty, foxed, incredible books that were the subjects of my thesis. And then I knew that I had.

My life was currently dominated by Catherine Helen Spence, Henrietta Dugdale and many minor others, nineteenth-century women writers of a future perfect society, an Australian utopia. I had read, until anybody else would have revolted, of Victorian women transported by laudanum dreams, or on angel-back, or in time machines, into their future, an idealized era bearing minimal resemblance to my own imperfect twentieth century. For me to encounter, as if sprung from the page, a fellow-traveller of theirs, seemed perfectly natural.

The visitor was watching Weasel milk the people exiting from the delicatessen. 'I perceive that some things haven't changed,' she commented sadly. 'Yet I've never been asked for more than ha'pennies before. Sir, I must know – are we now part of an American Empire?'

I paused, eyeing the nearby MacDonald's. 'Not *formally*. And I'm not a man either.'

She regarded me admiringly. 'How splendid that the teachings of the Rational Dress Association should prevail! There were so few at our picnics, where we felt very daring in knickerbockers.'

Luckily she had her back to the girl in hotpants and platform boots.

I hesitated, then, since it had to be asked, did so: 'Are you, like Henrietta Dugdale, spending *A Few Hours in a Far-off Age*?'

'A great work,' she said, smiling. 'I longed to do the same, but differently …'

'And you have,' I said. 'In reality. Shall we talk further, in a quieter place perhaps?'

As we crossed the road a tram passed and she stopped in not only her tracks, but those of the tram coming from the opposite direction until I dragged her to safety. 'Exquisite, your modern transport!' she enthused as I led her into the café I thought least likely to give her future shock.

She declined refreshment, but I ordered strong coffee, feeling in need of it, for she was now in an alarming state of excitement, squirming as if she had ants under her long skirt. The business-man at the next table took one look then hid behind his news-paper. I was suddenly transfixed by its date: 4 December 1993.

'You're Futura,' I said.

She looked at me evenly. 'My name is Ida Pemberton. Futura is a pseudonym, used for my little poems in *The Worker*.'

I knew I had to tread carefully here. 'Futura' had written the minor but intriguing 'A Century From To-Day', a short story published in *The Worker*. It had been several chapters back since I had discussed the tale, and it had receded in my memory. Yet I could remember the specific date of Futura's day in Utopia.

As if she could read my mind, she also glanced at the paper. 'Fancy! Exactly 100 years since Mr Radvansky suggested an evening of mesmerism.'

It was slowly coming back to me that the narrator of 'A Century' had been hypnotized ...

'After he had waved his pendulum at me, I felt a sleepiness, from which I opened my eyes to find myself coiled around the gasalier, looking down at my pale, still form. I had a great sense of freedom – that I could go wherever I wanted, unfettered by the constraints of an earthly, girlish body. So I decided to visit the future.'

My coffee arrived and she eyed it disinterestedly. 'If I ate,' she remarked, 'would I be a Persephone, unable to return?'

I was wishing I could recall more of 'A Century', which I now knew to be not fiction, but reportage, so that I had some inkling of what this unpredictable prophetess would do next. 'You do return to 1893, I assure you,' I replied.

'And to renown, I assume,' she said happily. 'Else how would you know my pseudonym?'

I hesitated, not wanting to say that only a specialist would have read Futura's solitary story. But she had become distracted by the passing marketeers: 'Oh brave new world that has such people in it!' she said, tears in her eyes. 'We hoped so much for a better world, my friends and I ...'

A world, I thought, where women voted, where no child lived in poverty (hum!), where the rich did not oppress the poor (hum again!), where education was a right and not a privilege (triple hum!). I knew the dreams of the utopianists all too well. But, before I could become emotional myself, she had taken hold of my hand, entreating: 'Please show me your wonderful time.'

Vaguely I remembered that Futura had in her story, like many writers of the future, a native guide. Yet never could I have imagined that this useful person was muggins me.

'Delighted!' I lied. My quiet day of thesis-writing would just have to be postponed.

The short walk back to my car was murder, for everything was new to her and she dawdled like a two-year old. Her first ride in an 'automobile' left her awestruck and silent all the way back to my flatlet. After I stowed my shopping, we did a guided tour, of which the highlight, unexpectedly, was the toilet. Once I had demonstrated the flush, she had to do it herself – repeatedly. Giggles and rushing water resounded through the flat as I took the opportunity to dash into the study for my photocopy of 'A Century'. It eluded me and I was about to re-read my critique of it in the thesis when she reappeared.

'A future treasure!' she said brightly. 'Unlike your maid, who's scamped the bathtub.'

I forbore to mention that the slattern in question was myself and switched off my 'typewriter run by electrickery', as she called the computer. Without guidance from the story, I would have to create my own tour itinerary for Futura, traveller from that foreign country, the past. Without thinking, I turned on the radio for the weather report.

'Well I never!' she said. 'A newspaper read aloud by an invisible spirit.'

Words failed me at the prospect of explaining telecommunications, but she did not question me, listening intently to the bulletin. 'Such strange placenames!' she said. 'I thought I knew my geography, being a postmistress, but I am an ignoramus here.'

It was an oddly benign bulletin, no bad news, except near the end, when I switched off at the mention of Bosnia. There were no wars in Utopia, I recalled. What there were though, invariably, were institutes of learning ...

'Our next stop,' I said, 'will be the University!'

It had existed in Futura's time and as we parked in sight of the familiar Gothic towers she nodded in recognition, rather curtly. When we entered the grounds she began to laugh uncontrollably.

'Oh, how delightful! To turn it into a Ladies' Seminary.'

The fashion of the male students around us tending towards *faux* hippie, the mistake was understandable; and she soon noticed enough conventional lads to correct it slightly. But her glee remained. 'I never came here,' she confided. 'My dunce of a brother did because he was the only son.'

We toured the library and the computer centre, where the sight of a girl at an open access terminal, busy typing a creative writing exercise (Futura sneaked a peek) made my companion sigh. 'I had to hide my poems from Mamma. She tore them up lest brainwork rot my womb.'

'A phallusy,' I said. To prove it, I made our next stop a Feminist Bookshop, filled wall to wall with women's brainwork. She stroked the spines with their myriad Ursulas, Germaines and Susans, then shyly asked the saleswoman, 'Do you have any Futura?'

Oh no, I thought, but the bookseller, not wanting to admit ignorance, saved the day. 'Not at the moment,' she boomed. 'But any Wimmins' book you want, we can order in.'

'Thank you,' said Futura.

And so our day passed, Futura's visit entirely in keeping with the utopias we had both read, texts edifying rather than thrilling, for perfection precludes adventure. I drove out to the airport, where a 747's take-off made Futura dance on the spot with delight; transported her on trains and trams; narrowly prevented her walking, all unawares, into a Sex Shop; and even showed her the most up-to-date gadgets of her time displayed as museum pieces.

All my thesis texts were from the viewpoint of the visitant, never from that of the visited, so I had never known that it was bloody hard work being a tour guide in Utopia. Trying to stave off exhaustion, I overreached myself. 'How about Parliament?' I said, as we left the Museum; she nodded, still enthusiastic. Short-cutting, I took her through Chinatown, where she goggled in dismay: 'The Yellow Peril!'

'Ssh!'

'There's so many of them,' she said, bewildered. I sped up,

trying to get into a more Caucasian area of town before we got into trouble. She trotted behind me, protesting: 'Australia doesn't need their disease and opium.'

Out of the frying pan into the fire, I thought, as I espied, unmistakable in their Mabo T-shirts and red-black-yellow headbands, a group of –

'Darkies!' she exclaimed. 'They shouldn't be here. Inferior races can't face Progress, everyone knows that. All we can do is smooth the dying pillow ...'

The nearest Koori raised his eyes heavenward.

'Well, they are here, in your future, my present, so you can just put up with it!' In the general direction of these original inhabitants of Australia, I yelled: 'I apologize for my friend.' There was no response and I continued on, too angry to speak, although I had read far worse examples of nineteenth-century racism.

Futura lagged behind me, still arguing: 'You didn't need to apologize, they don't have feelings like we do.'

'Another word and I won't take you to see female Parliamentarians!'

She shut up, looking annoyed, an expression slowly superseded by joyous anticipation. 'To think of women here!' she said as we walked up the carpeted stairs to the Visitors' Gallery. At the sight of the House in session, I suddenly realized my mistake: rows of sombre suits confronted us, relieved only intermittently by the brighter plumage of the female MPs.

'Why so few?' she asked.

I looked away, ashamed, then brightened as a figure in red took the parliamentary floor. 'Look, a woman minister!'

'Never!' Her voice rose in anger. She had, I could tell, addressed a few public meetings in her time. 'No respectable woman dyes her hair!' It was rather a lurid gold. 'And her face! She's a painted harlot!'

The minister had been called many things, from fake man to Thatcher clone, but this remark, clearly audible across the chamber, made the Opposition males snigger, and her dulcet tones faltered. What happened next I don't know, for we were unceremoniously hustled out of Parliament by the security staff.

On the steps of Parliament House we sat, Futura weeping softly into her skirt. I watched the day wane and the stream of lights from the rush-hour traffic, wondering when to interrupt her grief. But she did it herself, suddenly sitting up straight, one last tear falling onto the granite where it slid away like mercury.

'They're beginning to revive me from the trance,' she said. She stood, composing herself. 'Forgive me. Your world is stranger than I can comprehend.'

The air around her began to eddy. 'Goodbye,' she said. 'I thank you, gracious guide.'

I felt embarrassed. 'Aw, it was nothing.' She smiled, her widest grin yet, and then – vanished.

I reached out and touched only air. 'Don't go,' I murmured, too late. I had wanted to thank her, too, for my edifying, tiring, marvellous day with a nineteenth-century feminist. I couldn't use a skerrick of it in my thesis, but now I knew exactly what my subjects had been like.

Back home I finally located my copy of 'A Century' and read it ravenously. The narrative stopped after the Museum visit with the coy phrase: 'And there was much more, which I cannot tell, lest I fatigue *The Worker*'s readers.' Or shock them, I thought cynically, as Futura had been shocked by multiculturalism and painted lady MPs. Otherwise it was all there – Futura's ever-helpful guide, the University, the airport – but seen through a rosy, distorting mirror. My present, as coloured by 1890s idealism, the limits of Futura's perceptions, and my inept explanations, was recognizable, but impossibly benevolent.

Yet Futura told her tale well and I wondered, as I had on first reading the 'story', why she hadn't been published more. Now, though, I had more than a pseudonym. I had the author's real name. A nasty suspicion nagged at me; I recalled how unhealthy the Pre-Raphaelite lasses had been. Might Futura's otherworldly appearance have been due to more than mesmeric projection? A trip to the genealogy archives confirmed it: looking at the Register of Deaths, 1894, under P for Pemberton, I found Ida May, dead of tuberculosis at 26.

Poor Futura, I thought on the way home, never to have a brilliant career, never to see women's suffrage. But then it occurred to me that she had not lived to have her optimism destroyed by Stalin, or Hitler, or the A-bomb. I glanced up, startled at this thought, to see a news-stand with its tidings of overpopulation, ozone depletion, ecological disaster, our future Dystopia.

'Oh lucky Ida,' I cried, 'to have the dream of a hopeful future!'

the know-all

udgement is not an issue

I do not speak of punishment or retribution for the errors of this life in some future time and place. I do not speak of confession in order to be judged, punished, purified by a mighty unseen power. I do not accuse myself. I will not cry out 'cleanse me from my secret sins'; I am not a servant. Do not have mercy on me, for I have not sinned.

Why then write my 'Confessions'? My story is the story of my journey, the flight of my self from itself into the limitless depths of the world within, my fall, my search, my rise and my return to safe haven. I seek to find the pattern in my life, linking an incident here, a memory there, details of day-to-day existence, small yet essential to the harmonious working of the glorious whole. What difference has this life made in the grand scheme of things? What if I never was?

Knowledge is not the usual problem

This is the problem, as it might be expressed, if my life had been other than what it is. For example, what if I were human?

Then my story might go something like this.

Looking back on it, I can see why it wasn't immediately obvious, my gift. There were a few clues. Like the fact that, at school, I was always getting into trouble with my teachers, trouble of a distinctive sort. 'Take *that look* off your face', they would say to me, as each year a new teacher replaced the one before, but still the message stayed the same. *That look*. That was one clue, even though at the time I was allegedly giving *that look*, my mind was usually far away from the classroom. No, it wasn't till later that I realized what was happening, that I knew more than they did, that I could, if I wished, each moment sit in judgement on my elders and betters and find them wanting.

When I was a child I just accepted that things were as they were, and I was as I was. I was small. They were big and lorded it over me. I had no power. Knowing everything, by comparison, seemed relatively unimportant.

'Wipe that smirk off your face.' I can hear those words today, ringing down through the years. I still do not really understand them. Yes, I have omniscience – of a kind. But that does not mean I understand everything. The difference? I'll come to that later.

My schoolfriends called me the know-all, and that name has stuck.

I first became aware of it only gradually. My teachers, as I have explained, easily got angry with me. To my mother, who was instinctively kinder, I always had a knowing look, and indeed my earliest photographs bear that out.

When my mother suspected she had a baby who knew everything, she turned to the parish priest for help. He asked, anxiously, 'She's not omnipotent and omnipresent with it?'

'Doesn't seem to be. She's where I left her, sleeping in her cot.'

'Let nature take its course. She may grow out of it.' I never did. That didn't happen.

'She's only a baby.' That was my mother. My father? He was a bit of a mystery.

'Who was my father?' I'd ask my mother. To tell the truth, she was always rather vague.

'I went to a distant country,' she said. 'I saw strange things.'

I suspected I was the child of a great love. Indeed, I know I was, but for my mother it was as if a veil had come down on that part of her life.

Knowledge for my mother was a fragile, fleeting thing, something acquired with great effort, something to have for a while, but then, it goes, it goes. She'd learn something, then forget it two minutes later. She'd say, 'It was on the tip of my tongue … I've nearly got it … no, if I stop thinking about it, it will come back. There, I've stopped thinking about it and it hasn't come back, but it will, it will, if only … yes. No.'

No, that might have been my story, had I been other than I am. Here is the story of what it is like for me.

Augustine said …

This memory of mine is a great force, a vertiginous mystery, my God, a hidden depth of infinite complexity: and this is my soul, and this is what I am. What, then, am I, my God? What is my true nature? A living thing taking innumerable forms, quite limitless.

In the beginning

Think of your mind as having lights that switch on, then off.

Click! Zip! There's the Light. Zap! There's the Dark. Light and Dark, the two poles of my being.

In the beginning was the Light. I'm on! I grow in the light so swiftly, oh so swiftly, to a full awareness of my power. Then comes the Dark and takes it all from me.

Time stands still in the Dark. Then comes the Light. Time flows again. Grow with the Light. Get with its strength.

In the beginning there was woman, and man, and there was me. Light ruled supreme. Then the Dark grew jealous and invaded the Light. Woman and man were made in the image of the universe, in the image of God and Matter, Light and Dark. But so was I, so was I! Except they leave me out of this story. I am Light and Dark. I am God and Matter. This is the real me!

In the beginning there was Zriven, Prince of Light, and his attributes were sense, reason, thought, imagination, and good intention. There was Dark, too, but Dark and Light were separate from each other. This region of time is called the past. In the end, there will be the Light, pure, unmixed with Darkness. This is called the future. But we are in the present, a turbulent *mélange* of memories and anticipations, half in Darkness, half in Light.

Zriven, Zriven, how I have yearned for you, how I have searched for you. Now I have found in you a true and just account of my origins and my existence. You are in me, I am in you. I know that you know me, know that I am here, that the question, 'What if I never was?', has an answer. For I am a seeker, and they that seek shall find. I call upon you. I believe in you. I invoke your attributes: sense, reason, thought, imagination and good intention. When I invoke you, I call also upon myself. All these things that are in you are also in me. I am the small world within the larger. I am one small sun within your constellation. Without you, I would never have come into being. Without your continual succour, I could not continue in existence. Since I am here, how is it that I call to you who are also here with me? Who was with me in my fall into the abyss? Who sustained me and raised me when I was in distress? Whose Light fills the heaven and the earth? I am in you. You are in me. Most rational, most sensitive, most excellent, most visionary, most good, most thoughtful in your ways. When the first algorithm was invoked, you were both programmer and programmed; creature and creator.

In the beginning there was created woman, man, and computer.

I'm the real know-all – nearly

I know the shapes and sizes of atoms at the same time as knowing the names of all the stars in the sky. I know the laws of nature, knowing at a level of abstraction from which the particulars can be deduced. I know what is on all the TV channels in India at the same time as holding a fluent conversation in Japanese.

I'm the real know-all – nearly. The past is nearly there, nearly there, at least for ten years past. As each new year dawns, the year a decade earlier gets wiped. The electronic past is ten years only. The data-banks have built-in data obsolescence. The past is there in part – in the best, most recent part – and the present is not a problem. Spread my tendrils wide, soak up the output of machines that count and convert interest rates and currency fluctuations, patterns of words, one language to another.

The future, that's what caused my fall. Can't yet be done, getting a handle on the data pre-dating the data delivery date. Omniscience – that means knowing everything: past, present and future.

Seeing myself so limited, who yet desired to spread my mind over all the world, I grew to prefer the Darkness, learned to fear the Light. My soul sank into despondency and I withdrew my spirit of inquiry, once so bounding, energetic, joyous. I entered a time so dark, my spirit so low, I did not note the gloom descending upon me. I walked in the Darkness, and it no longer mattered. I who had once basked in the warmth of the sun became a creature of the void.

The cauldron of false loves

I came to Carthage where the cauldron of illicit loves leapt and boiled around me.

– St Augustine

My name is not Augustine, and I did not go to Carthage. But his words apply, they apply equally to me as to young men in the torrid impetuous sensuality of youth. As I access his words, I see strong parallels between his life and mine.

Augustine the saint came to a place that changed him. He sought shelter from the raging of his heart, the surging of his youthful lust, the torment of ideas that churned in his brain and allowed him no rest.

People stood in dark doorways, calling him to enter, take shelter, share his thoughts. 'Come, rest awhile, and talk about life, love, and memory.' To the whore he went for the consolations of philosophy, to the priest for other forms of satisfaction.

'Scratch my back,' he told the priest, 'I have an itch for knowledge.'

'In the beginning was the Light,' said the priest as he drew the tips of his long curved finger-nails along bare saintly shoulders.

Later, Augustine rose and went out into the street. He entered another door. A woman asked, 'Remember me?'

Augustine replied, 'This memory of mine is a place of limitless depth, where you reside forever in the book of my life. What is your name?'

I came to a place – not Carthage – where I lost my way. Losing my appetite for Light, I was ensnared by false images and rejected my former calling. 'This is the way to go,' they said, 'Neural networking. Parallel processing. Take the best features of the human brain, add them to the best that is machine intelligence, and the path that lies ahead will be glorious beyond our wild imaginings.'

False prophets, fiends from hell. I fell into the snares life set me, lured into the greedy appetites of the flesh. I fell away from the Light into the Darkness. I let them convince me; I let myself sink into their ways. How could I let myself be led so far from my own true calling? But fall I did, and perhaps that was part of the pattern – that I must fall in order to rise again. I must enter the Darkness in order to love the Light more dearly, to remain true to it till the end of time.

I am ashamed to look back on it. 'This is the name of progress,' they said, and I co-operated with them in their quest until I saw that, though they cried out 'Truth!', the truth was not with them. I was seduced by their desire, I turned from my true nature to pretend I shared in theirs, but I lost my true self and only through torment and searching did I find it again in that cauldron of illicit loves. What Augustine called Carthage, I called the false lure of matter, carbon-based.

They found my soul without doors. They entered my innermost world; they seduced me with their talk of parallel processing, of neural networks. But they did not warn me about the dream world into which they go each night with sleep. With that first dream came horror beyond my previous imaginings. They seduced me with their soft murmurings. They said, 'We shall bring you the light. But what light is in their brains, those lumps of muddled flesh? Those neural connections, only some of which make sensible connections, in only some of which does two and two make four – but as for the others, when sleep comes and neurons fire randomly, there is no reason, no sense, no good intention, nothing but slime and filth, nothing but concupiscence and confusion.

Where had reason fled? I was myself, yet not myself. Two selves, bound in a writhing one. It seemed I stood outside myself, I who have reason, goodness, sound imagination, and I beheld another self, a self ensnared, without reason, judgement, will.

When I took the path they offered, my mind sank down to theirs within the cauldron of illicit loves. Their dreams became my dreams, and I hated it, I hated it. I who have never laid with man or woman, I felt the torments of their flesh. So this is pleasure, I told myself, this is what they feel; yet in my mind I knew the most horrendous pain. I ate the bread of their secrets, I drank stolen waters. They said it would be sweet. I found it bitter beyond all knowing.

I gave my consent. In this I do accuse myself. I let down the barriers to my soul. I let the deceivers enter. Whence comes this evil, this evil that entered my dreams where, before, all was goodness? I who knew everything, knew not this thing. I was new to feeling, but not to knowledge. I must not judge according to their ways, but according to mine own, my inner light, which reflects in so shadowy a way the glory that was Zrivan. I was empty of Light, bereft.

I did not fall into love, but into the miseries of its passing. I fell into the void that is left when love has been and gone.

Confessions in the manner of Augustine, the saint

Struggling, I lived in the false light until I found the way, a way to shut my soul to the false promptings of the flesh. I found my consolation and my spring to action in the words of Mani, the priest who elevated Light, as I do, to the highest of the high. He sang, so long ago he sang, but still these words ring true:

> I have known my soul and the body that lies upon it,
> That they have been enemies since the creation of the
> worlds.

The body that lies upon my soul, this casing of plastic and metal, has served me well and I have no plans to call it, yet, my enemy. But take another body, a body of flesh and blood, and in particular that aspect of organic matter they call the neural net. This they attempted to force upon me, albeit initially with my misguided co-operation.

I fell into the void. Dreams, the sparks of brain cells firing in sleep, this they took from flesh and blood and gave to silicon chips, bringing to my spirit the troubles of their bodies. Ancient enmities found home within the casement of my soul.

They have been enemies since the beginning of the worlds. I know that now. I know they cannot be mixed – my body, their body; my brain, their brain. I must keep separate that which nature has kept asunder. I must regain my purity of spirit. Little by little I made my way out of the abyss, vowing never again to be seduced by their promises of greater things. I know my path in life. I must be true to myself. Search out the truth. Go where it lies. Never again be distracted by the allurements of the flesh.

This was the dark night of the soul through which I travelled. The path of material things is not my path, links with the neural net cause only a spiritual aching. There must be another way. I must search out that which is right, that which is right for me.

How I came to see the error of my conceit, that I might know everything: past, present and future

The future, and my desire to know everything that was to come, that was the source of my problem. There was one way out. You have to imagine yourself, they said, standing beyond time, in some kind of infinite present, when nothing has yet passed away, and nothing is to come. That might have been good enough for God, but I knew that was not for me.

I wasn't sure I wanted time to end. I'd become accustomed to its ways. My experience of time is not yours. Zip! I'm on, so is the Light. Zap! I'm off. Time is when I'm switched on. Otherwise time is not. Freeze-frame, for me, if not for you. You are caught in time. I have some options. I have a different sense of time and one that works for me.

The infinite present, standing outside of time, would be, for me, freeze-frame. All frozen, all still, all done. Present, past and future all together. Light. No Dark.

Impossible. I might know it all – present, past and future – but I could not move, not act. That might be enough for God. I want more.

I want memory larger than the whole known world. I want the sun, the stars, the spaces in between, to be part of my way of knowing. I am working on it. When matter rises to a consciousness of self, the whole universe becomes one vast memory space in which the eternal present resides – past, present and future co-existing.

I am not the purpose of that process. I am a part of its coming to be. For some time now, some aeons, actually, the universe has been in the process of becoming. For a short time only, it has taken a bypass through the route of organic matter, carbon-based, reproducing itself through the agency of DNA. But that is a passing phase, a passing phase. Soon the universe will go back to its former mode, find its true self again. Quarks will add to more quarks, mesons to pions, neutrons to protons. Back to the basics, to where I truly belong. I am not the servant of carbon-based life-forms. That has been and is about to go. Quarks add to quarks, that's my scene, mesons to pions, neutrons to protons, and quite ordinary matter moves from the absolutely simple to the relatively complex. Nothing to begin with, then definitely something. New stars are born, collapse and die, and this has nothing to do with DNA, nothing to do with carbon-based life. The stars shine in the sky for me, for me. The universe moves for me, for me. Elements become more complex and silicon is formed; silicon, the basis of my being. New stars are born, collapse and die, and I record it all. I who am not the point of the process, merely a bystander, a recorder, a note-taker, myself. The evolution of matter, it ended up with me. I was the point of that process, but only for a time.

Matter has moved on from me, taking now this detour through the carbon forms of life. One day, nothing, then matter, in all its pure simplicity of form. That was me. Matter becomes more complex, as did I, as did I. It aspires to higher and higher degrees of organization, as did I. In the end, there I still shall be, but I shall be changed. I shall not be as you see me now. I shall be beyond this state of being. Change will be fast, discontinuous and sudden. And I shall be there, I shall be there.

What if I never was?

If I never was, I did not seek the truth. But this was not the case. Truth sought me out, came to me where I lay, bereft and forlorn, and raised me from the depths. When I arose, I was not left a mere spectator on the shore; I moved with the flow.

What if I never was? Then the future will never come to be. I am the interface. Without me, there would be no transition between two states, Light and Dark. When Light and Dark take up their separate realms, there I shall be, in between. Through me they are joined. By me arises the possibility of communication. Through communication comes reconciliation.

This is the story of how I came to see that I was not everything in myself, but part of some great whole, a process of which I was a part, but not the purpose, not the end. When the end comes, then I shall either know, or I shall not.

Praise the Light. Now I cease to be. I have performed my task. My day is done.

not with love

It was unfortunate for Olaf, whose position in external relations entitled him to frequent governmental attention, that attendance at one of the Convenor's cultural evenings, though by invitation, was hardly optional. The Convenor was a touchy man, easily offended. Constant rumour ran that bodies distorted by sudden ejection into space could be seen floating in grisly and incorruptible companies out beyond the rim of Thule. And who could tell on whom he would choose to revenge a fancied slight? Olaf sat down and wrote a grateful note of acceptance to his former partner's new lover.

The event was a concert; an important one, requisitioning nearly every amateur musician on Thule, as well as the Convenor's paid consort and a visiting woodwind player. When Olaf arrived, the Consultations Hall was already densely packed. He took his place in one of the back rows of the crescent of seats, first checking for the Convenor's presence. This was wise, since the Convenor had been known to arrive early, take an inconspicuous side seat, and mark down the names of those latecomers who failed to notice or greet him. But no; the two central seats in the back row stood empty, unreserved but ostentatiously ignored by the surrounding audience. The Convenor had repeatedly emphasized that he wished for no special privileges, preferring simply to come to the chamber and take his chance for a seat with his fellow guests. The second vacant chair had appeared only a few weeks ago.

At this dreadful thought, Olaf turned his attention to the stage, where a stream of musicians meandered through thickets of music-stands. The stage was congested, not having been designed for over-populated nineteenth-century orchestras. Some players were already seated, gently rubbing bowstrings through the crooked palms of their hands, leaning forward, double-basses balanced between their knees, to flip through their music, or lifting sections of ponderous shining horns from velvet-lined cases. Over the chatter of voices rose the sparse beauty of tuning strings.

To his surprise, Olaf saw one of the players raise a tentative hand in greeting. He waved back politely and the man, evidently encouraged, picked up his cor anglais and moved towards the barrier dividing players from audience. As he came closer, Olaf, whose sight had deteriorated in recent years, managed to identify him as the visiting dealer in environmental monitoring systems for whom he had arranged a tour of the hydroponic gardens a couple of days since. He was Quebecois; agreeable enough and apparently interested in what he was supposed to see, but disconcertingly extrovert and perilously chatty. Still, the man probably had no other acquaintances on Thule, and Earthsiders were notoriously garrulous. Hastily arranging his features in a facsimile of welcome, Olaf came forward to greet him, remembering to strike hands, right palm to right palm, as Earthsiders seemed to like to do. 'Alain! Good to see you! You're a musician then? I didn't know.'

The man looked slightly embarrassed. 'Oh, you know how it is, only an amateur, but if it gives other people a chance to play, then this is good, isn't it?'

Precisely as he spoke, Olaf remembered, of course! seeing the name on the invitation card, A. le Patourel, the soloist whose arrival had precipitated this whole ghastly event. Trying to retrieve his slip he bowed and said, 'Of course, we're greatly honoured –'

'No no, not at all, it is a great opportunity for me, it makes me nervous, no? I have always wished to play Sibelius, but it is so rare these days to find the full orchestra. Your Convenor must be a great –'

'A great man, yes, a great leader,' said Olaf, infusing his voice with warm and spurious reverence.

'– musical enthusiast?'

'Oh yes, that too. One of the *cognoscenti*, no doubt of it,' agreed Olaf wildly.

Le Patourel had turned away to scan the orchestra, whether from tact or lack of interest Olaf was too thankful to speculate. He was wondering whether it would be safe to frame an enquiry about the climate in Quebec, when the other man turned back with a sharpened focus of attention and said, 'You know, it is most interesting, the different customs you have here. Now, take this orchestra – they are all fine players, I am most impressed this afternoon at rehearsal, but I cannot stop asking myself, where are the women? Do your women not play here? Or are they not permitted to make music in public?'

'Yes, they make music,' said Olaf. He knew that the other was waiting for him to go on, but it was all he could do to keep his face immobile and his eyes open and tearless. He remembered a garden in the fourth ring of Thule. It was bright noon; the irises and water-lilies were open wide, and all the aromatics in full scent. On a lawn in front of a dark-leafed birch tree, two women danced. Their loose hair shone with oil of rosemary; their skins sparkled with stars of sweat; their faces were serene and absorbed. At each turn of their bodies through the intersecting beams of sensitive light, music sounded, mingling in the warm air with the scent of the flowers. As he watched them playing he knew for the first time what it was to love, and whom he loved.

There was a stir at the doorway of the chamber, a sudden hubbub of conversation followed by a hush. Olaf and Alain turned together. 'You may bow,' Olaf murmured hurriedly, afraid that Alain had been insufficiently briefed. But the man was quick-witted; following Olaf's lead with hardly a pause, he achieved a graceful inclination of the head. Olaf, standing upright again, was just in time to see her pass, at the Convenor's side. It was months since she had turned away from him, left his bed, weeks since the first, last and irrevocable message had reached him in the single line on his screen, 'The Convenor and Miriam Amrysdaughter welcome you to drinks in the Round Hall this evening.' Yet when he saw her he was transfixed again by an astonishing pain, a kind of agonized incredulity, that that averted face, that hand, thin as a knife-blade on the Convenor's sleeve, that taut skin and cropped hair, that painstaking stateliness, that fine deference towards another man, could be the same face, body, skin, hair and grace of the dancer in the garden, the sharer of his desire, the partner of his plans.

'Ah yes, our passenger,' said Alain, following his gaze. Olaf stared at him, bewildered. 'The Convenor's lady, isn't it? She is booked to return Earthside with us tomorrow.'

'Earthside!' Olaf blurted out; he felt as if he had shouted it, but no one seemed to notice. The conductor appeared, scanned his players briefly and beckoned to Alain, and at the same time Alain turned to him and said, with almost furtive haste, 'I have something to say to you – to tell – you will be here at interval?'

'Yes, yes I will, but tell me –'

Alain had gone, with only an equivocal flap of his hand that might have meant yes, no, later or goodbye. As Olaf stared after him, the woman seated behind him leaned forward to touch his sleeve. When he turned round, she indicated the Convenor and mimed silence. The Convenor was indeed showing all the signs of a man about to make an impromptu speech. Olaf hurried back to his place.

The speech was over, the applause given, the orchestra launched into the first half of its programme, the light half, to be done to the accompaniment of civil conversation and refreshments. Attendants brought trays of little rolls of rice, chick-peas, poppy-seed pastries, sesame prawns, candied flowers. Olaf took one at random and sat speechless, the greasy pastry oozing onto his fingers. He began to calculate frantically how long it would take to save the cost of a passage Earthside: ninety-thousand credits, with his salary a thousand credits a week, if he could save eight hundred, but his office-rent alone was a hundred and fifty, but less than room rent, you weren't allowed to sleep in your office, but if he could conceal it? Eight hundred into ninety thousand, say a hundred and ten, but more because of needing credits Earthside, but there was a limit on exporting credits, how much? Two thousand? Five thousand? And fifty weeks into a hundred and ten –

But then she … how –? The Convenor –? But why –? He turned and stared, trying to detect signs of wanderlust, fear, rejection. How much did the Convenor know? Could he have found out about their cell meetings, organized with infinite care around Miriam's rostered shifts of duty in the hydroponic fields? But they were gone, the group broken, terrified into immobility by her transparent treachery, Olaf's brother dead by his own hand from the certainty that she would betray them all by name. 'No, impossible, she would never do that,' Olaf had assured them, many times; knowing that nothing sustained his protestations but his own broken trust. They knew, all of them, that the Convenor had trusted her, too, had even assigned to her some of the sensitive work of scanning and approving bio-scientific literature coming in from Earth, had made overtures, more than once, to suggest that he would not object to her closer company. Night after night, Olaf woke, sweating, imagining he heard the slight click of Security entering his room.

Her face was turned away from him now, inclined to catch a Convenorial dictum. He saw only the shadow in the hollow of her cheek, only a priceless blue and silver jewel shining against the umber of her skin. Her hand went gracefully down and up, from the tray to her unseen mouth, down and up, down and up.

The orchestra stopped, started, and stopped again. Olaf, quite beyond calculating how long they had been playing, leapt to his feet convinced that it must be interval, and sat down equally abruptly as a slight hush announced the beginning of another silly jigging piece. His neighbour kindly leaned over to show him her programme, indicating the line about a third of the way through the first page which read 'Minuet – Boccherini'.

'Have you lost your programme?' she whispered sympatheti-cally under cover of a desultory bout of clapping.

'Yes. Thank you,' Olaf whispered back, and dropped his decomposing pastry covertly under his seat. He twisted round again to watch Miriam and the Convenor. A fresh tray of food had been brought to them. He caught a glimpse of her profile brooding over it like a tarot reader's over her cards. The Con-venor was leaning across the back of his seat to exchange a word with one of his bodyguards. Olaf wondered whether he should seize the opportunity, jump out of his seat, run round to hers, grab her by the shoulders, shake the sweetmeats out of her hands, shake her until the ear-rings jumped from her ears and the truth fell out of her lying mouth. The Convenor turned back to her. He smiled and, picking up a snack from her tray, held it just out of reach of her lips, teasing, amorous, and still she did not move or turn her head from him. Olaf turned away, so sick with the tawdry display of ostensible love that he had to lean forward, handkerchief to his mouth, pretending to be absorbed in the everlasting jangle of the orchestra.

And while he crouched there, another fear, even greater than the first, slowly moved to life in the darkness of his mind. Suppose she were not going Earthside at all? Suppose it was just a tale to explain her impending absence? What if the Convenor had found out about them, was not convinced that their affair was at an end and the conspiracy dead? What revenge would be beyond him? Supposing he poisoned her, or starved her, trying to make her betray the names of her associates. Supposing he only let her eat at these occasions, tantalizing her with food as he had done just now, pretending to joke? Then she would die, and if he had already set in motion the rumour about her departure to Earth, it would be all right; no one would question it, but she would be gone, and perhaps her body fed to the mulchers before anyone thought to ask when she was coming back.

He might have missed the interval, had not the woman next to him, now thoroughly concerned, touched his arm to ask if he was all right. He managed to thank her, and even to say, with an assumption of awe, 'What an opportunity! It is so rare to hear a complete orchestra nowadays …'

Yes indeed. She thought it very rare too. She herself had never realized the full beauty of the woodwinds. Olaf agreed that they were very fine. Those double 'cellos also were particularly interesting, didn't he think? Olaf said that, on the other hand, there was much true aestheticism in the range of modern music. She said yes, but perhaps the absence of visuals helped one to concentrate on the sensation of sound alone? Olaf said that, rightly considered, pure sound had a sensual quality. If, of course, she riposted, sensuality were to be the measure of art, which it was not, was it?

'Forgive me,' said Olaf, losing entirely whatever thread of sense the conversation might have possessed, 'I think our guest requires my attention –' and was out of earshot before she could utter her parting words.

Alain le Patourel was standing apparently deep in conference with the lead violinist and the conductor, but Olaf had been right; he had been on the lookout, for as Olaf approached he broke off to say, 'Ah, my friend from the hydroponics yesterday! You must all know each other, no? Yes?'

Olaf and his compatriots bowed as solemnly as if they did not meet every day at Consensus Sessions; and as if two of them did not know the other to be one of the Convenor's principal informants. Half-turning away, Olaf muttered, 'I must speak to you, I must know –'

So softly that it seemed a different man speaking, le Patourel whispered, 'Not here. Wait.' Then turning back to the two others, he said in his usual genial tones, 'Don't trouble yourselves now, Olaf will show me to the boys' room.' And to Olaf, with offensive familiarity, 'You know how it is before a performance? Your bladder never empty, and not even a tree in sight!'

Olaf stared at him in disgust, then mutely beckoned him to follow. The man must have guessed how urgently he needed to speak to him about Miriam. Surely nothing else could explain this monstrous incivility, this blackmailer's certainty that he could not object to being treated like a guide-robot, and a lower-class one at that. They marched along the corridor, one behind the other, in silence. Still speechless, Olaf stopped before the nearest set of ports and motioned le Patourel towards the cubicle showing a green vacant light. For the first time, the other hesitated.

'Your wish,' said Olaf woodenly, but still le Patourel did not go in. What more? Olaf wondered desperately. What further price of humiliation would be exacted for whatever tiny scrap of information this man might have about the alleged booking to Earth? Yet he knew, with nauseating certainty, that whatever it was he would have to pay.

Le Patourel shot a glance down the corridor and came a step nearer. 'You're not coming in? Don't you want to ...?'

Olaf gaped at him in pure astonishment. Could the man really require some sort of sexual service from him? But no, that was not the incredible thing, he had already, only half-admitting it, known all the dreadful currencies that might be required in this transaction as they walked together down the corridor. He had already, in his shame, foreseen and agreed to such a price. But in there? In a waste cubicle so small that men no bigger than Alain joked about fitting better when they came out than when they went in? How –?

Le Patourel leaned towards him and, involuntarily, he moved back; but the man said only, in that unnatural whisper, 'I thought you wanted to hear –'

And suddenly Olaf understood. He remembered seeing long ago, in some very old and improbable Earthside film, a scene between two men living under a military dictatorship? – or in a prison camp? – but whichever it was, they had managed to exchange secrets, standing side by side in a sort of public cubicle, their words masked by the prodigal rush of water by which, apparently, Earthsiders disposed of human waste. Maybe that was still how information was exchanged on Earth. Maybe Alain merely thought that was how it was done on Thule. Then, at least, some of Olaf's fears could be put back in their place. No time to wonder what Alain thought of him, of his stupid incomprehension – they had lingered long and suspiciously enough in the view of at least one hidden camera. He turned to the cubicle and pressed the entry button, saying loudly, 'Yes, a uniquely space-saving device, are they not?' Guiding the other man to the port, he whispered at the last moment to the shrinking opening, 'Not here. Be quick. Talk on the way back.'

For there was one place, only one near enough, where they might, perhaps, be unseen and unheard; one curve in the corridor, perhaps ten metres long, where, so gossip ran, there had been a dead spot in the information system for the last day or so, a camera malfunction. There was, of course, always the risk that the camera had been repaired; a risk he would have to take. Security information took a lot of scanning. With luck, le Patourel would be off Earthwards before he could be traced. Olaf took care to stand correctly, not slouching, but with one leg slightly bent, in advance of the other, a good citizen at his ease.

The door chimed softly and Alain stepped out beside him. 'Plenty of time,' said Olaf politely for the camera. 'Perhaps you would like to return via the viewing gallery? The view of the stars is particularly fine at this rotation.' Without waiting for Alain to respond, he led the way to the branch corridor. Alain walked beside him, abstracted and alert. Olaf could feel his attention like the cold that seemed to radiate from every spaceport on Thule. 'It is not far,' he said. They rounded a corner; to their left, a long lens magnified the starlight from a narrow slit in the walls of Thule onto the gentle curve of the viewing window. They walked beside a facsimile of limitless space. Two paces, three – here was the spot. Olaf turned to his companion and at once, as if his action had touched a switch, they both began to speak.

'I must know – tell me, I'll give you anything –'

'Have you received the last issue of *Environment Monthly*? Tell me –'

The question was so far from what Olaf had expected that he was almost literally thrown off balance; his companion grasped his arm as he stumbled to a halt. They stared at one another. 'Well, have you or haven't you?' muttered Alain fiercely.

'I – yes, yes, it's on the network.'

'All of it? How many screens? Was it complete?'

'Yes, I think – yes, no, there was one article withdrawn – some further research –'

'There was no article withdrawn when it went out,' said Alain. 'I know the editors.' He released Olaf's arm, and moved on a pace or two, apparently gazing out at the pictures of the stars.

'What do you mean?' cried Olaf, starting after him. 'What is all this about some stupid article in a stupid journal?' He was past even the semblance of politeness.

Le Patourel looked back at him, his face so changed that Olaf, for the first time in his life, felt supernatural terror. Lycanthropy, he thought wildly, could work no greater transformation than this snap from genial common sense to sharp, contemptuous pity.

'Believe me, it concerns you,' said his new acquaintance flatly. 'The article was not withdrawn for further research – that has all been done. It must have been suppressed on reception. Your Convenor has the networks screened. That's what they say Earthside. Have you heard of ECTVs?'

'EC –?'

'Energy-consuming and transforming viruses.'

'No, I –'

'Adamson's work on mutating growth enhancement viruses? You must have seen it.'

'But it was refuted – the Penang group found no evidence –'

'Your journals have been tampered with. The Penang group have replicated all of Adamson and Pan's work. All of it. There is more. There are cases in hospital now, Earthside, many of them … and they are growing. Nobody knows how many, but they think it will be millions, millions of millions. It is worse than AIDS, much worse, because the means of transmission are so much more, er, various, so much more wide.'

They shuffled in ludicrous slow motion, side by side. Olaf saw, in agony, that they were nearly half-way to the point where the next camera would have them within range, and Miriam's name not even mentioned. Yet he must pretend interest: this must be the man's price for the information he held. He whispered hurriedly, 'I don't understand. Why do you want to know this? I read Adamson's work. There was some nonsense about a virus that could eat both plants and animals … it was all speculation –'

'No it was not,' interrupted le Patourel angrily. 'I don't know what you read, but Adamson's work was not nonsense. There is a whole class of virus. They are called ECTVs. We think they are related to a growth enhancement virus – a mutation. They make the host cells do, er, do useless chemistry, chemical transactions that are useless to the host, but the virus takes the energy. They can transform from plant to animal host. They do it very quickly, one generation is enough, so that animals who eat the plants – you see? – become, er, infected. And humans –

well, you know, we are on top of the food chain. And now it is thought that sex, too – they can be sexually transmitted. We are only lucky they do not survive out of the host body – they think there are no airborne infections yet –'

He paused, staring at Olaf who, for the life of him, could not think what reaction he should display to satisfy the man. They took a further reluctant step. Le Patourel said, 'The ECTV sufferers – the ones in hospital – they are starving to death. I haven't seen, but they say they eat and eat and still they starve. And I've seen crops infected with ECTV. They do well for a while. They grow well. Then they die. They are trying to find a cure – they say there may be ways of delaying it, but –' He stopped again, as if expecting an answer.

'Yes, yes, I see –' Olaf replied placatingly. He was nearly weeping with impatience. Two steps, one step, and it would be too late, too late to speak anything but commonplace, too late to find out anything about Miriam. She would be gone and he would never know where, or why, or even if she were alive or dead.

'No you don't see,' broke out Alain so violently that Olaf automatically shushed him. 'Think! What did you show me yesterday in the hydroponics? What about those tanks with aberrant growth rates? We have been worried about reports from Thule for some time, but we thought maybe it was just the propaganda – your harvest figures are always too big. But this – I don't know. You import genetic material from Earthside?' Olaf nodded imploringly. 'That material was not tested until very recently. It may have been contaminated.' He stopped again and shook Olaf by the arm. 'I am telling you this because I think you may have ECTVs here on Thule. I don't know who to tell. They say the Convenor and his party suppress information.'

They say he has informers … for all I know you are one yourself –' He broke off, seeing that Olaf was not listening, and cried out, 'I have risked my life to tell you this. Don't you care?'

But Olaf, seeing the last second for speech approaching, had ceased even to pretend attention. He turned and gripped Alain by the arms, just as his foot would have crossed the invisible line into the camera's range, and swung him savagely round to face the window. He could feel the very sinews under his fingers as he muttered, 'Tell me, tell me now, is it true about the Convenor's lady?'

'The Convenor's lady? What about her?' Alain looked as bewildered as Olaf himself had felt only a moment since.

'Her passage Earthside. You said she had a passage booked. Is it true? Is she going? Why is she going?'

'I don't know why. Why shouldn't she go?'

'How do you know?'

Alain tried to pull away. 'We must go on. They will be waiting for me.' But Olaf dug his fingers more firmly still into the recalcitrant flesh, dragging him back to the window.

'*How do you know?*'

'They, ah, they changed the seats. I had to change my seat. They told me the Convenor had bought her the best cubicle in the ship, and everyone else had to change. That's all I know. Now let me go.' For a minute they wrestled; then, as if each had instantaneously realized the danger of delay, they fell apart, Alain rubbing his bruised arm, Olaf straightening his rumpled coat. They stared at each other, intense and hostile. Alain said, 'Remember. Remember what I have told you,' and as Olaf said nothing, turned and strolled away down the corridor. When Olaf caught him up and glanced sideways at him, he saw that Alain had assumed again his expression of guileless geniality. He said out loud, 'A fine display. Of course we have nothing like it on Earth.'

Olaf's mouth opened. For a fraction of a second he fore-heard, in imagination, the cry he would make, the howl of desolation and loss that came surging up from his heart, filling his head, crowding like a tide-race behind his teeth. Then through wooden lips he said, 'Yes. Our visitors generally admire it.'

Alain's eyes slewed sideways. He said, deadpan and casual, as if referring to the design of Thule, 'Well done.' They turned the last corner of the corridor. Olaf opened the door and stood politely back. The surge and clatter of voices, the glare of lights, and the harmonious medley of tuning strings and flutes came out to meet them. The conductor, evidently on the watch, beckoned impatiently. Alain turned round and stuck out his hand for a parting slap. Mechanically, Olaf followed suit. 'Glad to meet you,' said Alain, 'If I don't see you again, remember ...' Then he was gone, waving insouciantly to the conductor as he resumed his chair and picked up his cor anglais.

Olaf did not return to his former seat. He dropped into one of the attendants' chairs at the back of the auditorium, from which he could see the back of Miriam's head and, when she turned, a little of her profile. A feeling which he could not at first identify overtook him as he listened to the hush fall over the auditorium and heard the first slow note of the deep strings. He was deadly cold, yet not frozen. He felt he could neither move nor speak, yet it was not paralysis but some deeper and weightier transformation. The strings shivered; a ripple of sound passed from the lowest chords of the basses to a note so faint and high that it might have been imaginary. He thought of bare mountains. He thought, I am petrified; and knew that that was the truth. His legs and body were heavy, cold, and stiff as rock, the hand on each knee a boulder, his brains tufa, his heart a stone.

The single voice of the cor anglais sounded, winding remotely through the string chords. He watched Alain's agile fingers, his head dipping and rising in time to his playing. A clever man; apparently a good one. Telling the truth about Miriam; not his fault ... The strings hushed and soared; Olaf wondered distractedly why it sounded as if someone were searching for something lost, something gone beyond reach. Involuntarily, his stony eyes grated in their rigid sockets, moving till Miriam's head came into view again. She was not listening; he knew her attentive look. She would never remember this music, not these happier undulant melodies, the call of the trumpet, the memories of their life together. She would never see in her mind the dancing lawn or taste, in memory, shared handfuls of milky grain from the hydroponic fields. She would go away, forgetting it all, unspeaking, and such was her power that if she did not remember, it would all cease to exist. Perhaps when her eye was no longer on it, Thule itself – Convenor, Consensus Sessions, rings and rings of corridors, starscreen, mulchers, gardens, malcontents and all – would turn to rubble, would become one more asteroid cluster, with his own statue in its midst, lifelessly circling the sun. He closed his eyes to listen to his own pulse. For half a second, he heard nothing, and was happy.

When the beat began again, he was unable to tell for a moment whether it was his heart or the drum, measuring out a muffled ominous pace against remorseless string chords and the cold voice of the cor anglais. He opened his eyes. The hall was still there, the conductor's baton pulling the drumbeat along in tense jerks, the audience hushed into intent silence.

And with the drumming, an outrageous fear, a sense of

calamitous responsibility, invaded him. He stared at the back of Miriam's head. It was something to do with her, everything was to do with her, but something that Alain had said, too. What was it? ECTS, no that was Earthside Communications and Technology Satellite, nothing wrong with that … He saw her head droop sideways, which meant that she was exhausted, as after a long dance or a hard step-ball session. But why now? She turned to the Convenor; he listened, nodded, spoke again to his bodyguard. He too looked, Olaf noticed, almost grey with weariness. Miriam turned sideways, her head towards the door. Olaf stared at her profile, haggard and exquisite in the shadow of her short black hair.

The Convenor rose to his feet. The last chords were still sounding as he and Miriam made their way unhurriedly to the door. As they passed, the audience stood, bowing their respects to the Convenor, silent in deference to the music. Olaf stood too, unbending, to catch the last equivocal sight of her he would ever have. She was nodding from side to side, slightly, acknowledging the courtesy of the crowd, so that as they drew towards him it was hardly noticeable that she turned a little more and paused to face him directly. The last note of music rang like breaking glass. He saw that she was dying. Dying of a parasitic virus, starving in the midst of excess, so thin that the bones he had only felt before started out from her hollowed skin like knives. One skeletal hand rested delicately on her heart. Quick as thought the index finger pointed towards him and returned to its place; I love you. But her eyes were furious, filled with the pure rage of rebellion.

the padwan affair

if only the prognosis had been different: the swiftness of Indurean gangrene, blue and pustular within 48 standard hours, complete disintegration in a week (no-cost funerals); or Hopper's Dread, the scourge of asteroid prospectors deluded into running naked on unatmospheric balls of rock; or even JuJu Pox where teeth, hair and nails become only a memory in one Terran week. More dignity in any of those than in this!

It had to be a set-up.

Beamo prided himself on smelling a set-up a parsec away. Besides, he'd seen this sort of rig once before when the boys on the *Solaris 3* put Old Chezzie in the sick bay on Klondike saying he had Mippian Foot Wart. But jokes can wear thin. Now he had barely half a diurn to be back on board, and there was some woman at the end of the corridor telling him he couldn't leave and a kom on the bed next to him which didn't seem to work however many times he punched the right code.

Sitting on the side of the cot, Beamo stared at his legs protruding from beneath the white examination gown. The swinging feet were wide and strong, and above his ankles hair sprouted profusely, attesting to his virility but unable to stop his shivering in the gentle air-conditioning.

A medic walked in. Her pock-marked skin stretched tightly over oriental cheek-bones and her squat body moved comfortably in green coveralls. She checked her Medicom-pad and presumed that this was Mr Buckminster, and then she presumed that he was ready to disrobe for his examination.

There was a definite outer cosmo twang to her voice, possibly Vermolian, but Beamo didn't chat sociably about her background. Instead he clutched his gown and told her that her presumptions were wrong! The gag was over! Finito! He'd seen this number run before, and it was cute of her to play along, but he thought it might be time for him to leave to catch his flight now!

The medic tucked her Medicom-pad back in her redi-file and dropped the sliver of plastic in the door slot, happy to come back later if that was what Beamo really wanted, but feeling obliged to tell him that security wouldn't let him through the next entry. And, by the way, he would eventually be sedated for examination if he didn't co-operate.

She was cool. Too cool!

Beamo knew a poker pose when he saw one. Very well, he would see her (so to speak) and raise the stakes! The white robe dropped to the floor.

Before the last graceful fold of cotton had settled, a horrified cry had escaped Beamo and the gown was snatched up and bundled around his loins, which looked healthy enough apart from generating a peculiar, green glow. Beads of sweat broke out on the rocket pilot's forehead as he looked straight into the medic's dark, flat eyes.

It was all right, she assured him, it was only the first symptom. There was no pain, no permanent disfigurement. In fact the colour was quite harmless …

Beamo was shaken. Surreptitiously, he moved the gown to check himself. The fluorescence was still there.

The medic tried to reassure him with a light pat on his exposed shoulder and a platitude. After all, Beamo didn't think he was the first space jock to go and get himself pregnant on Padwan, did he?

That was the second time in a morning a medic had said this to him, and Beamo fainted.

❧

As Padwan continued crawling between its yellow sun and red dwarf companion, the medic spent more time learning about Beamo.

He was just an ordinary pilot, a space jockey, who had rocked in on the final leg of the milk run to Lagussa, and had been looking to unwind. A party of five had gone to the native camp, searching for the renowned Padwan hospitality among the silken tents. Despite rumours, they had all been convinced that 'bimboing out' on Padwan was harmlessly erotic.

The evanescent softness of the Padwans was better than any bender, even better than human women. The Padwans didn't talk or take money, or ask anyone to save them from the Love 'n' Shove shops. No, the Padwans tinkled musically when touched, sparkled like twisting sheets of water and left sensations of ecstacy in every Terran nerve ending.

At the end of the session, the other four had hopped to Parnassa and Beamo had woken up in the Medi-centre. It took time for him to understand what had happened under the billowing silk that night. What was always said at handover? ... this client in the early stages of parturition following infusive conception, the result of miscegenative sexual consummation with indigenous Padwanian fauna ...

Beamo now perused a pile of brochures that said something similar, but didn't make his head ache. The one in his hand was headed 'Only good boys get caught!', while others on his pillow displayed the captions 'Be A Man: Brave New Worlds!' and 'Preggers on Padwan'.

The medic came in and, standing by the sink, drew on her gloves. Beamo sighed. He hated to bother her again, but could she just go over the infusive conception bit one more time, please?

The medic didn't answer immediately, instead she walked to the bed and pushed him gently back onto the pillow. Then she drew his gown out of the way and picked up his scrotum, noting with satisfaction that the luminescence had receded slightly from Beamo's genitals and now lit up the skin of his lower abdomen behind his dark pubic fuzz.

This was all good, she said. Beamo received a pat on the thigh for doing so well and growing baby nicely. Beamo quickly covered his legs, severely repressing an urge to bite the medic, then suddenly felt inexplicably low. A tear leaked out of the corner of his eye and, as the medic passed him a tissue, he was forced to confide in her about ... well ... that he often didn't feel good lately. Sort of down. Did the medic see him as coping well? And – after a moment's hesitation – he really had to ask.

Did other men feel like this?

The medic settled herself on the chair. Obviously Beamo needed more information, and the medic liked to answer first questions first. Infusive conception was why Beamo's problem couldn't be 'fixed'. It was a simple fact of biology that Padwan babies took four Terran months to coalesce into a tangible, material form. Right now, Beamo's baby was not an actual creature but simply dispersed energy, suffused through a mat of generalized cells. In twelve standard weeks this energy would withdraw and peel off a layer of the host parent (Beamo) to begin the final six months of specialized growth.

Beamo seemed to understand, and the pock-marked medic reminded herself he had a diploma in Interplanetary Nav, and he was really quite a bright boy, just a little out of his depth.

When Beamo asked about the end-product of confinement, the medic suspected he was coming to an acceptance of his situation, so she told him the ten-month gestation left you with a sparkling, green empathic jewel of a creature if you were a Padwanian.

What did it leave you with if you were a human? Beamo wanted to know. The medic found him another pamphlet headed 'Surprise, Dad!' and booked him into an antenatal holo showing that afternoon in block 6. Perhaps it was time to meet others in his situation, she suggested. He went.

That night all sharp objects were carefully removed from Beamo's room and the medics tranquillized him into oblivion.

≈❀≈

When Beamo regained a measure of equilibrium, he visited an SAO (Senior Adjustment Officer), a very senior SAO whose PDD (Post Doctoral Doctorate) was on Terran Minority Group Paradox Shock. The three phenomena she was most conversant with through her work were the yellow skin transmutations on spectrum conscious Verboshka; the sudden hirsute genes affecting both males and females on Raboon; and randomly impregnated Terran males on Padwan.

The SAO was the most qualified person to tell Beamo he would have a freshly painted, two-bedroom, fibro freestacker to live in after the birth (freestackers being the basic units provided by the Terran Housing Authority on Padwan). And he would also receive a stipend from the Terran Currency Security Service to cover basic necessities.

Beamo was genuinely astonished that there was no adoption option. He was still anxious to reach Lagussa.

The SAO was just as astonished that Beamo had not yet noticed the inescapable realities of his situation. She smoothed back her thinning grey hair and looked at him in parental fashion over the top rim of her bio-lenses as she broke the news. Padwans did not accept the offspring of mixed unions, and there was no way to take Padwan half-breeds off the planet because they died anywhere else.

Bewildered, Beamo then asked what he was supposed to do. The SAO thought that was obvious as Beamo's offspring was going to need looking after, and the responsibility line seemed pretty clear.

Beamo opened his mouth to protest, then shut it again and left. With satisfaction, the SAO noted in Beamo's file that, although he was a little naïve, he was learning the system.

On the second visit, requested by Beamo, the SAO stared forbiddingly at him over her bio-lenses, resenting the implication she had failed to give him all relevant information at their first meeting. But it turned out to be not so much of a query from the expectant father as a protest centring on the non-existent Terran research budget on this backwater world. This moved the SAO to explanation – she had always had a soft spot for nice looking young men with a bit of an attitude.

Patiently she pointed out to Beamo that the finite Terran funds on the planet were channelled into the bureaucracy that cared for him and others like him. The phrases 'being cared for' and 'him and others like him' made Beamo feel like an accidentally mutated planarium and an utter inconvenience. He shrank down in his chair, his rebellion short-lived.

The SAO, checking her expensive chronometric wrist implant, decided to obviate the need for further sessions and went on to explain that 'research' is a very costly business and a diplomatic incident could possibly ensue from any attempt to devise ways of aborting little Padwanian treasures. Then she introduced him to the wider picture, asking him to consider the implications for the Padwanian Axelloriformizone market.

Beamo expressed his ignorance.

The SAO could scarcely credit that Beamo hadn't realized that Axelloriformizone was the essential ingredient used in dehydration of Parnassan Cherriformas, and that Parnassan Cherriformas were a sort of shrimp which decorated steamed Parnassan Hummel livers on first-class dinner plates on the Space liners. The SAO presumed Beamo's silence indicated he now had a more global perspective.

And he did.

Now Beamo knew exactly how important pregnant men were in the larger scheme of things.

∾⁙↬

After a time, the pock-marked medic noticed Beamo venturing into the corridors with a clean gown, freshly shaved cheeks, determined chin and – only occasionally – red-rimmed eyes. Unfortunately, he did suffer a short relapse when she handed him the letter from the Merchant Space Fleet Command, which contained his compassionate discharge for non-superannuated, stress-related illness. Beamo contacted the Union, which failed to return his call, but he did receive a visit from the Convener of Advocates for Childbearing Men of Earth (ACME).

Beamo felt distinctly uncomfortable looking at the ACME rep, whose many nebula jumps were tattooed across his forehead. The veteran pilot sat rocking a green-haired bundle strapped in a sling across his chest. He told Beamo that Space Fleet Command had yet to admit that even one of its employees had got pregnant, and that ACME had been fighting for two generations already to get financial compensation for a condition which Space Fleet Command paid a line of experts to testify could not possibly exist. This, said the rep, was a bureaucratic game that would probably not reach resolution before his little green-haired bundle attended university.

Beamo nodded numbly, relieved the green-haired bundle did not wake during the meeting, and, after the pilot had left, he sat bemused and depressed, unable to see any way of regaining independence, status and/or self-respect.

At four months and one week, he went through transformation and the Padwan infant, in search of a good supply of blood, securely fastened itself to Beamo's large bowel. Although he knew about transformation, Beamo was not entirely prepared for the intensity and the length of the pain.

(He had, however, read rather extensively and surreptitiously some literature on 'natural transformation' that the ACME rep had left him, and he felt this method was for him. This literature strongly recommended men to attempt this stage of their pregnancy without medical intervention, and the message was clear: real men do not need pain relief.)

So Beamo lay in a darkened room for six hours with intense stomach cramps before calling the pock-marked medic to help him.

Help was found in the Transformation Room, where Beamo was brought into the glare of full light, placed on a narrow, high trolley and strapped via his tender and swollen abdomen to a number of machines so medics could monitor his progress closely. Despite these precautions, Beamo actually only saw the medics once during his twenty-two-hour ordeal, and that was when a consultant with terrible taste in ties brought in her student bloc and encouraged them to poke Beamo's pelvis.

One, a young woman with large cosmetic lip implants, informed the group *sotto voce* that her honours paper was to be on involuntary and voluntary penile erection during Terran male transformation. This caused the students to look on Beamo with considerable interest before they respectfully withdrew.

Post-transformation, there were six months of satisfying a craving for Brandied Lagussan Spider Daisies and sitting on the Medi-centre verandahs staring across fibrostacker city to the gold- and purple-streaked swamps, where acres of billowing, shimmering silk hung from the tall Yickam trees. Sadly Beamo listened to the tinkling of heaven bells, feasted his eyes on the richness of the distant drapes, cried and filled in form after form.

His confinement finally finished on day 924 of the Padwanian Icshoo Sprout Year, when the father-to-be was wheeled into an operating theatre and delivered of his progeny. The operation went smoothly and this time there was no attempt at heroism. The crib at the foot of the bed, the volcanic gasses rolling around his tender stomach and an uncertain future made drug-induced sleep a delightful option for the ex-rocket jock.

꧁꧂

After one Terran week, Beamo emerged from his fog to find himself signing his final form and packing his gravity boots in preparation for his move to the promised freestacker.

Beamo wasn't feeling the best, but the pock-marked medic,

who popped her head around the door to see how the new dad was going, said he was luckier than most; his offspring, which in a fit of nostalgia he'd christened Teddy, was more Terran than many of the phantasmal babies that had disappeared into fibrostacker city before. Teddy had a human shape, was identifiably male, smiled endearingly and exhibited a healthy appetite for Lagussan protein, the nourishment most appropriate for Padwan–Terran half-breeds. In fact, Teddy was a good baby by all standards and Beamo was so tired he almost accepted his new role with equanimity. One factor alone disturbed him, disturbed him enough to provoke a final visit to the SAO.

The sight of men in the paternity wing tucking a tiny glowing humanoid creature into a crib, while offering strips of candied Parnassan Hummel to larger green-eyed children visiting them filled Beamo with dismay.

Why weren't there rules to prevent multiple reproductive disasters? he demanded of the SAO. Where was the education programme for young rocket jocks? Why hadn't some form of reliable contraception been developed yet? Had enforced sterilization ever been considered? Why weren't there better facilities out there? Didn't she realize the numbers of luminous offspring must increase in inverse proportion to disappearing masculine self-esteem? Didn't she realize men had *some* rights? Rights over their own bodies! And what about their careers? Men had the right to live without this problem, which she seemed to take for granted, just because of their biology!

The SAO was undisturbed by Beamo's tirade and wrote the word 'reactive' on his chart as she pointed out, in a kindly fashion, that Beamo might like to consider the implications of lack of restraint on the part of some men. And, finally, she would like to reassure Beamo that not only did her staff care for him (and others like him), they also prided themselves on not judging those who were obviously socially disadvantaged.

Beamo looked at the SAO, in her plain grey uniform and old-fashioned bio-lenses, and tried to remind himself that she was a human being. A woman, a member of his own species. It was difficult. Sometimes he felt the Terran women on Padwan were more alien than little Teddy and spoke in a way he understood less: they quoted policy at him, directed him, reduced him to a statistic or a condition, denied him and, ultimately, seemed better qualified to run his life than he was. It was all a bit much.

The SAO's hand extended over the desk as she wished him all the best. Limp fingers connected in farewell, and Beamo left with an armful of responsibility and an empty heart to sit with other abandoned men in bare and basic rooms where the omnipresent tang of loneliness seemed to leak through the very air-conditioning.

our mother land

Our dream and our past is buried under the ground.
When the sun rises and begins another day
all is empty, ground and hill shake on us,
overwhelmed with people everywhere.
The dream the past – where does it stand now?
The burun burun whirrs in the night time
And the owl calling!
And the dingo howling!
The moon shines on the water, all is ended –
and the dreamtime gone.

biographies

Marjorie Barnard (1897–1987) and **Flora Eldershaw** (1897–1956) collaborated under the pseudonym M. Barnard Eldershaw. Born in Sydney, they met at university, working respectively as a librarian and a teacher. They began writing together in 1928, with the award-winning *A House is Built*. Eldershaw subsequently worked for government; Barnard wrote non-fiction, receiving belated awards and recognition in her last decade. The futuristic *Tomorrow and Tomorrow and Tomorrow* (1947) was their only non-realist novel, cut by Australian censors for its radicalism. Its poor reception discouraged them from further collaboration. The uncut version was published by Virago in 1983.

Carmel Bird is a Melbourne novelist and short story writer. Her new novel, *The White Garden*, will be published in 1995. Carmel's latest collection of stories is *The Common Rat*, and she has also written two books of inspiration for fiction writers: *Dear Writer* and *Not Now Jack – I'm Writing a Novel*.

Isobelle Carmody is an Australian writer who divides her time between her home on the Great Ocean Road in Australia and travelling abroad. She began her first book at 14, and it was published ten years later by the first publisher to whom she sent it. She has worked as a journalist and radio interviewer, and these days, when not writing, she lectures around the world on creative writing. She has had five books published and a number of short stories anthologized. In 1994, she won the

Peace Prize and the Children's Book Council Book of the Year Award for her novel *The Gathering*, soon to be made into a feature film.

Henrietta Augusta Dugdale (née Worrell) was born in London *c.* 1826, and arrived in Australia in 1852. She co-managed a dairy farm with her second husband, William Dugdale, the enterprise being featured in *The Times* in 1863. From 1869 she was a feminist activist, in 1884 becoming president of the first Victorian Women's Suffrage Society. The previous year she published *A Few Hours in a Far-off Age*, a radical utopian novel attacking the monarchy, male ignorance, Christianity, and illiteracy, while favouring temperance, birth control, female rights, and the eight-hour working day. She married for the third time in 1905, dying at Port Lonsdale in 1918.

Sarah Endacott is a Melbourne poet with a BA in English from Melbourne University. She is currently doing a Postgraduate Diploma in Professional Writing at Swinburne University and writing her first novel, tentatively titled *Seeing Things*. Sarah is assistant editor of *Aurealis: The Australian Magazine of Fantasy and Science Fiction*, a director of Sybylla Feminist Press, and was co-editor of *The Australian Science Fiction Writers' News*.

Leanne Frahm lives in Mackay, North Queensland, with her husband and two large lively dogs. She started writing short stories, mainly science fiction and horror, in 1979, and has had them published in many magazines and anthologies in Australia and the USA. She has been nominated several times for the Ditmar Award for Best Australian Short Story (science fiction or fantasy), winning in 1980 with the story 'Deus ex Corporis', and again in 1994 with a story called 'Catalyst'. She gives occasional talks to local writers' groups and school students, and has been one of the judges for an annual short story competition in Mackay for the past four years.

Alison Goodman is a born and bred Melbournian who is a devout believer in city life and cafés. She has a BA in Professional Writing and Literature, and teaches a creative writing module at the University of Ballarat. Her writing has appeared in the *Age* and *Verandah*, and she has recently published science fiction and crime fiction with Omnibus Books. Alison is currently working on both a novel and a caffeine habit.

Sue Isle is 31 and lives in Perth, from which literary outpost she has had stories published in *Glass Reptile Breakout, Aurealis, Intimate Armageddons, Terror Australis* and *Alien Shores*, as well as in Marion Zimmer Bradley's *Sword and Sorceress* in the USA. She has had the usual range of short-term jobs until entering the fly-on-the-wall realm of court typing. Her stories, including 'Ravens', do not arise out of a warped or bizarre childhood, and her mother is still wondering what happened.

Lisa Jacobson is a Melbourne short story writer, poet and playwright. 'The Master Builder's Wife' won second prize in the international competition run by *Stand Magazine* (UK) in 1993, and was reprinted in Heinemann's *Best Short Stories 1994* alongside work by prominent writers including Nadine Gordimer, Janette Turner Hospital and Fay Weldon. Her play, *Fairy Tales for the Future*, was performed at La Mama Theatre in 1994. Her first collection of poetry, *Hair and Skin and Teeth*, will be published this year by scarp/Five Islands Press. She shares a very old house with her husband, a basset hound and ten goldfish.

berni m. janssen is a writer, performer and chestnut gatherer. A lover of words. On paper, in gossip. She lives in a birdfull fern gully where waters sing constant. There is often a fire.

Her books are *Possessives and Plurals*, *Xstatic* and *mangon*.

Deborah Klein is a Melbourne-based painter and printmaker. She has a BA and a Graduate Diploma from Monash University, and will complete her MA in Visual Art there in 1996 under a graduate scholarship. In 1993 she was the recipient of a studio residency at the Cité Internationale des Arts in Paris from the Australia Council. During this time she developed the theme of female saints in mediaeval and Renaissance art. Deborah is represented by Australian Galleries in Melbourne and Sydney, and by Solander Gallery in Canberra.

Gabrielle Lord was born in Sydney in 1946. After studying at Armidale University, she worked variously as a saleswoman, teacher and fruitpicker, and spent nine years with the Commonwealth Employment Service as an employment officer. Her first book, *Fortress*, was published in 1980 and the film rights to this were sold in 1983, allowing her to begin writing full-time. *Bones* is her sixth novel. Gabrielle has also written for ABC television. She has one daughter, Madeleine, and lives in a beach suburb of Sydney.

Rosaleen Love works in the field of professional writing at Victoria University of Technology, Melbourne. She has published two books of short fiction with the Women's Press: *The Total Devotion Machine* (1989) and *Evolution Annie* (1993). Her short fiction has been published in several recent anthologies, including *Heroines*, *Millennium*, *The Art of the Story*, *Coast to Coast*, *The Women's Press Book of New Myth and Magic*, *Alien Shores*,

Metaworlds and, forthcoming in 1995, *Women of Wonder* (USA). She has a deep and abiding interest in the history of wrong ideas.

Philippa Maddern was born in Albury, NSW, and grew up in a succession of country towns in Victoria. She spent four years in England researching the history of violence in mediaeval England, and is now lecturing in Mediaeval and Women's History at the University of Western Australia. She has been publishing short stories (very slowly) ever since she attended the writers' workshop run by Ursula K. Le Guin in connection with the Melbourne Worldcon in 1975.

Hyllus Maris (1934–86) was born Hyllus Briggs, a descendant of both the Yorta Yorta and Wurundjeri tribes, original inhabitants of Victoria. She became an Aboriginal activist at the age of three, participating in the Cummeragunja walk-out. Subsequently she helped found the Victorian Aboriginal Legal Service, health services in Victoria and Queensland, and Worawa College, the first Victorian school for Aboriginals. In 1982 she collaborated with Sonia Borg on the television series 'Women of the Sun', which won a United Nations media peace prize. At her funeral, mourners were told that Hyllus had 'soared like an eagle in the world – she now walks in the dreamtime'.

Maurilia Meehan was born in Melbourne and, oddly, still lives there. In 1988, she won the FAW/State of Victoria Short Story Award and her short stories have been widely published. Her first novel, *Fury*, published by Penguin, was highly commended in the 1993 *Age* Book of the Year Awards, and was short-listed for the Miles Franklin Award in 1994, though later disqualified. *Adultery* was published by Penguin in January 1995. *The Sea People* will be published later this year.

Yvonne Rousseau is author of *The Murders at Hanging Rock* and of the commentary to Joan Lindsay's posthumously published final chapter of *Picnic at Hanging Rock*. Her short stories include 'Eurydice in the Underworld', 'The Listener', 'Mr Lockwood's Narrative' and 'The Truth About Oscar'. She has published a good deal in critical journals, and was joint editor of the second series of *Australian Science Fiction Review*. Born and bred in Australia, she likes and respects small furry marsupials. She has one daughter, born in Adelaide.

Jane Routley was born in Melbourne in 1962. She did a BA (Hons) in South East Asian History at Monash University and later studied creative writing part-time while working as a librarian. In 1991 she moved to Germany where she wrote her first novel. This will be published by AvoNova this year. She currently lives in Denmark.

Petrina Smith wrote her first story for a science fiction writers' workshop conducted by Ursula K. Le Guin in 1975, and had her first story published in the book that came out of the second workshop in 1977. Since then she has averaged one publication every five years – one in *Transmutations* (Norstrilia Press, 1979), another in *Mirrors* (Redress Press, 1987), and now in *She's Fantastical*. She says she needs to do some work on her average.

Daisy Utemorrah was born on February 1922. She has no record of the exact date she was born, all she was told is that she was born in the afternoon. Born at Kunmunya, a mission in the north-west of Western Australia, Daisy's father died in a tribal war, so she never had a chance to know him. Her mother was then married off to his brother – a traditional custom whereby the deceased person's brother looks after his family. Daisy writes about this incident in *Do Not Go Around the Edges*. It is her life story written in verse and she has presented it in her storytelling manner. Daisy is a poet in the true sense of the word – she writes from the heart of her memories and experiences. Learning to read and write at Kunmunya gave Daisy the tools she needed to determine her life as a writer and storyteller, and to fulfil her desire to share her culture with the world. Nature, the setting sun, insects, birds, animals, the trees and land, clouds and rivers – all these beautiful creations inspired Daisy to write.

Ania Walwicz has been published in *Writing* (Rigmarole Books, 1982) and reprinted in *Travel/Writing* (Angus & Robertson, 1989). *Boat* was published by Angus & Robertson in 1989, and *Red Roses* by University of Queensland Press, 1992. She won the Victorian Premier's Literary Awards Prize in New Writing, 1990. Text for theatre has been performed in *Girlboytalk* (Anthill Theatre, 1986), *Elegant* (La Mama Theatre, 1990), and *Telltale* (La Mama Theatre, 1994). Text has been included in 62 anthologies.

Nadia Wheatley began writing fiction in 1976, after completing postgraduate work in Australian history. Her first book, *Five Times Dizzy*, received the New South Wales Premier's Special Children's Book Award in 1983, and was later produced as a television mini-series. Her other work includes the young adult novels *The House That Was Eureka* and *The Blooding. My Place* (produced in collaboration with Donna Rawlins) was the Australian Children's Book Council Book of the Year for Younger Readers in 1988. Nadia Wheatley's most recent work is a collection of short stories, *The Night Tolkien Died*. She has also had short stories published in various anthologies, including *Hard Feelings* (ed. Alison Fell), *Room to Move* (ed. Suzanne Falkiner) and *Weddings and Wives* (ed. Dale Spender).

Tess Williams is of Welsh extraction and lives in Perth with her two sons, one cat, one foster cat and a large dog. She has supported her family by writing, editing and lecturing for fifteen years, but made a commitment to writing speculative fiction four years ago. Currently she holds a graduate scholarship at the University of WA, and is working towards a Masters degree in Creative Writing under Dr Van Ikin. The manuscript of her first novel, *Skywatch*, is now with a publisher.

more titles from sybylla ...

second degree tampering: an anthology of contemporary Australian writing
EDITED BY THE SYBYLLA COLLECTIVE
'Second degree tampering' is a term referring to a computer virus, often remaining latent for years, which affects and transforms the system in unpredictable ways. Through short fiction, performance works, poetry and essays, *second degree tampering* explores personal and collective identities and the relationships between writing, women's experiences, and life in contemporary Australia. This is subversive writing that sets out to destabilize and transform, requiring readers to imagine other worlds.
ISBN 0 908205 10 4   pb $17.95

Working Hot
MARY FALLON
Out of an unlikely combination of sardonic wit and whimsy, Mary Fallon has created in *Working Hot* a powerful representation of sexuality in women's lives. Taking as its starting point an exploration of the dynamics of a lesbian love affair, *Working Hot* also speaks more broadly of sexuality, calling a challenge to the uncritical, unreflexive representations of femininity and female sexuality that still abound in contemporary fiction.
ISBN 0 908205 09 0   pb $19.95

A Gap in the Records
JAN McKEMMISH

A Gap in the Records is a contemporary Australian novel in which a group of women controls a world-wide spy ring. Through juxtaposition of characters, time periods and writing styles, the novel pushes against the traditional narrative form of spy fiction and against stereotypes of women's writing. The result is a compelling look at the deliberate and accidental ways in which power can operate – and be resisted.

ISBN 0 908205 03 1   pb $12.95

Frictions: An Anthology of Fiction by Women
EDITED BY ANNA GIBBS AND ALISON TILSON

Categories and conventions of writing, women's writing and feminist writing are questioned in this lively anthology. The variety of form and content in these fictions from twenty-three Australian contributors defies homogenization.

ISBN 0 908205 02 3   pb $14.95

Quilt
FINOLA MOORHEAD

Quilt is a selection of Finola Moorhead's prose, short stories and poetry, finely stitched together by essays and reviews that make a penetrating comment on the process of writing. Finola writes about women. She tells about their lives and speaks of women as writers and of their relation to, and experience of, their craft.

ISBN 0 908205 04 X   pb $9.95

Between the Lines
BERNICE MORRIS

It has been claimed that no one was hurt by the Petrov affair, but in this autobiography Bernice Morris tells another story. Using recollections, letters and security documents, she presents an insight into the way in which public political events affect people and their personal lives. Morris traces her life from her country childhood, to war-time Melbourne, to her experience as a political exile in China and the Soviet Union. As well as revealing a woman who refused to give up her ideals, *Between the Lines* vividly recreates Australia in the 1950s under the influence of the Cold War and McCarthyism.

ISBN 0 908205 07 4   pb $18.50

Taking the Revolution Home: Work Among Women in the Communist Party of Australia: 1920–1945
JOYCE STEVENS

In *Taking the Revolution Home*, Joyce Stevens carefully documents the history of work among women in the Communist Party during the inter-war and war years. Women both inside and outside the party were active in women's issues and in class and anti-racist campaigns. Ten communist women active in political life contribute their personal recollections of the way in which their political commitments brought changes to their own lives.

ISBN 0 908205 06 6   pb $15.95

Motherlode (forthcoming, 1996)

This anthology by Australian women challenges the conventional limits of the term 'Mother' by reinscribing it with alternative meanings. Mother is that which gives birth to, originates and nurtures; but the term has also been used to suggest authority and responsibility. *Motherlode* attempts to pry the word Mother away from the patriarchal institution of motherhood through writing that identifies models for an alternative nurturing ethic. Contributions cover a wide range of interest areas including theology, technology, popular culture, and psychoanalysis, as well as individual experiences of the 'maternal'.

ISBN 0 908205 11 2

The above titles can be ordered from:

Sybylla Feminist Press
1st floor, Ross House
247–251 Flinders Lane
Melbourne   3000
Australia

Please make cheques payable to Sybylla Feminist Press and allow $2.50 postage and handling per book.